THE WEREWOLF'S ASSISTANT

Phoenyx J. Rose

For the little girl I once was - who wrote to find escape, hope, and magic. Thank you for believing in stories long before you knew they could heal.

Table of Contents

Enter the Wolf's Den

Elias

From the moment Linda Myers stepped into my office, I knew this conversation would end badly. The scent of her anxiety drifted toward me, sharp and unpleasant, mingling with the faint fragrance of her lavender perfume. She was nervous, and her fear was palpable, hanging thickly between us like fog rolling silently through a forest at dusk.

Linda's dark hair was meticulously pinned back, her makeup impeccable, yet her hands betrayed her carefully composed facade, clutching the edges of her tablet with white-knuckled desperation. Her heartbeat thrummed erratically beneath the surface of her controlled exterior, betraying every attempt she made to appear calm. Humans had always been easy to read, their bodies an open book filled with secrets they wished they could hide.

Silence settled between us, heavy and thick, stretching on until it became almost suffocating. It was a tactic I'd honed over centuries, an effortless power play, and I knew exactly how long to let it linger until it became unbearable.

Linda finally cleared her throat, a brittle sound breaking the oppressive quiet.

"Sir," she began, meeting my gaze with practiced bravery, "we've completed the hiring of your new executive assistant."

I arched a brow, allowing my gaze to linger, holding her captive in its intensity. "You mean to tell me that after combing through thousands of qualified supernatural candidates, you've selected a human to handle my affairs?" My voice was deceptively soft, each word dripping with quiet menace.

Linda shifted in her seat, clearly uncomfortable under my scrutiny.

She straightened, lifting her chin just a fraction higher, a futile attempt at dignity. "She's the best candidate we could find, Mr. Blackwell. Her resume is impeccable, her references glowing, and frankly, sir, we've exhausted all other options. The internal candidates, they uh…know your reputation. They refuse to work with you."

I smiled faintly, the expression cold and without humor. It was true. I was notoriously difficult. Ruthless, even. But my power, my control, came from demanding absolute perfection. Weaknesses were intolerable, hesitation unacceptable. Yet now, this woman—this *human*—was being thrust into my carefully constructed world, a world she could neither handle nor comprehend.

"You understand, Linda - she won't last," I murmured finally, leaning back in my chair, fingers steepled beneath my chin. "She'll quit within the month, likely less."

Linda hesitated, choosing her words carefully. "If that happens, sir, we'll replace her immediately."

I studied her face, watching the barely perceptible tremor at the corner of her lips. She wasn't confident in her choice, merely resigned. I exhaled slowly, turning my gaze toward the windows, looking out over the sprawling city below—a city that existed at my mercy, though none of them realized it.

"Fine," I murmured at last, dismissing her with a flick of my wrist. "Send her in on Monday. We'll see how long this one survives."

Linda rose swiftly, nearly stumbling in her hurry to escape from my office, and as she closed the door behind her, I leaned back in my chair, eyes closing briefly. Something stirred deep within my chest, a subtle unease that whispered a warning I couldn't quite name.

A human assistant. Perhaps, for the first time in a very long while, my life was about to get interesting.

Harper

Standing in aisle six of Brooklyn's Discount Grocery Depot, I stared blankly at the half-empty shopping basket dangling from my elbow, silently calculating how much I'd already spent. The harsh fluorescent lights hummed overhead, casting an unflattering glow on the rows of generic cereals and cans of off-brand tuna. I sighed heavily, scanning my meager haul—store-brand macaroni and cheese, instant noodles, and a suspiciously discounted loaf of bread.

I reached reluctantly for a box of cereal—*Fruity O's*, definitely not the good stuff—but paused midway, spotting the price beneath it.

"Four bucks?" I muttered to no one in particular. "Seriously?"

With a resigned sigh, I placed the box back on the shelf. Maybe next paycheck, Harper. My pride stung slightly as I discreetly glanced around, making sure no one had noticed the pathetic exchange. But thankfully, the aisles were nearly deserted, aside from a weary-looking mother arguing quietly with her toddler about sugary cereals.

At the checkout, I watched anxiously as each item rang up, the numbers climbing painfully closer to the sad, lonely twenty-dollar bill crumpled in my hand. "$19.87," the cashier finally announced, barely looking up as I handed over my carefully counted cash.

Outside, the chilly evening air wrapped around me as I gathered the flimsy plastic bags and began the short yet dreaded walk back to my tiny apartment. Each step seemed heavier than the last, and I silently cursed the third-floor walk-up I'd chosen for its cheap rent, forgetting the daily challenge it presented whenever I had groceries. The brown paper bag strained under the weight of my provisions, threatening to tear at any moment.

"Here, Miss Wells, let me give you a hand with that," a familiar voice called from behind me.

I turned to see Tom, the aging but kind building security guard, approaching with an amused but sympathetic grin. "Hey, Tom. Thanks, you're a lifesaver."

"Just doing my civic duty," he joked lightly, easily taking the heavier bag from my arms as we ascended the creaking staircase. "You ever think of ordering delivery?"

"You think if I could afford delivery, I'd be lugging groceries up three flights of stairs?" I shot back, laughing despite my embarrassment. "Besides, I'd miss our bonding moments."

"Right, right," Tom chuckled as we finally reached my door. "I'd miss them too. It's the highlight of my day, really."

I opened my door, taking the bag back and offering a grateful smile. "You're a lifesaver. I owe you."

"Just pay your rent on time and don't get evicted," he teased. "I've gotten used to you around here."

"Deal," I said warmly as I shut the door behind me.

I'd barely set the groceries down when my phone began buzzing loudly from the kitchen counter. I glanced curiously at the unknown number, a nervous flutter settling deep in my chest. Taking a deep breath, I swiped to answer.

"Hello?"

"Miss Harper Wells?" a crisp, authoritative voice inquired.

"Speaking," I replied hesitantly, instantly straightening my posture as if she could see my slouch through the phone.

"This is Linda Myers from Blackwell Industries. I'm calling to inform you that your application has been approved. Mr. Blackwell has personally selected you as his new assistant."

I stared blankly at the wall, my mouth hanging open as the words sank in. My heart immediately hammered violently, skipping several beats. "Blackwell Industries?" I repeated slowly, blinking like an idiot, as if saying it again might magically make it sound less terrifying. Spoiler alert: it didn't.

"Yes, Miss Wells," Linda replied patiently, clearly fighting the urge to sigh. "You'll be reporting directly to Mr. Elias Blackwell himself. Your first day is this Monday. Please be punctual—he doesn't tolerate lateness."

"Oh. Cool, cool. Monday. Seven sharp. Totally got it," I babbled, nodding vigorously as if she could somehow see through the phone. "No lateness. Understood. Thank you so much. Really. You're amazing."

She hung up without another word, probably eager to get away from my awkward over sharing—and I just stood there staring blankly at my screen, replaying the conversation in disbelief. Elias freaking Blackwell. How in the actual universe had I, queen of microwave burritos and missed due dates, landed a job as his assistant?

My gaze shifted helplessly to my kitchen counter, piled high with overdue bills, student loan reminders, and my embarrassingly small grocery haul. Well, desperate times and all that. My tiny apartment suddenly felt way smaller, the walls squeezing in like they knew I was freaking out.

But hey, maybe I'd finally be able to afford brand-name cereal again.

Baby steps, Harper. Baby steps toward glory—or, more realistically, inevitable humiliation and unemployment.

Elias

The expansive boardroom was cloaked in tension as I moved deliberately toward the head of the long, polished mahogany table. Massive floor-to-ceiling windows stretched imposingly behind me, framing a sweeping view of the city skyline—a deliberate reminder of the vast empire under my control. Ornate portraits of generations past lined the walls, each stern, watchful gaze reinforcing the weight of expectation and dominance.

My executives shifted nervously in their seats, none daring to meet my gaze. Morrison, directly to my right, adjusted his tie for the third time, sweat beading visibly at his temples.

"I assume," I began, my voice smooth and measured, slicing through the heavy silence, "you have an explanation for today's failure."

Morrison's face paled visibly, his nervous gaze darting around the table, searching for support that would never come. He cleared his throat awkwardly. "There were unforeseen complications, sir. Our contact backed out at the last minute, citing... personal reasons."

"Personal reasons," I echoed softly, deliberately allowing skepticism to seep into each syllable. "How inconvenient."

"I—I'll rectify the matter immediately, Mr. Blackwell," he hurriedly stammered, voice quivering slightly under my scrutiny. "I already have an alternative solution in mind."

"See that you do," I warned quietly, my voice a velvet-covered threat. "Your alternatives are rapidly dwindling, Morrison."

He swallowed audibly, nodding quickly. Beside him, Eleanor Bradford—a seasoned, stoic executive who rarely showed emotion—

shifted subtly in her seat, glancing down at her notes to avoid any association with Morrison's failure.

"Understood, sir," Morrison murmured, shrinking slightly beneath my stare.

I let my gaze drift slowly around the table, relishing the subtle scent of unease permeating the room, a raw satisfaction stirring beneath the surface.

"Now," I continued coolly, "if there's nothing else—"

An unfamiliar scent suddenly teased my senses—soft, warm, unmistakably human. Vanilla and lavender danced beneath something sweeter, brighter. It distracted me completely, intriguing and irritating me simultaneously. My wolf stirred with unexpected curiosity, immediately alert.

Turning slightly, my gaze fixed on the young woman hesitating at the doorway. Clearly flustered, strands of chestnut hair had escaped from her hastily tied ponytail, framing a face flushed deeply with embarrassment. The simplicity and slight dishevelment of her appearance stood in stark contrast to the carefully curated elegance of the boardroom.

When she realized I'd noticed her, she stepped forward awkwardly, gripping a battered file folder tightly in one hand. Her heart hammered visibly beneath the surface of her throat, sending another faint wave of that tempting scent drifting toward me.

"I—um, hi," she stammered, managing a forced, awkward smile as her gaze darted nervously around the luxurious room, clearly overwhelmed. "Sorry to interrupt. I'm Harper Wells. Your new assistant?"

I raised one eyebrow slowly, allowing my silence to stretch just long enough for her discomfort to deepen. Her scent intensified slightly, a tantalizing mix of nervous adrenaline and bold defiance. It stirred something feral deep within my chest, something far more dangerous than mere curiosity.

"You were expected fifteen minutes ago, Miss Wells," I finally spoke, voice deliberately calm yet edged with disapproval.

Her cheeks flushed an even deeper shade of scarlet. She opened her mouth to speak, closed it, then tried again. "Yes. About that—I'm really sorry. I got lost. Twice, actually. This building is..." She gestured vaguely, visibly floundering, eyes briefly widening at the imposing artwork and sheer scale around her. "It's huge. Like, unreasonably huge."

Morrison coughed, clearly suppressing an ill-timed laugh. I shot him a sharp glance, and he immediately dropped his gaze, color draining from his face again. Eleanor, however, allowed a rare moment of quiet amusement to flicker behind her otherwise impassive eyes, her lips twitching slightly before she hastily looked down at her notes.

Returning my gaze to Harper, I allowed myself a brief moment of curiosity at her sheer audacity—or perhaps reckless bravery—in being so openly candid. Her scent continued to tease, sweet and inviting, a dangerously tempting distraction.

"I'm sure your sense of direction will improve," I replied coolly, a faint edge of warning in my tone. "Quickly."

Her eyes widened briefly, and for a heartbeat, genuine defiance flared beneath the embarrassment, intensifying her scent even more enticingly. "Oh, absolutely," she said with forced brightness, holding my gaze firmly despite her obvious discomfort. "I'm already making mental notes. Landmarks, breadcrumbs...maybe I'll start carrying flares."

A stunned silence blanketed the room. Nobody had spoken to me like that, especially in front of my executives—in decades. Perhaps centuries. I narrowed my eyes slightly, studying her more closely, feeling a grudging respect beginning to form despite myself.

"Indeed," I murmured softly, thoughtfully, voice holding just a hint of intrigue. "I look forward to witnessing your improvement. Starting immediately."

"Right. Yes. Immediately," she echoed hastily, bobbing her head quickly. "Again, sorry for interrupting."

"Don't apologize," I replied smoothly, tilting my head slightly as I studied her flushed features, taking in every subtle nuance of her expressive face. "Just don't make it a habit."

Her shoulders straightened slightly, the defiant spark resurfacing as she met my gaze squarely for one daring second. "I won't."

"Good." I inclined my head slightly, signaling the end of our exchange. "Wait outside, Miss Wells. We'll speak further after this meeting."

She backed out quickly, pulling the heavy oak door closed behind her with perhaps more force than necessary, the loud thud resonating sharply in the ensuing silence.

For a long moment, nobody spoke, as though collectively holding their breath, waiting cautiously for my reaction.

I allowed a faint, deliberate smile to curve my lips—cold and calculated, devoid of warmth. "Well then. Where were we?"

As my executives hastily resumed their reports, my thoughts lingered unexpectedly on Harper Wells—human, late, irreverent. Her scent continued to tease my senses, sweet and reckless, disrupting centuries of careful self-control.

Perhaps this particular assistant would last longer than anticipated.

Yes. Perhaps she just might.

Harper

My heart was basically doing a drum solo in my chest as I speed-walked away from Elias's office. I collapsed into the ridiculously fancy leather chair at the small, super-organized desk they'd assigned me, trying to wrap my head around what had just happened.

"Cool, cool, totally nailed it," I muttered to myself, rolling my eyes at my epic ability to make the world's worst first impression. Nothing like sass-talking the CEO on day one. *Real smooth, Harper.*

Everything around me was polished, expensive, and *way* too clean—a stark reminder that I was probably going to break something irreplaceable by lunchtime. Compared to the tornado aftermath of my apartment, this place was practically an art gallery. And I did not belong in an art gallery.

A pang twisted sharply in my chest as memories of my cluttered, tiny apartment flooded in—stacks of unpaid bills, the eviction notice I'd narrowly avoided last month, the crushing sense of never quite being enough. The bitter taste of past failures still lingered, whispering doubts into my ear: 'You'll screw this up too, Harper. Just wait.'

Before I could spiral too deep into how spectacularly unqualified I was for this job, the phone rang, nearly sending me out of my skin.

I fumbled for the receiver, barely managing not to drop it. "Harper Wells," I squeaked, then cleared my throat to sound less like a panicked mouse. "I mean, hello. Harper Wells speaking."

Silence. Awkward, uncomfortable silence. Then his voice came through—smooth, deep, and annoyingly calm.

"Miss Wells, I need you in my office. Now."

The line clicked dead before I could answer. "Cool, cool. On my way," I muttered to absolutely no one.

Taking a deep breath, I smoothed my skirt and whispered a quick prayer to whatever deity handled awkward office interactions, hoping Elias Blackwell wouldn't eat me alive. Or fire me on my first day. Either seemed totally possible at this point.

"Okay, Harper," I whispered to myself, standing shakily and forcing my feet toward his door. "Time to fake it till you make it—or get fired spectacularly. Whichever comes first."

The door felt approximately six thousand pounds heavier this time as I shoved it open, stumbling awkwardly into Elias's domain like an uninvited house guest. Awesome. Elias stood by the massive windows, broad shoulders outlined dramatically against the fading afternoon sunlight, looking annoyingly perfect and totally intimidating. For a solid minute, he didn't even turn around, leaving me hanging in that awkward limbo of *'Do I say something, or do I just stand here and try not to breathe too loudly?'*

Finally, he spoke, still staring dramatically into the distance. "Miss Wells. Do you have any experience organizing corporate events? Specifically, high-stakes negotiations involving parties who dislike one another intensely?"

My eyes widened. What kind of question was that? "Uh, corporate events? High stakes?" I echoed brilliantly; brain-to-mouth filter officially disengaged. "Not exactly. Unless refereeing arguments between my best friends about who wore the outfit better counts—but I'm guessing that doesn't qualify, huh?"

He turned slightly, eyebrow raised, and I swear I saw something almost like amusement flicker across his usually unreadable face.

"Oddly enough," he said, voice low and annoyingly smooth, "it just might."

Wait, what? Seriously?

He moved deliberately to his desk, picked up a folder, and extended it toward me. I took a cautious step forward, grabbing the folder like it might bite, and definitely noticed the annoying flutter of nerves in my stomach when our fingers briefly brushed. Because of course. *Classic Harper.*

"These are the details you'll need," he continued, voice silky smooth but laced with an obvious warning. "I trust you'll handle it competently.

My reputation—and now yours—depends on it."

I swallowed hard, mouth moving without permission. "Right. Absolutely. No pressure at all."

His eyebrow arched higher. *Cue internal screaming.* "I mean—I'll do my best," I amended quickly, face heating up in a full-blown blush.

"See that you do, Miss Wells," Elias said, his tone dangerously gentle.

Clutching the folder against my chest like a shield, I bolted from his office for the second time today, heart pounding from nerves, embarrassment, and the lingering weirdness that came from Elias Blackwell actually kind-of-sort-of smiling at me.

Yeah, Monday was off to a great start.

Elias

As the door clicked shut behind Harper, I stared at the empty space she'd occupied moments before, a scowl forming slowly. Something about the lingering warmth of her presence grated on me, disrupting the carefully balanced control I'd perfected over centuries. Her casual irreverence, that oddly charming blend of awkwardness and humor—it was like a pebble lodged beneath layers of meticulously crafted armor, impossible to ignore and irritatingly persistent.

Her scent still lingered faintly in the air—warm, sweet vanilla mingled with something uniquely bright, like fresh citrus after a rainstorm. It stirred something deep within me, deep-rooted and unsettling, a reaction I hadn't experienced with any assistant in recent memory. The countless others who'd passed through these halls had come and gone without leaving so much as a ripple. Their fear had been palpable, predictable, easily dismissed. But Harper Wells, with her unfiltered mouth, nervous courage, and intoxicating scent, had managed to unsettle me in mere minutes.

I rubbed the bridge of my nose, deeply irritated at myself for noticing such trivial details. It was absurd—unacceptable, even. Dangerous.

My thoughts were abruptly interrupted by the harsh buzz of the phone on my desk. With a low growl of annoyance, I snatched up the receiver, answering sharply. "Blackwell."

"Sir." Lucien's voice was measured and calm as always, but today there was an unmistakable undercurrent of urgency that immediately sharpened my attention. "We've received credible intelligence about a potential threat to the upcoming negotiations. I strongly advise postponing any events or speaking engagements. Just for the time being, sir. The risk is significantly higher than anticipated."

I leaned back slowly, my jaw tightening with barely concealed irritation. It was always something. For centuries, threats had come and gone—rivals, enemies, those hungry for power or vengeance. I'd built this empire stone by stone, spilling blood when necessary, wielding fear as expertly as a blade. Danger was part of my existence, ingrained deeply into my bones. It was exhausting, but retreat was never an option.

"Who's behind this?" I asked quietly, eyes narrowing as I stared out the expansive windows at the sprawling city, deceptively peaceful beneath the golden glow of evening lights.

"Unknown," Lucien admitted reluctantly. "But whoever it is, they're targeting you specifically, Elias. This isn't about the business—it's personal."

Of course it was. It always was. Centuries had taught me that personal vendettas ran deeper than greed, burned hotter than ambition. For a fleeting moment, my mind wandered inexplicably back to Harper—her wide eyes, her awkward defiance, entirely out of her depth—and irritation surged anew. It wasn't my responsibility to concern myself with her ignorance. She'd either survive, or she'd fail spectacularly. Either outcome is inconsequential.

"We proceed," I said finally, voice cold and absolute, leaving no room for argument. "Increase security—double it. But we will not retreat. Whoever seeks to challenge me will quickly learn their error."

Lucien hesitated only briefly before answering. "Understood, sir."

The line disconnected, plunging my office back into silence, now heavy with my own unease. My gaze lingered on the spot where Harper had stood—nervous, defiant, reckless—utterly unaware of the perilous world she'd entered. Humans were fragile creatures, temporary sparks against the vast darkness of immortality, fleeting as stars in an eternal sky.

I rubbed the bridge of my nose again, releasing a slow, controlled breath as fatigue pressed down upon me. Harper Wells was a distraction I couldn't afford, a complication in an existence that demanded clarity and absolute control. Yet, for reasons I couldn't fathom, her intrusion into my life didn't feel entirely unwelcome.

I exhaled harshly; my jaw clenched. This was unacceptable. She was a temporary assistant, nothing more—a fleeting presence easily replaced.

But even as I reassured myself of that simple fact, I knew deep down Harper Wells already had complicated matters far more than I cared to admit.

Chapter 2

Settling Into Chaos

Harper

Three weeks at Blackwell Industries had felt like three entire lifetimes—and not the fun kind. Every morning, I was there by exactly 6:45 AM, twenty minutes before anyone actually expected me. Not because I was suddenly a punctual person (I wasn't), but because the thought of strolling in late and facing Elias Blackwell's death glare was enough to make me set alarms in triplicate. Seriously, the rumors about my boss? Totally undersold. He wasn't just intense; he was next-level scary.

Today, though, the crushing anxiety eased up a bit, thanks to the life-changing magic of payday. I clutched the thin envelope reverently, grinning stupidly at it like it contained a love letter rather than a bank statement. It felt almost criminal to earn this much money after just a few weeks of mostly trying not to break stuff—but hey, if it was wrong, lock me up. Who knew keeping a billionaire's coffee intact was such lucrative work?

"Miss Wells," a familiar voice suddenly said, jolting me out of my happy little fantasy and nearly causing my coffee mug to die a tragic death by gravity. I scrambled to catch it, clutching the paycheck guiltily to my chest.

"Oh! Linda, hey," I blurted, smiling sheepishly up at her.

Linda Myers stood there; tablet hugged tightly to her chest. Her warm chestnut hair, carefully styled into a neat, flawless bob, framed a face softened by gentle laugh lines and patient hazel eyes. Today, her usual cautious half-smile was warmer, friendlier, and the kindness radiating from her felt genuinely comforting. Something about Linda had always vaguely reminded me of my mother—maybe it was the quiet patience, the gentle warmth she offered freely, or just the unspoken sense that she understood more than she let on.

"Enjoying payday?" she asked gently, eyes twinkling knowingly as she glanced at the check still clutched protectively against my chest.

"Oh my god, you have no idea," I said, exhaling dramatically. I leaned forward conspiratorially, lowering my voice like it was some grand secret. "I'm officially upgrading from ramen to—wait for it—takeout. And not even the cheapest takeout. I'm talking full-price sushi rolls. Fancy, right?"

Linda laughed softly, shaking her head with genuine amusement, though the warmth in her gaze carried an unmistakable note of sympathy. "You're lasting longer than most of his assistants. Trust me, that's impressive."

"Oh, great. That's not unnerving at all," I joked weakly, giving her a thumbs-up that felt embarrassingly forced. "But hey, at least he hasn't fired me yet, right?"

She smiled gently, her eyes filled with empathy that reminded me again of my mother—patient and warm, never judgmental. "Trust me, the absence of a complaint from Mr. Blackwell is practically a glowing review."

"Fantastic," I said dryly, my voice dripping with sarcasm, though I couldn't stop the grateful smile tugging at my lips. "My greatest professional accomplishment is literally 'not annoying him enough to get fired.' Good to know I'm setting the bar nice and high."

Linda chuckled again, offering a reassuring pat on my shoulder as she turned to leave. "Keep it up, Harper. You're doing fine."

I watched her go, momentarily comforted, yet also strangely uneasy. I wasn't sure whether to feel proud or mildly concerned that simply surviving nearly a month without a formal complaint from my boss counted as success. But for now, I'd take it.

Go me, I guess.

By the time I packed up at the end of the day, I was already mentally mapping out my evening. The paycheck in my wallet felt like a tiny beacon of hope, and I had a plan: I'd drive the three hours to my parents' house, hand over a little cash to Mom and Dad, and maybe—just maybe—eat something that didn't come from a microwave.

The drive was a familiar one, though it had been months since I'd last made it. As I merged onto the highway, the city skyline faded into the rear-view mirror, replaced by rolling hills and the occasional grove of trees. The sun hung low in the sky, casting a golden glow over the landscape. I rolled down the windows, letting the crisp autumn air fill the car. The scent of fallen leaves and distant wood smoke brought a wave of nostalgia so sharp it almost hurt.

I hadn't been home in months. Not since the whole "moving to the city to chase my dreams" thing. My parents had been supportive, of course—Mom with her endless optimism and Dad with his quiet, brooding nods. But I knew they missed me. I missed them too, even if I didn't say it often enough.

The three-hour drive flew by in a blur of memories. I passed the old diner where I'd worked my first summer job, slinging pancakes and dodging flirtatious truckers. There was the gas station where my high school friends and I would buy candy bars and gossip about who was dating whom. And then, finally, the turn onto the gravel road that led to the house I grew up in.

The house itself was exactly as I remembered it: a cozy, slightly lopsided farmhouse with a wraparound porch and a roof that sagged just enough to give it character. The brown paint was peeling in places, and the garden out front was overgrown, but it was home. I pulled into the driveway, my tires crunching over the gravel, and sat there for a moment, just taking it all in.

The front door swung open before I could even get out of the car. Mom stood there, her hands on her hips and a wide grin on her face. She was wearing her favorite apron—the one with the daisies—and her hair was a little messier than usual, like she'd been baking all afternoon.

"Well, look who finally decided to grace us with her presence!" she called, her voice dripping with mock indignation. "Harper Wells, city girl extraordinaire!"

I laughed, climbing out of the car and grabbing my bag. "Hey, Mom. Miss me?"

"Oh, just a little," she said, pulling me into a tight hug. She smelled like cinnamon and vanilla, and for a moment, I felt like a kid again. "Your dad's inside. He's been brooding by the fireplace all day, pretending he's not excited to see you."

I grinned. "Sounds about right."

The inside of the house was just as I remembered it too. The walls were covered in family photos—me as a baby, me as an awkward teenager, me graduating from college—and the air smelled like wood smoke and freshly baked bread. Dad was, indeed, brooding by the fireplace, though he looked up when I walked in and gave me a small nod.

"Hey, kiddo," he said, his voice gruff but warm. "How's the city treating you?"

"Oh, you know," I said, dropping my bag by the door. "Same old, same old. Boss is still terrifying, but at least I'm not starving anymore."

Mom laughed, shaking her head. "Well, you're home now. And I made your favorite—pot roast."

I followed her into the kitchen, where the table was already set, and the smell of dinner was making my stomach growl. As we sat down to eat, I pulled out the envelope with the cash I'd brought for them and slid it across the table.

"Here," I said, trying to sound casual. "Just a little something to help out."

Mom's eyes softened, and she reached over to squeeze my hand. "Oh, honey, you don't have to do that."

"I know," I said, shrugging. "But I want to."

Dad didn't say anything, but he gave me one of his rare smiles, and that was enough.

As we ate, Mom filled me in on all the local gossip—who was getting married, who was getting divorced, who had accidentally set their garage on fire—and I found myself laughing harder than I had in weeks. Dad chimed in occasionally with his dry, sarcastic comments, and for the first time in a long time, I felt like I could breathe.

It's good to be home.

Elias

When Linda stepped into my office later that morning, she seemed noticeably less terrified than usual—almost composed, even—which was both curious and mildly irritating. Humans tended to wear their emotions openly, easily decipherable. Linda's fear was reliable, predictable, and, frankly, convenient. Today, though, something had shifted. Her posture was straighter, her tone steadier, and her eyes held a glimmer of something I couldn't immediately place. Confidence? Amusement? Whatever it was, it didn't belong there.

She hovered near the doorway, waiting politely for my invitation. I inclined my head slightly, signaling her forward, and she stepped inside with the kind of cautious grace that suggested she was still aware of the precariousness of her position. Good. She should be.

"How is Miss Wells working out, sir?" she asked carefully, clearly trying to keep her tone professionally neutral.

I silently regarded her for a moment, fingers steepled beneath my chin. "Define 'working out,' Linda," I replied dryly. "If you mean her ability to spill coffee, trip over nothing, and destroy expensive antiques, then I'd say she's performing exceptionally well."

Linda's cheeks flushed slightly, but she pressed onward bravely. "But beyond those minor incidents, sir?"

"Minor?" I echoed sharply, eyebrow arching. "Two coffee machines and a priceless Ming vase aren't exactly minor."

Linda visibly swallowed, regrouping quickly. "Of course, sir. My apologies. I'll replace them immediately."

"See that you do," I murmured, leaning back into my chair, irritation still simmering beneath the surface. "As for Miss Wells—she's…unusual."

Linda tilted her head, curiosity winning over caution. "Unusual in a good way, sir?"

"In an exceedingly irritating way," I corrected quietly, my gaze shifting to the window. The city sprawled below, a chaotic mess of humanity that I had long since learned to navigate with precision. Harper Wells, however, was a different kind of chaos—one I couldn't seem to control. "She's irreverent, clumsy, completely inappropriate—and yet strangely competent enough that firing her would seem premature. At least for now."

Linda's expression softened into something almost like amusement, quickly hidden behind professional neutrality. "So, you're satisfied, then?"

"I'm tolerant," I corrected sharply, my voice cutting through the air like a blade. "For the moment."

She nodded, lips twitching despite her best efforts. "I'll let Miss Wells know you're pleased."

"Do no such thing," I snapped sharply, irritation flaring. "Tell her instead to keep her chaos contained to her own desk."

Linda inclined her head quickly. "Understood, sir. I'll remind her we have a limited supply of antiques."

"You do that," I muttered darkly as she retreated, closing the door behind her with careful precision.

Alone again, I released a frustrated breath, jaw tightening as I stared out the window at the bustling city below. Harper Wells had captured my attention—an exceedingly rare feat—and it grated against every carefully controlled instinct I possessed. She was reckless, a walking disaster wrapped in awkward charm, and her presence was a growing annoyance, a fracture in my centuries-old façade.

It wasn't just her clumsiness, though that was certainly a factor. It was the way she seemed entirely unfazed by my presence, as though my reputation—my very existence—was nothing more than a mild inconvenience. She laughed too loudly, spoke too freely, and had a habit of looking at me as though she could see straight through the carefully constructed walls I had spent lifetimes building. It was infuriating.

And yet, there was something about her that I couldn't quite dismiss.

Her incompetence was undeniable, but so was her determination. She showed up early every day, despite her obvious disdain for mornings. She apologized profusely for every mistake, even as she made new ones. And, most baffling of all, she seemed genuinely unafraid of me. Not in the way Linda was unafraid today—no, Harper's lack of fear was born of something else entirely. Something I couldn't quite name.

It was profoundly unsettling, and yet, despite myself, undeniably intriguing.

As I stared out the window, my mind drifted back to a time I rarely allowed myself to revisit. Centuries ago, when the world was simpler and my walls were not yet so high, there had been another woman like Harper. Her name was Eleanora, and she had been a force of nature— wild, unpredictable, and utterly fearless. She had laughed in the face of danger, danced in the rain, and looked at me as though I were just a man, not the immortal creature I had become.

The memory came unbidden, sharp and vivid, as though it had happened yesterday. We were standing in a moonlit garden, the air thick with the scent of jasmine and the distant hum of cicadas. Eleanora's laughter rang out, bright and unrestrained, as she twirled in the grass, her bare feet leaving imprints in the dew.

"Eliaston," she called, her voice teasing, "are you just going to stand there like a statue, or are you going to dance with me?"

I leaned against a tree, arms crossed, watching her with a mixture of amusement and exasperation. "Dancing is hardly a productive use of time, Eleanora."

She stopped mid-twirl, her hands on her hips, and fixed me with a look that was equal parts challenge and mischief. "And brooding in the shadows is? Come on, live a little. You're not going to crumble into dust if you let yourself have fun for once."

I raised an eyebrow, my lips twitching despite myself. "You have a remarkable talent for oversimplifying things."

"And you have a remarkable talent for over complicating them," she shot back, grinning. She strode over to me, her dress swishing around her ankles, and grabbed my hand before I could protest. "One dance, Eliaston. That's all I'm asking. Unless you're afraid?"

I scoffed, but I didn't pull away. "Afraid? Of you?"

"Of letting go," she said softly, her tone shifting. Her eyes, usually so full of laughter, were suddenly serious. "You carry the weight of the world on your shoulders, Eliaston. But you don't have to. Not with me."

For a moment, I was speechless. Eleanora had a way of cutting through my defenses, of seeing the parts of me I kept hidden even from myself. It was equal parts terrifying and exhilarating.

"You don't know what you're asking," I said finally, my voice low.

"I do," she insisted, her grip on my hand tightening. "I'm asking you to trust me. To let me in. Just for a moment."

I hesitated, torn between the instinct to pull away and the overwhelming desire to give in. In the end, it was her smile that decided it—bright, unwavering, and filled with a warmth I hadn't realized I was craving.

"One dance," I conceded, and her face lit up like the sun.

She pulled me into the clearing, her laughter ringing out again as we moved together under the moonlight. For the first time in centuries, I felt alive. Truly alive.

That night was one of the few moments in my long existence where I had allowed myself to be vulnerable. And it had cost me everything.

Eleanora's fearlessness had been her undoing. She had died because of me, because of the world I inhabited, and I had sworn never to let anyone close again. The pain of losing her had been unbearable, a wound that never fully healed. And so, I had built walls—thick, impenetrable walls—to ensure that no one could ever hurt me like that again.

And yet, here was Harper Wells, with her irreverent humor and clumsy charm, stirring up memories I had buried long ago. She was nothing like Eleanora, and yet she was everything like her. The way she laughed, the way she looked at me—it was all too familiar, and it made my chest ache with a pain I hadn't felt in centuries.

I turned away from the window, shaking my head, forcing the memory away. Harper Wells was not Eleanora. She was a nuisance, a distraction, and nothing more but a problem. But she was a problem I wasn't ready to solve. Not yet. For now, I would tolerate her presence, if only to satisfy my own curiosity. But the moment she became more trouble than she was worth, I would remove her from my life without a second thought.

Until then, I would watch. And wait. And, perhaps, learn.

Harper

Lunch break finally arrived, saving me from another four hours of accidentally destroying priceless artifacts and narrowly avoiding Elias Blackwell's signature death-glare. I practically bolted out of the building, stepping into the sunlight with a relieved gasp, like someone who'd just survived a hostage negotiation. The city buzzed around me—chaotic, loud, and blissfully normal after the sterile intensity of Blackwell Industries.

I spotted her immediately. Sophie was impossible to miss, even in a crowd. Her vivid red hair glinted in the sunlight like a warning beacon, and she was lounging dramatically at our favorite café, her arms thrown wide as if she were auditioning for a soap opera.

"Oh my God, you survived three whole weeks!" she cried, enveloping me in an unnecessarily dramatic hug. "Honestly, Harp, I lost money betting against you!"

"Wow, Soph, your support is overwhelming," I deadpanned, but I couldn't hide my grin as we sat down. "Seriously, though, it's a miracle. But hey, I'm determined to keep this job—at least until I can afford groceries that aren't store-brand ramen and sadness-flavored coffee."

Sophie's eyes widened dramatically as I slid the menu toward her, savoring the moment. "Lunch is totally on me," I declared proudly, gesturing grandly like a game-show host. "That's right, I'm officially rich enough for avocado toast and stupidly overpriced iced coffees. Maybe even extra guac, if you're feeling fancy."

She gasped, clutching her imaginary pearls dramatically. "Who are you and what have you done with my perpetually broke best friend?"

"Oh, her?" I grinned, shrugging dramatically. "Yeah, she sold her soul to corporate America. Turns out, the devil doesn't wear Prada, he wears Armani, hates coffee stains with a fiery passion, and has perfected RMF to a terrifying degree."

Sophie tilted her head, confused. "RMF?"

"Resting Murder Face," I explained, dead serious. "It's like resting bitch face, but way scarier, and probably lethal."

Sophie burst into laughter, leaning forward conspiratorially. "Seriously, how scary is Elias Blackwell up close? Is it as bad as they say?"

"Worse," I said immediately, lowering my voice dramatically. "He can probably set fires with his stare. I accidentally broke two coffee machines and an antique vase already—and I swear, every time, he looks at me like he's mentally picturing creative ways to hide my body."

Sophie snorted, her eyes dancing with laughter. "Well, at least you're still employed. That's gotta mean something, right?"

"Yeah, like maybe he's waiting to fire me spectacularly in front of everyone," I mused aloud. "He's probably just biding his time, thinking of the perfect way to ruin my life."

We laughed together, and for a few minutes, the weight of debt, overdue bills, and Elias Blackwell's intimidating presence faded into the background. But even as we joked, my mind stubbornly replayed his piercing golden gaze, wondering just how long my newfound good fortune would last.

Sophie and I had been inseparable since we were kids, but it wasn't just because we were best friends. She was my sister in every way that mattered. When we were thirteen, her parents died in a car accident, and mine didn't hesitate to take her in. "Family's family," my mom had said, like it was the simplest thing in the world. And just like that, Sophie became a permanent fixture in our lives—loud, chaotic, and utterly irreplaceable.

She'd always been the dramatic one, the one who could turn even the most mundane moment into a scene from a movie. I, on the other hand, was the cautious one, the one who overthought everything and tried to keep us out of trouble. It didn't always work. Sophie had a knack for dragging me into her schemes, but somehow, we balanced each other out.

"Remember that time you tried to bake cookies for Mom's birthday and set the kitchen on fire?" Sophie asked, as if reading my mind. She smirked, stirring her iced coffee with a straw. "And I convinced you to tell her it was a science experiment gone wrong?"

"Yeah, and she totally bought it," I said, rolling my eyes. "Until Dad found the recipe book with 'Happy Birthday Mom' written on the cover."

Sophie laughed, the sound bright and familiar. "God, your parents were saints for putting up with us."

"They still are," I said, smiling. "Mom still calls you her 'bonus daughter,' you know."

Sophie's expression softened, and for a moment, she looked almost serious. "I don't know what I would've done without them. Without you."

I reached across the table and squeezed her hand. "You'd have been fine. You're Sophie freaking Carter. You'd have charmed your way into someone else's family by now."

She grinned, her usual bravado returning. "True. But I'm glad I didn't have to."

We spent the rest of lunch swapping stories and catching up, the way we always did. Sophie told me about her latest art project—a series of paintings inspired by "the existential dread of modern capitalism"— and I filled her in on the latest Blackwell Industries drama. By the time we finished our overpriced avocado toast, I felt almost human again.

But as we said goodbye and I headed back to the office, the weight of my new reality settled over me once more. Elias Blackwell's golden eyes seemed to follow me everywhere, a constant reminder that my newfound stability was fragile at best. Still, as I stepped into the elevator, I couldn't help but smile.

Elias

I sat at the head of the expansive mahogany conference table, fingertips pressed lightly together, watching in cool silence as my security team argued among themselves. The air in the room was thick with tension, a familiar, almost comforting discomfort. Lucien stood near the door, arms crossed rigidly, his eyes scanning the room with practiced vigilance. Marcus sat silently to my right, a stone fortress of calm, listening intently but betraying no reaction.

Across from me, Isabella leaned forward sharply, her voice low and edged with frustration. "This isn't an idle threat, Elias. Someone out there wants blood—yours specifically. We need to reconsider your public engagements. Limit your exposure."

I let her words linger, staring impassively back at her. "We have never cowered before. Doing so now would signal weakness."

Her eyes narrowed. "And ignoring this could get you killed."

I raised an eyebrow, my voice deceptively soft. "Many have tried. Yet here I am."

A strained silence settled over the table, thick and unyielding. Finally, Lucien cleared his throat cautiously. "Security has already been increased, sir. We have installed additional checkpoints, cameras, and a second perimeter. There's little more we can do without severely disrupting the negotiations."

"Then triple it," I ordered, coldly dismissive. "I want eyes and ears everywhere. Leave nothing unchecked."

Lucien inclined his head respectfully. "Of course, sir."

Isabella rose swiftly, her posture rigid. "Just remember, Elias.

Confidence is admirable. Arrogance is deadly."

"Noted," I replied coldly, dismissing her with my tone as much as my words. She stood, clearly irritated, and exited without another word.

One by one, they filed out, leaving me alone in the oppressive silence of the glass-walled conference room. I exhaled slowly, the weight of centuries pressing on my shoulders. How many more threats would I need to extinguish before this existence became unbearably tedious? How many more betrayals, how much more blood?

The room fell silent as the last of my team filed out, leaving me alone with the weight of their warnings. I exhaled slowly, my gaze drifting to the glass walls of the conference room. Beyond them, the office buzzed with its usual rhythm—mundane, predictable, and utterly human.

Then I caught it: a faint, warm scent cutting through the sterile air. Sweet, like sugar and sunlight, and entirely out of place in my world. Harper.

I turned just in time to see her walk past, oblivious to the tension she'd interrupted. She was clutching a small bakery bag, her face lit up with that infuriatingly cheerful smile. For a moment, I allowed myself to watch her, torn between irritation and something I refused to name.

A gentle knock startled me from my thoughts, and before I could respond, the door swung open. Harper stepped tentatively inside, her cautious expression slipping instantly into something brighter when she saw I was alone. Her scent filled the space again, rich with sweetness and warmth. Infuriatingly pleasant.

"Hey," she started awkwardly, holding up the bakery bag as though it were an offering. "So, uh, I brought you something. It's a pastry—a danish, actually. It's kind of amazing and way too overpriced, but like, worth it. Thought maybe you'd, you know… want one."

I stared at her silently, momentarily speechless by the sheer audacity of her gesture. Her smile faltered slightly under my scrutiny, her cheeks turning a faint pink as she shifted nervously, obviously second-guessing herself.

"Did I interrupt something super important?" she asked hesitantly. "Because I saw the whole intimidating crew leaving. Definitely looked like serious, end-of-the-world stuff."

I arched an eyebrow at her blunt assessment. "End-of-the-world stuff," I echoed dryly. "Interesting phrasing."

She shrugged, sheepish yet undeterred. "You just have that look—

y'know, 'we're planning world domination and possibly crushing our enemies by lunch' type of vibe."

For a long moment, I stared at her, the absurdity of the moment slowly sinking in. This woman, utterly oblivious to the shadowy complexities of my life, had waltzed into a conversation about potential assassination attempts with…pastries. Her audacity was either astonishingly brave or dangerously naïve. Perhaps both.

I reached out and took the bakery bag from her grasp, deliberately ignoring the brief, electric warmth of her fingertips brushing mine. Opening it, I glanced down at the pastry nestled within—golden, flaky, dusted lightly with powdered sugar. Ridiculous.

Yet I found myself murmuring, almost grudgingly, "Thank you, Miss Wells."

Her expression brightened instantly, her smile wide and disarmingly sincere. "No problem, Boss. Figured maybe carbs would lighten your whole broody situation. Everyone's nicer after sugar. It's science."

I stared at her blankly, torn between genuine annoyance and the faint stirrings of amusement I refused to acknowledge. "My 'broody situation'?"

She grinned broadly, entirely undeterred by my tone. "Yep. You know—whole intimidating-boss-vibe thing you've got going on."

I shook my head slightly, irritation warring with reluctant amusement. "Careful, Miss Wells. You're skating dangerously close to insubordination."

She flashed me a quick, playful salute. "Noted, Boss. Enjoy the pastry."

With a final cheerful wave, she spun around and walked out of the conference room, leaving behind the lingering scent of sugar, warmth, and reckless optimism.

I sat back, staring down at the danish in its delicately crinkled paper bag. For a moment, a fraction of a second, my resolve softened—before I quickly snapped it shut again, irritated by the slip. Harper Wells was trouble, a brightly burning ember tossed carelessly into a centuries-old darkness. If I wasn't careful, she might just ignite something I wasn't prepared to extinguish.

I sighed heavily, taking a reluctant bite of the pastry and grimacing at how annoyingly delicious it was. That woman was going to be the absolute death of me, one way or another.

I worked through the night, my office lit only by the muted glow of my computer screen and the faint pulse of city lights that bled through the wide, panoramic windows. Time meant little—minutes stretched into hours without notice, the darkness deepening around me until even the city's heartbeat seemed distant, subdued.

A faint sound—a scrape, barely audible—caught my attention. My body went still, every nerve alert, senses sharpening instinctively. I lifted my head, inhaling deeply, drawing the air slowly into my lungs. My nostrils flared slightly. There it was: sweat, adrenaline, and the sharp, bitter tang of silver.

Danger.

Before the attacker even emerged from the shadows, I was on my feet, eyes narrowing, a low growl building deep in my chest. The wolf within me woke instantly, uncoiling from beneath layers of human restraint, pacing restlessly beneath my skin.

He stepped out from behind the cabinet by the far wall, swift and silent, dressed in black tactical gear, his face partially obscured by a dark mask. He lunged forward, silver blade glinting in the pale, artificial glow of my desk lamp. The wolf snarled louder, demanding blood, and my body responded instantly, moving fluidly to intercept him.

He swung the blade viciously toward my chest, and I twisted sideways, narrowly avoiding the deadly arc. The tip caught me just below my collarbone, slicing through fabric and flesh in one sharp, white-hot flash of pain. I growled through gritted teeth, my vision sharpening as anger surged through my veins, the familiar heat of the wound intensifying my fury.

Instinct took over. In one swift motion, I caught his wrist, twisting hard until the bones strained beneath my grip. His breath hissed through clenched teeth, eyes wide, the pain evident despite his attempts to suppress it.

"Who sent you?" I snarled, voice low, rumbling with raw menace.

He jerked violently, desperate, pulling another blade from his belt and driving it toward my ribs. Anticipating the move, I spun him around and slammed him brutally against the glass wall. The weapon fell from his grip, clattering sharply to the floor.

"Who?" I demanded again, tightening my grip until his pulse fluttered helplessly beneath my fingers. His eyes burned with defiance, but fear lurked behind it—a prey's terror, unmistakable.

"Kill me," he spat through his mask, breath ragged. "I won't talk."

My lips pulled back slightly, exposing teeth sharp enough to make him flinch. "You're nothing but a pawn," I growled, disgust creeping into my voice. "A messenger sent by a coward. You're not even worth killing."

For a moment he stared at me, uncertainty flickering across his face. Seeing the hesitation, I loosened my grip just enough, baiting him. Predictably, he seized the chance, breaking free and stumbling toward the shattered window, his desperation overtaking his pride.

He glanced back once, eyes wide, his breath fogging rapidly in the cool morning air.

"Tell whoever sent you," I said quietly, coldly, "that next time, I won't let their messenger live."

Without another word, he threw himself from the window, disappearing into the pre dawn shadows below.

Blood trickled hotly down my chest, soaking through the torn fabric, pooling silently on the polished marble floor beneath me. I stood there in silence, listening to my furious heartbeat echoing in my ears.

Someone had made their intentions clear tonight. It was a challenge—a direct threat to me and my pack. To my territory.

I bared my teeth slightly, tasting the copper tang of blood and betrayal.

"Let them come."

Harper

I didn't normally do this whole "getting to work at ungodly hours" thing, but insomnia was kicking my butt lately, and honestly, there were only so many episodes of bad reality TV I could watch before I started questioning my life choices. So here I was, strolling into Blackwell Industries at 5:15 AM, my coffee held like a precious lifeline as I yawned into my sleeve, eyes barely open.

The building was eerily quiet at this hour—no bustling footsteps, no ringing phones, no terrifyingly stern assistants stalking through the corridors. Just me and the faint hum of fluorescent lights, flickering half-heartedly as though annoyed I'd interrupted their nap time.

I stepped out of the elevator onto Elias's floor, immediately noticing something was off. First clue: the distinct chill in the air, courtesy of a broken window at the far end of the hall. Glass shards sparkled on the marble floor, catching the pale glow of morning twilight and creating a scene straight out of one of those true-crime documentaries I always regretted watching at midnight.

"Oh, that's comforting," I muttered, clutching my coffee tighter and stepping gingerly over the glass. "Just your everyday shattered window. Totally normal."

The closer I got to Elias's office, the faster my pulse ticked up, intuition screaming that something was very, very wrong. His door hung slightly ajar, another clear warning sign because Elias Blackwell did not do casual entrances.

I hesitated, my hand hovering over the door handle. "Don't be a coward, Harper," I whispered to myself, pushing the door slowly open.

The sight in front of me froze me solid. Broken glass scattered across the floor in Elias's office, glittering under the dim lights like ice crystals strewn carelessly across black water. My pulse skipped instantly into a frantic rhythm. I swallowed hard, hesitating for just a heartbeat before stepping gingerly through the chaos, dread building with every careful step.

Elias sat at his desk, chair pushed back slightly, head tilted back in obvious pain. His normally flawless shirt was shredded and hanging open, stained with dark red that glistened sickeningly against his chest. Beneath the ruined fabric, inked patterns curled and twisted vividly across his skin—dark, elegant tattoos covering the smooth, muscular planes of his torso, traveling upward toward his collarbones in a symphony of intricate designs I couldn't quite decipher in the dimness. Symbols and shapes seemed to twist gracefully across his chest and collarbones, accentuating his defined muscles, tracing down toward his ribs.

For a heartbeat, I couldn't look away—captivated and horrified in equal measure. His breathing was slow, controlled, but shallow. My pulse kicked up another notch, worry slicing through my curiosity.

He hadn't noticed me yet—his eyes were closed tightly, jaw clenched, and even in pain, his face retained that dark, dangerous beauty that always made my stomach flip in confusing ways. I swallowed nervously, taking a cautious step forward.

"Um, Mr. Blackwell?" I finally managed, voice barely above a whisper. "Is that your blood or someone else's? Because, uh…either way, it looks pretty bad."

His eyes snapped open instantly, fixing me with an intense stare, golden irises blazing in a way that left me feeling suddenly vulnerable and completely out of my depth.

The Attack

Elias

My eyes snapped open, instantly alert at the faint sound of Harper's voice. Pain radiated sharply from the wound just beneath my collarbone—a burning sensation that burrowed deep beneath my skin, searing and relentless. Silver. It felt like molten metal twisting brutally through muscle and bone, the familiar agony threatening to shred whatever remained of my composure. I bit back a growl, pressing a hand firmly against the jagged tear, desperately hoping sheer pressure could dull the torture enough to think clearly.

It couldn't.

The door stood open, and Harper hovered uncertainly in the doorway, eyes wide, frozen mid-step like a deer caught in headlights. Her expression rapidly shifted between shock, embarrassment, and genuine concern; emotions so plainly visible on her face that they felt almost tangible in the thick air. Her heartbeat echoed frantically—fast, erratic, panicked—filling my senses until it was nearly deafening. I could smell the adrenaline pouring off her, mingled with her usual scent of vanilla and lavender, creating a heady cocktail of fear and fascination that threatened to overwhelm my already strained self-control.

Her gaze traced downward slowly, clearly without conscious thought, lingering on the complex dark tattoos inked across my exposed chest. The intricate symbols woven carefully across muscle and sinew spoke silently of centuries past wars won, losses endured, memories buried deep. Harper's cheeks flushed vividly as she stared, the heat of arousal adding a new dimension to the tantalizing mixture swirling around her.

She shifted awkwardly from one foot to the other, clutching a cardboard pastry box and steaming cup of coffee as if they were shields against whatever darkness she'd unwittingly entered.

"Is that…your blood, or someone else's?" she asked once more, her voice shaking, stubborn determination pushing through fear, refusing to let silence linger.

I straightened slowly, swallowing a fresh wave of agony that surged viciously through me. I drew on centuries of practiced restraint, carefully masking my discomfort behind a cold, indifferent façade.

"It's mine," I said evenly, voice deceptively calm despite the storm raging beneath my skin. "You shouldn't be here yet, Miss Wells."

She blinked, clearly thrown off-balance by my matter-of-fact tone. Yet, against all reason, she took another tentative step forward, eyes darting nervously between my bloodied shirt, the shattered glass littering the floor, and the now obvious weapon embedded just beneath my skin.

"Right. Right." Her head nodding uncontrollably. "Okay. But you look, like…seriously hurt," she persisted awkwardly, her voice wavering slightly. "Should I call someone? An ambulance? Security? Maybe your mom?"

Despite the pain, the absurdity of her final suggestion nearly drew a bitter laugh from me. My mother had been dead nearly four centuries, but Harper couldn't possibly understand that. She couldn't understand any of this—and that was precisely why she shouldn't be here.

"No," I snapped sharply, immediately regretting the venomous edge as she flinched slightly, startled by my harshness. I exhaled slowly, forcing my voice to be softer, gentler, though only slightly. "That won't be necessary."

Her eyes narrowed, suspicion mingling stubbornly with concern. "But you're bleeding everywhere. I'm no doctor, but I'm pretty sure that's not normal."

Normal. How little she knew.

I glanced down at the wound, frustration simmering dangerously beneath the surface. The blade remained partially buried, its silver edges biting viciously, preventing any chance of immediate healing. Without hesitation, I wrapped my fingers firmly around the hilt and, gritting my teeth, pulled it free with a single brutal, practiced motion.

Blood sprayed in a dark crimson arc, splattering across my pristine desk, mingling obscenely with paperwork and expensive stationery. The sharp metallic scent filled my nostrils, dizzying and coppery. Pain roared through me, white-hot, nearly blinding. Yet, aside from a tightly controlled exhale, I offered no reaction, no hint of weakness.

"Oh my God—" Harper gasped, stumbling backward, her hands shaking so violently the coffee sloshed dangerously close to spilling. Her face drained instantly of color, leaving her eyes enormous and bright with horror. "You just—are you serious? Who does that?"

"Someone who doesn't have the luxury of waiting," I growled, breath hitching involuntarily as I pressed the palm of my hand firmly against the gushing wound. I stared at her, eyes narrowing. "I told you, Miss Wells—leave."

For a heartbeat, I thought she might obey. But instead, her chin lifted stubbornly, defiance burning behind the fear. "You know what? No. You can't just sit here bleeding all over your fancy furniture and expect me to pretend this is fine. Because it's definitely not fine."

She stepped closer, her voice trembling with bravery she clearly didn't fully feel. "Let me help, Mr. Blackwell. Please."

For the first time, I hesitated, feeling the subtle cracks form in the armor I'd built so carefully over centuries. I watched her closely, studying her face, searching for deceit, finding only genuine, stubborn kindness.

"Miss Wells," I finally said, voice lowered dangerously, soft yet edged with warning. "If you insist on staying, make yourself useful. Otherwise, leave me."

Harper

I stared at Elias for another long, stunned moment, the bloody dagger gleaming ominously against the polished wood of his desk. My mind felt stuck, looping the same useless thought on repeat: *He just pulled a freaking knife out of his own chest.*

I mean, who even does that?

Shaking myself out of the shocked trance, I stepped forward, setting my coffee and pastry box carefully onto his wrecked, blood-spattered desk. The rich scent of coffee and raspberry pastry mixed bizarrely with the sharp tang of blood and sweat, twisting my stomach into knots.

"Useful it is, then," I muttered nervously, mostly to myself, needing the sound of my voice to anchor me to reality. Elias simply stared at me, eyes narrowed, clearly unimpressed by my awkward bravery.

I spun quickly on my heels, forcing my shaking legs into action. My breath came in short bursts as I hurried toward the small kitchen at the far end of the hallway. Adrenaline buzzed through me, mixing uneasily with the surreal disbelief that this was my life now—fetching first-aid kits for my bleeding, insanely intimidating boss at five-thirty in the morning.

I rummaged frantically through the cabinets, finally pulling out the white plastic case marked with a bold red cross. Grabbing a handful of napkins, I wet them hastily under cold water, trying to keep myself steady even as my heart raced wildly in my chest. With one final deep breath, I closed my eyes, forcing some composure into my chaotic thoughts.

"You've got this, Harper," I whispered shakily to myself, clutching the kit tightly. "Just breathe. It's just your boss—covered in tattoos, bleeding all over his expensive office, and acting way too calm about the knife he just ripped out of his chest. Totally normal. Completely fine."

I exhaled sharply, squared my shoulders, and hurried back toward the madness I'd left behind.

My heart thundered as I walked back into Elias's office, gripping the first aid kit in one hand and damp towels in the other. He sat perfectly still, leaning back heavily in his chair. His eyes were closed, his jaw tightly clenched, and it was evident from the doorway that pain had prominently marked his features, accentuating every angle.

I froze momentarily, taking in the raw vulnerability of his posture. His torn shirt revealed intricate tattoos woven across his powerful chest and shoulders—dark lines and strange symbols etched into bronzed skin, winding gracefully through dried trails of crimson blood. I swallowed hard, pulse fluttering anxiously, and gathered every scrap of courage I had left.

"Okay," I said softly, clearing my throat as I approached hesitantly. "I found a first-aid kit. It looks...official enough." My voice wavered awkwardly, the joke falling flat in the heavy silence. Elias glanced up slowly, eyes piercing and wary, watching me carefully as I moved toward him.

"You don't have to do this, Miss Wells," he muttered quietly, clearly uncomfortable beneath the thin veneer of control he struggled to maintain.

"Yeah, well, you look like you just fought a war," I said gently, kneeling cautiously beside him. "I'm guessing you lost—badly."

He gave a short, humorless laugh, eyes darkening slightly with something unreadable. "Not quite."

I pulled out antiseptic wipes and gauze pads, then paused, eyeing the wound apprehensively. Blood had congealed around the jagged cut, angry and raw, and something silverish glinted faintly in the torn flesh. My stomach twisted sharply, but I swallowed hard, forcing my hands to remain steady.

"So, um," I started nervously, trying to distract myself from fainting or throwing up—both equally likely at this point— "you wanna tell me what happened here?"

He stayed silent a beat too long, and I glanced up to find him staring intently at my face, assessing something I couldn't read.

"A minor disagreement," he finally answered coolly.

I raised an eyebrow skeptically, dabbing cautiously at the dried blood around his wound. "Yeah, clearly just a casual office spat. Does HR know about your disagreements?"

Another flicker of reluctant amusement crossed his face before he masked it. "You'd be surprised."

I bit my lip, focusing back on the wound, trying desperately to keep my hands steady despite the unsettling intensity of his gaze. "Look, I know it's not exactly my place—but are you sure you don't want me to call someone? Security? A doctor? Your mom?"

"My mother's been dead for centuries, Miss Wells," Elias replied dryly, a faint smirk tugging at the corner of his lips. "But thank you for the thoughtful suggestion."

I blinked, stunned into silence for a heartbeat, then shook my head slightly. "Oh—right, cool. Centuries. Got it. Totally normal thing to say." I swallowed nervously, refocusing on cleaning the wound. "Do you always make a habit of fighting at the crack of dawn?"

"Trouble rarely keeps convenient hours," he murmured darkly, muscles tightening slightly under my fingertips.

Carefully, with far more tenderness than I'd thought myself capable of, I began gently wiping away the dried blood, trying desperately not to flinch as I felt his muscles tense further beneath my touch. Elias inhaled sharply, jaw clenching tightly in stoic silence.

"Almost done," I whispered softly, glancing upward anxiously, meeting his gaze for just a brief moment.

His eyes were intense, shadowed by something that looked suspiciously like vulnerability, something clearly unfamiliar to him. He nodded slowly, jaw tightening again as I gently pressed gauze firmly against the wound.

"There," I said softly, stepping back, slightly breathless. "You're, uh, patched up. Not pretty, but better than bleeding all over your super fancy floor."

He exhaled slowly, tension draining slightly from his shoulders. "Thank you, Miss Wells."

I blinked, startled by the quiet sincerity in his voice. He wasn't exactly the kind of guy who threw around casual thank-you's. My mouth moved faster than my brain, desperate to fill the silence.

"You could probably just call me Harper now—or Harps, or Miss Harper...or" I rambled awkwardly, immediately regretting every syllable as heat flooded my cheeks. "You know what, scratch that. Forget I said anything."

Elias exhaled slowly, a faint flicker of amusement briefly breaking through his usual icy composure. "Harper." His voice softened unexpectedly, carrying a faint, reluctant warmth I'd never heard from him before. For the briefest second, his eyes met mine directly, piercing and unguarded, revealing a vulnerability he usually hid behind walls of ice and authority. But just as quickly, his gaze slid away, the familiar mask slipping back into place as he quietly said, "That'll be all."

"Right. Great. Cool, cool—I'll just, uh, leave now."

I hurried from his office, heart hammering wildly, fully aware that his gaze followed me every clumsy step of the way.

Elias

I watched Harper hurry from my office, her heartbeat thundering in my ears until it gradually faded into silence. Her scent lingered stubbornly, weaving itself into the fabric of my senses—a mixture of nervousness, coffee, and the unmistakable sweetness of raspberry pastry. It was disturbingly pleasant, irritatingly so. I growled softly to myself, fighting back the lingering urge to follow after her, to ensure she hadn't inadvertently drawn any more danger upon herself.

Pain pulsed insistently beneath the bandages she'd carefully applied, the silver-inflicted wound already beginning its slow, agonizing healing process. Silver always took its time, the burn deeper than skin and muscle, sinking right down to my bones. But Harper's hesitant, gentle touch had somehow eased a deeper ache, leaving behind an unsettling calm. I rubbed a hand roughly over my face, irritated by my own weakness.

She was reckless, impulsive—everything I despised and yet inexplicably craved. The thought of her stumbling blindly into danger again sent a spike of fear through me, sharp and unrelenting. I couldn't let it happen again. Not to her.

"Get it together," I muttered darkly, scolding myself for indulging such thoughts. Harper was a temporary presence—human, fragile, and far too innocent for the dangerous games already at play. Allowing her to remain close was a risk I couldn't afford.

Yet even as I warned myself against attachment, my eyes fell on the small box she'd left behind, still resting on the blood-smeared desk. With a sigh of reluctant curiosity, I reached over and opened it. Inside sat the raspberry Danish, the scent sugary and tantalizing, mixing absurdly with the copper tang of dried blood.

Shaking my head, I tore off a small piece, tasting it slowly. My jaw tightened in annoyance even as I savored it. I took another reluctant bite, savoring it slowly, a subtle warmth spreading through my chest. The sweetness reminded me of her—unwelcome yet strangely comforting. I growled under my breath, irritated by how effortlessly she'd slipped past my defenses.

"Damn it," I muttered, pinching the bridge of my nose, frustration battling with reluctant appreciation. "Still delicious."

For just a moment, I allowed myself to rest, placing my head against the cool, hard surface of the desk. Exhaustion swept through me, a bone-deep weariness clawing at my senses, more relentless than I'd ever admit aloud. Closing my eyes, I surrendered briefly to the slow, steady rhythm of my own breathing, allowing my body time to knit back together.

It felt like only moments later when the sound of hushed voices and careful footsteps stirred me awake. My eyes snapped open immediately, instincts sharp, senses flooding back to full alertness. Sunlight streamed harshly through the cracked window, illuminating shattered glass scattered across the floor, glittering like fractured stars.

Lucien stood at the threshold of my office, grim faced, assessing the damage with narrow eyes. Beside him, two members of housekeeping hovered nervously, brooms and dustpans in hand, glancing uncertainly between him and me.

"Lucien," I growled hoarsely, sitting up straight. "What is the meaning of this?"

"Harper called," he said smoothly, tone carefully neutral, though his eyes betrayed mild curiosity. "She said your office had been…compromised. Asked us to come immediately."

I scowled, irritation flaring briefly before fading into reluctant acceptance. Of course she had. Leave it to Harper Wells, reckless and impulsive, to take matters into her own hands.

"How thoughtful," I muttered dryly, rising stiffly to my feet. "Remind me to thank her for her…initiative."

Lucien's brow lifted subtly. "You seem to be recovering well, given the extent of the damage."

"Yes," I murmured sharply, glancing down at the fresh bandages that now concealed my tattoos and the wound beneath. "It could have been worse."

Lucien's gaze sharpened slightly, stepping closer as he lowered his voice, concern threading through his carefully chosen words. "Elias, whoever did this clearly knows your vulnerabilities—knows exactly how to hurt you."

"Yes," I murmured darkly, my jaw tightening with quiet fury. "And I intend to find out exactly who told them."

Lucien's eyes narrowed thoughtfully, considering my words carefully before speaking again. "The attacker?"

I sighed, exhaustion returning like a weight across my shoulders. "Gone. He was only a messenger. But he's delivered his message."

"And our response?" Lucien asked carefully, watching me closely.

My gaze drifted toward the doorway Harper had passed through earlier, remembering the hesitant courage in her touch and the warmth of her concern. An uneasy heaviness settled in my chest as the realization struck me—had she arrived just moments earlier, she would have walked straight into danger, entirely unprepared and vulnerable. My jaw tightened, and I felt an unsettling surge of protectiveness mingling with my growing irritation.

She was already becoming a liability; one I couldn't afford. My expression hardened sharply, pushing back the unwanted emotion.

"Our response," I said darkly, "will make it abundantly clear that this...was a mistake."

Lucien inclined his head solemnly, understanding the gravity behind my words. He turned toward the housekeeping staff, waving them silently forward, the broom bristles softly sweeping the broken shards of glass away.

As they began their work, Lucien lingered, observing me silently for another moment, his expression cautious. "Elias, about Harper—"

I shot him with a warning glare, cutting him off swiftly. "Leave it."

Lucien hesitated only briefly, understanding flashing behind his calm exterior. He nodded curtly, retreating silently from my office without another word, leaving me alone amidst the lingering aftermath.

I sank slowly into my chair, fingertips brushing lightly against the remnants of dried blood staining the polished wood of my desk. Harper's presence had already begun unraveling centuries of careful control, stirring something fierce and dangerous beneath the disciplined surface I maintained.

With a low growl of frustration, I pushed away from the desk and moved toward the cracked window, staring grimly at the sprawling city beneath. The world stretched below filled with allies, enemies, threats, and secrets. It had always been a precarious balance, one carefully managed through ruthless discipline and cold detachment.

Yet Harper Wells threatened to tilt everything, destabilizing the order I'd worked centuries to establish. I knew what I should do—dismiss her, push her away before the situation spiraled further out of control. But even as I thought it, the taste of raspberry pastry lingered stubbornly on my tongue, a sweet reminder of her defiant warmth, of her stubborn courage.

"Damn it," I whispered once more, frustration darkening my voice. I clenched my fists at my sides, forcing the unsettling emotions deeper beneath the surface. "This can't happen. It won't happen."

Harper

My hands wouldn't stop shaking, even after I'd scrubbed the blood off them twice. My nerves buzzed frantically beneath my skin, adrenaline still humming like a live wire. I stared blankly into the bathroom mirror, wondering how my day had spiraled from breakfast pastries to…whatever that was.

I mean, seriously—knives, tattoos, blood? Definitely not part of the job description HR had given me.

It's fine, I told myself firmly, splashing more cold water on my flushed face. *Totally normal first-job experience. Almost getting murdered. Cleaning wounds off your insanely attractive, terrifyingly intimidating boss. Sure. Why not?*

I took another deep breath, releasing it slowly, trying and failing to settle my nerves. The image of Elias's tattooed chest flashed vividly through my mind again, followed closely by the unsettling intensity of his golden gaze. Those symbols, intricate and strange, had looked so…ancient. Mysterious. Almost as intriguing as the man himself.

"Focus, Harper," I whispered sharply, forcing my reflection into a stern glare. "You almost walked into a literal murder scene. Get a grip."

But that thought immediately led to another, more alarming realization. If I'd arrived just a few minutes earlier, would the attacker still have been there? My blood went cold, goosebumps rising sharply along my arms. I'd been so caught up in Elias's wounds, I hadn't even stopped to think about my own safety.

I gripped the edge of the sink, knuckles turning white. This wasn't just nerves—this was a full-blown panic. Memories of previous failures, moments of vulnerability and helplessness, flashed through my mind. The fear of being unable to handle something important, something serious, was all too familiar.

"Pull yourself together," I whispered harshly, feeling slightly pathetic but not caring. "You survived today. That counts for something, right?"

The bathroom door swung open abruptly, nearly sending me jumping out of my skin. Linda stood in the doorway; her brows knitted tightly together in concern. She looked poised, as always—her elegant blouse impeccably pressed, her dark hair pulled into a smooth bun. Something about her gentle, yet fiercely protective demeanor calmed me a bit.

"Harper," she said softly, clearly trying not to startle me further. "Are you alright?"

I turned toward her with a shaky laugh. "Define 'alright.' Because if 'alright' means currently questioning all my life decisions, then yes, I'm great."

Linda's expression softened slightly, sympathy mixing with the lingering worry in her eyes. She stepped fully into the bathroom, closing the door behind her gently. "I heard about what happened. Mr. Blackwell asked me to make sure you're safe and unharmed."

I blinked, caught off-guard by that unexpected detail. Elias Blackwell—stoic, cold, intimidating Elias Blackwell—was worried about me? Warmth suddenly bloomed in my chest, chasing away a bit of the lingering chill, followed quickly by confusion and curiosity.

"He did?" I asked incredulously, my voice higher than I'd intended. "Elias Blackwell, my terrifying, practically emotionless boss? Are you sure we're talking about the same person?"

Linda's lips twitched with amusement, though her eyes remained serious. "He's difficult to read, I know. But Elias cares more deeply than he lets on. Especially when it comes to the safety of those around him."

I shook my head slowly, struggling to process that surprising bit of information. "So, this…is normal here? Knives, blood, random violence before sunrise?"

"Unfortunately," Linda sighed, gently squeezing my shoulder. "But I promise, Harper, you're not alone. We're all here, and we take care of each other."

"Good to know," I said weakly, mustering a small smile. "Because my backup plan was just hiding under my desk indefinitely."

Linda laughed softly, giving my shoulder another reassuring squeeze. "Well, if it comes to that, I'll bring you snacks."

"Perfect," I joked, feeling slightly better despite myself. "Just make sure they're stress-eating approved."

She smiled warmly, nodding once. "Take your time. If you need anything—coffee, pastries, a therapist—let me know."

"Will do," I murmured, genuinely grateful for her quiet reassurance.

Linda left quietly, the door clicking softly shut behind her, leaving me alone again. I exhaled slowly, squaring my shoulders. Whatever I'd stepped into—whatever secrets Elias Blackwell was hiding—I had a feeling I'd only just skimmed the surface.

I glanced at my reflection once more, wincing slightly at the sight staring back at me. My hair was a disaster—strands of chestnut escaping from a ponytail that had long ago given up trying. A faint smudge of Elias's blood stained my cheekbone, a stark reminder of how quickly everything had spiraled out of control. My shirt, once crisply ironed for my "big professional day," was wrinkled, dotted here and there with blood spots, coffee splashes, and pastry crumbs.

I looked like I'd just survived a street fight with a barista.

Yet beneath the messy hair, the exhausted eyes, and the evidence of the morning's chaos, there was something new—a stubborn, unfamiliar strength in the set of my jaw, a fierce determination staring defiantly back at me. Elias was dangerous, complicated, and clearly hiding a dozen secrets I wasn't remotely qualified to handle. And yeah, the logical part of my brain was practically screaming at me to run, to quit, to find something—anything—safer and simpler.

But something deeper—some reckless, stubborn curiosity—urged me to stay. Maybe it was because, despite the fear, I'd managed to help Elias to hold my own against his intimidating presence. Maybe it was the thrill of finally stepping out from my comfortable little box, even if it meant occasionally dodging knives and bloodstains.

"Congratulations, Harper," I told my reflection sarcastically, reaching up to wipe the stubborn smudge of blood from my face, succeeding only in spreading it further. With a resigned sigh, I tugged my hair back into a slightly neater ponytail. "You're officially addicted to chaos. Good luck surviving this one."

With one last deep breath, I straightened my shoulders, turned away from the mirror, and walked back out into whatever madness awaited me next.

Elias

Hours later, long after Harper had rushed from my office in a whirlwind of confusion and awkward bravery, the reality of the attack still lingered, a stark reminder of my own vulnerability. My chest ached relentlessly where the silver blade had torn through muscle and flesh, its poisonous touch lingering deep beneath the skin. Gloria, our healer, had come swiftly at Lucien's request, her soothing presence a temporary balm against the searing pain.

"You're fortunate, Elias," Gloria murmured softly, her aged hands moving gently but firmly across my wound, spreading her herbal concoctions—pungent mixtures of crushed herbs, oils, and magic—over the angry, silver-burned gash. Her gray eyes watched me carefully from beneath wisps of silvery-white hair that framed her weathered face, revealing quiet concern. "The blade missed your heart by mere inches."

"Yes," I muttered bitterly, jaw clenched tight against another wave of pain as she pressed a fresh poultice into the wound. "Fortunate."

"Hold still," Gloria chided softly, her voice carrying gentle authority. "The more you fight, the slower you'll heal."

Lucien stood near the doorway, arms crossed, watching me carefully. His dark eyes betrayed his worry, even as he maintained his typical mask of cool composure. His silence, more than anything else, told me he was still processing how close I'd come to true harm.

"Lucien," I said through gritted teeth, gaze flickering toward the ruined office behind him. "I want this cleaned immediately—before Harper returns tomorrow. She doesn't need reminders."

Lucien nodded solemnly. "Already arranged, sir."

"And Harper?" I asked, an unexpected urgency creeping into my tone. The thought of her wandering home alone after everything she'd seen twisted uncomfortably in my chest. "Did you arrange transportation?"

"Of course," Lucien replied steadily, his expression carefully neutral, though his eyes flashed briefly with understanding. "I sent Thomas personally."

Relief tightened my throat, and I nodded once, appreciating Lucien's foresight. I trusted him implicitly—especially when my own judgment felt compromised. My mind stubbornly replayed the sight of Harper's wide-eyed horror when she'd entered the office, her fumbling courage as she'd tended my wound. She'd been terrified, but she'd stayed, defying both her own instincts and my explicit warnings. That reckless bravery—her reckless bravery—was as fascinating as it was infuriating.

Gloria finally stepped back, wiping her hands on a soft cloth, offering me a faint smile. "Rest tonight, Elias. Your strength will return quickly—but your pride might take longer."

I offered her a wry, humorless chuckle. "My pride has survived worse."

"True enough." Gloria's eyes twinkled knowingly as she packed away her herbs and bandages. "But you're stubborn enough to test even the limits of immortality."

As she left, silence settled heavily in her wake, broken only by Lucien's quiet movements as he supervised the cleanup crew who had begun meticulously removing the shattered remnants of glass and bloodied artifacts. Watching my office slowly return to order—erasing every trace of violence—felt strangely hollow. I couldn't erase the memory of Harper's trembling hands or her stubborn defiance, nor the vulnerability I'd shown her, whether intentional or not.

"You should rest, Elias," Lucien urged quietly, concern shadowing his features. "The wound may heal quickly, but the silver's poison will linger for a bit."

I exhaled slowly, leaning back against my chair, exhaustion finally overtaking the last vestiges of adrenaline. "Later," I murmured, knowing rest would prove elusive anyway. "Check with security again—confirm the building is fully secure."

Lucien nodded sharply. "Understood. I'll personally see to it."

"And Harper?" I asked softly, almost unwillingly, meeting Lucien's watchful gaze. "Did Thomas confirm she arrived home safely?"

Lucien's lips twitched slightly, fighting back a faint, knowing smile. "Yes, sir. Thomas escorted her to her door himself. She's unharmed—if somewhat rattled."

"Good." The tension eased slightly from my shoulders, but the faint unease lingered stubbornly in my gut. I leaned back, pinching the bridge of my nose, exhaustion pulling heavily at every muscle.

Lucien lingered a moment longer, his hesitation palpable. "She handled herself surprisingly well, Elias. Especially given the circumstances."

"Yes," I agreed quietly, a reluctant note of admiration coloring my tone. "Better than she realizes. Gather everyone at the house tonight. We need to have a family meeting."

"Of course, sir."

With Lucien's quiet exit, silence returned to my office, heavy and thick, broken only by the rhythmic tick of an antique clock. My gaze fell again to the now-clean desk where Harper's raspberry Danish still sat mostly untouched in its box—a silent, ridiculous reminder of her unexpected intrusion into my meticulously controlled life.

Finally surrendering to fatigue, I closed my laptop, exhaling a long, weary breath. The drive home passed in silence, the familiar streets a blur of shadow and neon beneath the restless glow of streetlights. My muscles ached, my thoughts tangled hopelessly between anger, worry, and an unsettling sense of vulnerability. The city passed by in a hushed blur, indifferent to the turmoil that raged beneath my carefully maintained exterior.

As I stepped through the heavy front doors of my home, the quiet instantly settled around me, thick and oppressive. I moved through the darkened halls toward my room, hoping that a moment's sleep might quiet, even briefly, the chaos in my mind before the family arrives.

The expansive drawing room of my home was cloaked in heavy shadows, lit only by the flickering flames dancing restlessly within the stone fireplace. The faint crackle of burning wood punctuated the tense silence as my closest confidants and pack sat around the ancient oak table, their faces etched sharply with the weight of unspoken fears and simmering accusations.

Lucien sat to my right, his posture rigid and disciplined—a silent testament to his long service as my second-in-command. Centuries earlier, I'd found him half-dead in the forests of Bavaria, a victim of betrayal from his own bloodline. He was thirty, but even then, the strength behind his quiet resolve was unmistakable. His dark eyes now narrowed, meticulously examining the blade I'd removed from my chest hours before, the silver gleam beneath the firelight a stark reminder of our shared vulnerability.

Across from me, Isabella perched stiffly in her chair, her dark curls cascading down her shoulders like waves of midnight silk, her sharp, penetrating gaze never wavering from my face. My younger sister had always been fiercely independent, even before our lives had been irreversibly altered in the streets of old Venice. We'd navigated this immortal existence together—often as allies, occasionally as adversaries—but always bound by blood, loyalty, and stubborn pride. Isabella's ruthless scrutiny was something I'd come to both rely upon and dread, as her criticisms cut swiftly to the heart of any argument, she deemed reckless or foolish.

Marcus sat quietly beside Isabella, his broad shoulders and muscular frame dominating the space around him. A warrior from the ancient northern clans, Marcus had survived battles that would have broken lesser men. He'd fought alongside me in countless wars, a silent guardian whose loyalty had never once wavered. His dark skin gleamed faintly in the flickering firelight, and though his deep eyes revealed little, I knew he absorbed every word, every movement, constantly prepared to strike without hesitation or remorse.

Beside Marcus, Seraphina shifted anxiously, delicate fingers tracing restless patterns over the polished oak table. Her long, auburn curls and pale skin spoke to her Celtic heritage, her beauty both ethereal and disarmingly fragile. She'd been a healer, a keeper of ancient knowledge and quiet power. Though physically the smallest among us, Seraphina's gifts were formidable in their uniqueness—she was an empath, capable of sensing and influencing the emotions of those around her. Her power allowed her to diffuse conflicts before they began or turn allies into adversaries with a mere shift of intent. Yet, despite her profound strength, the weight of constantly experiencing the raw, unfiltered emotions of others often left her anxious and unsettled.

The tension stretched heavily between us, a silent undercurrent of centuries shared, battles won and lost, alliances forged and broken. They were my pack, my family by choice rather than blood—a bond stronger than mere lineage, built from shared secrets, battles fought side by side, and loyalty forged through fire and sacrifice. And tonight, that loyalty was being tested in ways none of us had foreseen.

Isabella broke the silence first, her voice edged with irritation. "I suppose you realize how close you came this morning, Elias. How close we all came." Her words were sharp, slicing through the stillness of the room. "Every reckless decision you make invites our enemies closer. Do you genuinely think it's wise to carry on with events and lavish parties when you're practically painting a target on your chest? They attacked you in your own self-proclaimed fortress of an office."

I exhaled slowly, ignoring the lingering throb of pain beneath my carefully buttoned shirt, my expression cold and unyielding as I held her stare. "If we show weakness, Isabella, even for a moment, we hand our enemies exactly what they seek…a foothold. You know as well as I do that retreat isn't an option."

She scoffed softly, shaking her head in frustration, her voice dropping to a pained whisper. "We've buried enough people we care about, Elias. Don't make me stand over another grave because of your stubborn pride. There's a line between strength and sheer arrogance. You've forgotten where it lies, and it's going to cost us dearly. You're endangering us—endangering yourself—and now you've brought a human directly into the line of fire. Which goes against all our principles.

My jaw tightened imperceptibly at the mention of Harper. Thirty impossibly thin minutes separated Harper from a fate I refused to imagine. Her frightened yet defiant eyes haunted her scent still lingered stubbornly on my skin, a relentless reminder of my mistake in allowing her close. The thought sent a cold twist of dread through my chest.

Lucien intervened smoothly, breaking the brief tension. "Isabella raises a fair point, Elias. This attack wasn't some haphazard attempt, it was precise, carefully orchestrated. Whoever is behind this knows us, and they're clearly organized enough to gain access and attempt a direct strike.

Lucien's voice tightened with controlled frustration. "Victor Ambrose has held a grudge since Paris. His alliances have grown over the last century. And the Greyson Coven—our truce with them was fragile at best. Either way, this move was planned meticulously. They knew exactly how to hurt us."

I rubbed the bridge of my nose, exhaustion pressing heavily against centuries of carefully constructed composure. "Do we have names yet?"

Lucien shook his head gravely, the firelight casting harsh shadows over his expression. "No confirmation yet, but surveillance footage from this morning might hold some answers."

I straightened instantly, the muscles in my back tightening in response. "Show me."

Lucien moved swiftly, placing a tablet on the table, the glowing screen harsh against the room's dim atmosphere. He tapped the play button, and grainy security footage from the lobby appeared, casting an eerie blue glow over our tense faces.

"There," Lucien murmured, pointing sharply. "Watch closely."

I leaned forward, the scene unfolding with chilling clarity. Our security guard, normally alert and reliable, stood conversing quietly with a figure whose face was mostly hidden beneath the shadow of a dark hood. Even from this distance, something in the man's posture—casual yet predatory—set off warning bells in my mind.

After a brief exchange, the guard glanced around before nodding, stepping aside and discreetly allowing a second hooded figure through the security doors. My fists clenched tightly as first man briefly stepped into view beneath the lobby lights, his face half-hidden by shadow, but his arrogant, self-assured smirk was unmistakable. He exchanged a casual handshake with the guard before calmly disappearing back into the darkness.

My voice trembled with barely suppressed rage. "Who is he? Do we know him?"

Lucien shook his head grimly, replaying the footage to study the figure again. "Not yet. We've never seen him before, but he's clearly involved."

Seraphina's delicate fingers stopped abruptly, her voice soft and cautious, trembling slightly as she spoke. "Elias, whoever these men are, they may not be working alone. Someone powerful is pulling strings here—and they're watching us closely, perhaps even from inside our own walls. We need to consider every possibility."

Marcus, who'd remained silent until now, shifted forward slightly, his deep voice steady as granite. "Then we remind whoever it is exactly who they're dealing with. We strengthen our defenses, tighten our grip, and make our stance perfectly clear." He leaned further forward, eyes unwavering as they held mine. "We've faced worse and survived, Elias. We'll handle this—together, like we always have."

I nodded slowly, appreciating Marcus's unwavering steadiness, drawing strength from his calm assurance. "Lucien, triple building security immediately. Replace the guard involved tonight and thoroughly vet all new personnel personally. Marcus, have the pack on high alert—no one moves without our knowledge. Seraphina, quietly leverage every contact you have. I want to know exactly who we're facing and precisely what they intend."

My gaze flickered back to Isabella. Her expression had softened slightly, but her eyes still burned with quiet defiance. "Isabella," I conceded quietly, allowing rare vulnerability to slip briefly through my carefully constructed façade, "your warnings are not ignored. We'll adjust our approach—but we do not yield. Not now, not ever."

She held my gaze for a long, tense moment before finally nodding slowly, reluctant acceptance etched into her features. "Be careful, Elias. Pride has ended better men than you."

Her words lingered heavily in the air long after they'd departed, leaving me alone once more in the room's oppressive darkness. Shadows pooled thickly in every corner, clawing hungrily toward the center of the room, drawn by our unease. Above, ancestral portraits watched silently from the walls, their painted eyes heavy with judgment, witnesses to generations of violence and secrecy.

I leaned heavily against the table, centuries of violence and responsibility pressing on my shoulders, heavier tonight than they'd felt in decades. Beneath my carefully maintained façade, a bone-deep weariness ached, pulling at the edges of my resolve.

My eyes drifted once more to the gleaming silver dagger lying on the table—bloodstained, dangerous, symbolic of a threat far greater than I'd anticipated. The intruder's casual confidence, Harper's dangerously close encounter, and the chilling revelation of betrayal within my own ranks all tightened my chest with fresh anger.

Sleep tonight would continue to be elusive, I knew, but I had to find some semblance of rest. Tomorrow would demand answers, and I needed my strength if I was to face them.

Moving through the darkened halls toward my room, I hoped the coming morning would bring clarity—but deep down, I knew this was only the beginning of something far darker and infinitely more dangerous.

Harper

The office was utter chaos.

The elegant, pristine halls of Blackwell Industries were suddenly a hive of activity and tension. Police officers moved quickly through the corridors, their faces stern, eyes carefully avoiding anyone else's gaze. Detectives in muted suits exchanged clipped conversations in hushed tones, taking notes on small pads of paper or snapping photographs of random objects. Security personnel I'd never seen before hovered at every doorway; their dark jackets pulled tight around them as they whispered urgently into earpieces.

And then there were the others, the hooded figures. Men and women whose faces remained obscured, hoods drawn low, eyes flickering in shadows as they moved silently, efficiently, radiating a kind of quiet authority that felt distinctly unsettling. They weren't police, I knew that much. They weren't employees, either. No one else seemed to know exactly who they were, and no one was brave enough—or stupid enough—to ask.

I sat rigid at my small desk, desperately trying to focus on literally anything other than the echoing whispers and speculative glances that kept landing directly on me. Apparently, news of the boss's bloody knife wound and his very flustered assistant who'd discovered him had traveled fast. Fantastic. I could practically feel the weight of every judgmental stare, every whispered conversation.

"Did you hear she found him?" "Poor thing, look at her—she must be terrified." "Do you think she knows something?"

I kept my head down, eyes locked stubbornly on my laptop screen, even though I'd been staring at the same email draft for two hours without typing a single word. My hands trembled slightly in my lap, and exhaustion clawed at my bones, making every second that passed feel like an eternity.

When the police finally told me I could leave, I grabbed my purse and practically ran for the exit, desperate to escape the suffocating atmosphere. The sleek black SUV they'd provided for the ride home—presumably arranged by Lucien or maybe even Elias himself—only made the entire experience feel more surreal. It glided through the city streets quietly, smoothly, with dark-tinted windows hiding my confusion and distress from the world.

The lights of the city blurred past, reds and blues mixing together in a hypnotic dance. I pressed my forehead against the cold window glass, grateful for its soothing chill against my overheated skin. My reflection stared back at me, pale and haunted, the dark circles under my eyes already prominent.

By the time I reached my apartment, all traces of adrenaline had drained completely away, replaced by bone-deep weariness. I dragged myself upstairs, my legs feeling impossibly heavy as I forced each step. The lock clicked behind me, the sound echoing strangely through my cramped, quiet apartment.

For a long moment, I stood unmoving just inside the doorway, staring blankly at the messy collection of my life: clothes draped carelessly over chairs, takeout containers balanced precariously in overflowing trash bins, a mountain of bills stacked accusingly on the counter. It all felt so incredibly distant and meaningless after today.

I sank down onto my couch, gazing numbly at the cracked ceiling above. The walls pressed inward, the silence thickening with every passing second. My mind looped helplessly back through everything I'd witnessed, everything I'd seen in Elias's eyes—pain, strength, an unspoken depth of secrets. The blood, the knife, the tattooed mysteries hidden beneath his shirt—all of it tangled together into an overwhelming, exhausting knot of confusion.

I don't know how long I sat like that, frozen in thought, before finally forcing myself toward my bed. Sleep seemed like a logical step, something that should have been easy given the sheer exhaustion weighing me down.

Instead, here I was.

It was nearly three in the morning, and apparently, my body had officially decided sleep was overrated. I lay in bed, eyes glued to the ceiling, watching as shadows twisted into creepy little monsters every time headlights flashed across the room. Honestly, if my insomnia kept this up, I'd probably have a full-blown mental breakdown by sunrise, complete with shadow puppet hallucinations.

I flipped onto my side, groaning dramatically into my pillow, but my brain refused to shut off, looping relentlessly over the absolute insanity that was yesterday. I mean, let's recap, shall we? Pastries, coffee, casual stroll back to work… then boom: boss bleeding out at his desk, casually pulling knives from his chest like it was no big deal. Just your average Wednesday.

"Why can't you just have a normal job?" I muttered into the darkness, waving my hand vaguely at the ceiling as if it could answer me. "Like, oh, I don't know…a librarian? Or an ice cream scooper?"

I rolled my eyes at my own rambling, kicked off the sheets with a sigh, and dragged myself out of bed. My bare feet hit the cold wooden floor, sending a shiver up my spine as I shuffled toward the tiny kitchen, navigating piles of unfolded laundry and empty takeout boxes with expert precision.

My laptop sat accusingly on my cluttered kitchen table, practically glowing in the dark like a neon sign reading *"Welcome to Harper's Terrible Life Choices!"* With a heavy sigh, I sank into the chair, the plastic squeaking indignantly beneath me. I flipped the screen open, the harsh blue-white glow lighting up my tired face and emphasizing exactly how much I needed sleep. Spoiler: it was a lot.

I stared at the blinking cursor, its constant rhythm mocking me. After a long, tense silence broken only by the hum of the refrigerator (probably judging my life decisions too), I forced my fingers onto the keyboard. Each keystroke felt uncomfortably permanent, like I was carving the words into stone instead of typing an email.

Dear Mr. Blackwell,

Please accept this letter as my formal resignation. Due to personal circumstances, I feel it is necessary to step down from my position as your assistant, effective immediately. Thank you for this opportunity.

I read the words again. And again. And then a third time, just for funsies. My stomach twisted tighter with every repetition. It felt so…final. Also, weirdly formal. I briefly considered adding a *"P.S.: Sorry about the whole knife-in-chest situation, hope you're doing great!"* but decided it was probably best to leave that out.

My finger hovered over the send button, trembling like a leaf. "Come on, Harp, just do it," I coached myself softly. "Rip off the Band-Aid. He'll probably just hire someone else tomorrow anyway—someone less clumsy, more qualified, and probably less likely to faint at the sight of blood."

I closed my eyes tight, sucked in a deep breath, and jabbed the button with way too much force. The quiet ping of the email leaving my outbox felt louder than a freaking cannon blast. I slumped back in my chair, the tension draining out of me faster than air from a balloon.

"Congrats, Harper," I whispered into the empty room. "You've officially quit the weirdest—and highest-paying—job you've ever had. Hope you're proud."

But I wasn't proud. I was nauseous. Anxiety curled uncomfortably in my stomach, whispering doubts in my ear. Had I just made the smartest move of my life—or possibly the dumbest?

I glanced at the dark shadows still swirling across my ceiling, silently mocking my inability to make adult decisions. *Yeah. Sleep definitely wasn't coming now.*

Chapter 4

The Failed Resignation

Elias

The home office felt unusually confined tonight, cloaked in the stark silence that only deepened at this ungodly hour. Outside, the sprawling city lay hushed beneath a velvet-dark sky, skyscrapers reduced to mere silhouettes punctuated by distant pinpricks of golden light. At 3 AM, the world felt suspended, reality softened and uncertain. The thick, panoramic glass windows offered no warmth tonight, only the illusion of openness, amplifying my sense of solitude. The silence of the night pressed heavily against me, thick with an uncomfortable solitude I'd rarely allowed myself to acknowledge.

Sleep had abandoned me entirely. Restless energy thrummed relentlessly beneath my skin, an agitated rhythm I'd long grown accustomed to—yet tonight, it felt unbearable, a relentless itch deep within my bones. My tie lay discarded, draped loosely over the edge of the desk; my shirt hung open, sleeves rolled roughly to my elbows, exposing the dark ink swirling across my skin, marks of a past I seldom allowed myself to revisit. I ran a hand through my hair, frustration seeping into a heavy sigh.

Just as I reached forward to finally closing my laptop, eager to shut away the digital demands that never seemed to end, a quiet ping echoed sharply in the heavy silence. My gaze snapped sharply to the screen, irritation tightening my jaw at the sight of her name—Harper Wells. Instantly, an inexplicable tightening gripped my chest, heart rate increasing as I read the short, ominous subject line:

"Resignation."

Pulse quickening, I opened it without hesitation, eyes rapidly scanning each brief, maddeningly polite sentence:

Dear Mr. Blackwell,

Please accept this letter as my formal resignation. Due to personal circumstances, I feel it is necessary to step down from my position as your assistant, effective immediately. Thank you for this opportunity.

My jaw tightened painfully, every muscle in my body coiling sharply with disbelief, irritation swiftly spiraling into something far more intense panic, laced with a stubborn, unfamiliar possessiveness. I stared blankly at the screen, grappling with the sharp pang of anxiety that clenched my chest like a vise. Harper Wells wasn't just leaving, she was cutting herself entirely from my life without explanation. The thought was infuriating, unacceptable.

How dare she walk away now? Now, when she'd begun slipping effortlessly beneath layers of carefully crafted defenses, unsettling my world with her reckless candor, her bright eyes, her infuriatingly distracting presence? My frustration boiled into something deeper, darker—a raw, vulnerable desperation I'd never admit to anyone, least of all myself.

Restless, I pushed violently away from the desk, pacing with tense agitation across the chilled hardwood floors. Each step echoed the chaos within, muscles coiled tight, adrenaline burning through my veins with nowhere to go.

I remembered vividly the defiance she'd shown while tending my wounds, how her gentle touch had unraveled something within me I'd long thought untouchable. Harper Wells was utterly infuriating, dangerously naïve, impossibly captivating, and now inexplicably essential.

"Damn it, Harper," I muttered darkly, fist clenched tightly on the desk. "You can't just—"

I didn't finish the thought. Couldn't finish it. Instead, driven purely by uncontrollable impulse and frustration, my fingers moved quickly over the keyboard, each keystroke heavy with barely concealed irritation and the unmistakable edge of desperation:

"No."

The email sent immediately, the stark confirmation blinking mockingly at me. I leaned back, stunned at my own recklessness, fighting a sudden, irrational urge to hurl the laptop across the room. I'd crossed a line I'd sworn never to approach, revealing a weakness and need I refused to admit.

The silence following my impulsive reply stretched unbearably, punctuated only by the steady, rhythmic ticking of the antique clock perched elegantly on the nearby shelf. My thoughts spiraled rapidly, circling around her infuriating presence, her awkward jokes, her fearless gaze—Harper Wells, human and reckless, a distraction I'd neither expected nor wanted, but one I'd come dangerously close to craving.

And yet, despite every reason to push her away, to let her disappear quietly from my life and return my existence to order and logic, I couldn't deny the surge of fierce possessiveness I felt.

I knew I'd probably just complicated matters further risking both my carefully maintained authority and my meticulously structured control. Yet even knowing the danger Harper represented, I found myself unwilling, perhaps unable, to relinquish my hold on her. Not yet.

Harper

I had barely pushed away from my desk, fully intending to stumble back to bed and salvage whatever scraps of sleep my insomnia-addled brain might generously allow, when my phone vibrated sharply. The sudden buzz nearly launched me into orbit, my heart hammering like it had personally taken offense at the rude awakening. Casting a wary glance at the clock—3:14 AM, really? —I reached toward the glowing screen cautiously, half-expecting an emergency alert or some cryptic text from Sophie about her latest existential art crisis.

But then I saw his name.

Elias Blackwell.

"Oh god," I groaned aloud, dragging a shaky hand down my face. Against every shred of better judgment, my thumb hovered over the notification before finally clicking open the email. Instantly, dread pooled heavily in my stomach, cold and sickly-sweet like melted ice cream. His reply was short—ridiculously short:

"No."

My mouth literally fell open. I stared at the screen, eyes wide in complete disbelief. No explanation, no polite request to reconsider, not even a full freaking sentence—just an infuriatingly arrogant, single-syllable shutdown.

"'No'?" I whispered incredulously into my darkened apartment, my voice wavering somewhere between outrage and slightly hysterical amusement. "Who does this guy think he is? Freaking Batman?"

A laugh bubbled up involuntarily, sharp and slightly unhinged, and I quickly slapped a hand over my mouth. Great, now I was officially losing my mind. And Elias Blackwell was the catalyst. Even better.

Beneath the irritation bubbling up my chest, though, was something else—something annoyingly, alarmingly close to excitement. I felt my cheeks warm traitorously and scowled into the shadows of my apartment, sternly reminding myself that this was the man who'd casually pulled a knife from his own chest. Not exactly ideal boss material—definitely not boyfriend material, either. But despite the logical protests echoing in my head, my pulse quickened just remembering the intensity of his golden eyes, the ripple of tattoos across his chest, the inexplicable magnetism of his dangerous presence.

"Okay, Harper, down girl," I muttered sternly, forcing myself back under the tangled covers. But sleep, elusive to begin with, was now utterly out of reach. Instead, my traitorous brain decided to replay that stupid, infuriating, and frustratingly intriguing single-word email on a maddening loop.

Two miserably restless hours later, I dragged myself out of bed, stumbling through my cluttered apartment as exhaustion hung from my limbs like lead weights. Showering didn't help, caffeine barely registered, and by the time I printed out the physical copy of my resignation letter, my carefully rehearsed speech had twisted itself into knots of anxiety and confusion.

Still, armed with determination (and about six cups of coffee), I marched into Blackwell Industries, mentally replaying my planned confrontation: a calm, cool, professional take-down designed specifically to put Elias firmly in his place.

But as I approached his office door, before my hand even lifted to knock, it swung open abruptly. There stood Elias Blackwell—composed, irritatingly confident, looking impossibly well-rested for someone who'd nearly bled out on his own desk less than twenty-four hours ago.

"No," he repeated smoothly, without preamble, his voice carrying the infuriating certainty of someone used to having his every command obeyed.

I blinked stupidly, my carefully prepared speech evaporating like mist under the intensity of his gaze.

"No?" I echoed weakly, my voice coming out embarrassingly squeaky. Recovering quickly, I straightened my spine, thrusting the neatly printed resignation letter toward him with renewed determination. "Take the letter, Mr. Blackwell. Or… Sir. Whatever you prefer."

His eyebrow arched, a slight curve of his mouth indicating a hint of amusement as his gaze flicked dismissively down to the letter, then slowly back up to mine. Arms folded across his irritatingly impressive chest—tattoos hidden now beneath an impeccably tailored white shirt, yet seared irrevocably into my memory—he simply tilted his head slightly, as if genuinely considering my demand, before replying in a voice that brooked no argument:

"No," he repeated, softer this time, yet somehow even more absolute. "I have a meeting in ten minutes. Conference room in five, Miss Wells."

Without another word, he turned and vanished smoothly into his office, the door clicking shut behind him with a finality that reverberated mockingly through my bones. I stood frozen in place, mouth hanging open yet again, resignation letter still dangling pathetically from my fingertips, forgotten and ignored.

"Great talk," I muttered sarcastically to the empty hallway, feeling irrationally like a scolded child. "So glad we did this. Super productive."

Determined not to surrender entirely to his stubbornness, I waited until Elias disappeared into his meeting and then quietly slipped into his empty office. With a victorious flourish, I placed my resignation letter prominently in the center of his desk—his pristine, irritatingly organized desk—smiling triumphantly at the tiny rebellion.

"There. Ignore that, *boss-man*."

Feeling a surge of fleeting pride but mostly just bone-deep exhaustion, I headed straight toward HR, hoping Linda could offer clarity or, at the very least, some validation that I hadn't completely lost my grip on sanity.

Elias

The expansive conference room was suffused with the harsh, sterile glow of fluorescent lights, casting clinical illumination across every polished glass surface. The grand, elongated table stretched imposingly down the center, lined by anxious executives who shifted nervously, the air heavy with expectation. Their eyes flicked discreetly toward the empty chair at my right—the place reserved explicitly for Harper Wells, who had yet to grace us with her chaotic presence.

I sat rigidly at the head of the table, posture deceptively calm, my fingers steepled tightly in front of me, tension radiating outward. Each passing moment tightened the coil of impatience deep in my chest, frustration building like the slow accumulation of a storm. Harper was inexperienced, reckless even, but obsessively punctual—her habitual early arrivals had become predictable, even oddly reassuring. This sudden absence felt wrong, unsettling in ways I refused to openly acknowledge.

A low hum of whispered conversation rippled nervously around the table, grating against my nerves. My jaw clenched tightly, irritation flaring sharply within me.

I cleared my throat, a quiet yet dangerously authoritative sound that immediately sliced through the murmuring, leaving a thick silence in its wake.

"Where is Harp—Miss Wells?" I corrected myself sharply, the informal slip drawing raised brows and exchanged glances among those present. My voice carried a razor edge, colder and more severe than I'd intended. Instantly, every gaze dropped, becoming intensely interested in laptops, paperwork, or the polished wood grain of the table—anything to avoid my direct stare.

The silence stretched uncomfortably, broken only by the faint ticking of an antique wall clock that marked each awkward second.

Shannon, positioned closest to me, shifted uneasily, her usually composed demeanor slipping momentarily as she gathered the nerve to speak. "I'm…not certain, sir," she finally ventured, meeting my gaze hesitantly. "Miss Wells didn't check in this morning."

I narrowed my eyes, a muscle in my jaw twitching involuntarily. It wasn't merely irritation now—it was a slowly simmering unease. Harper had seemed unsettled, certainly, but not enough to disappear entirely. My gut tightened with an unfamiliar pang—concern, sharper and more invasive than I'd ever admit aloud.

"Maybe she's sick?" Morrison suggested weakly from halfway down the table, his voice thin and hesitant, clearly anticipating my displeasure.

"Perhaps," Isabella interjected smoothly, a faintly amused curve lifting her lips. She met my eyes directly, her expression carrying an undercurrent of challenging defiance. "Or perhaps she's reconsidered her role here."

My gaze sharpened immediately, locking onto Isabella's face with a barely concealed warning. "And what makes you say that?"

Isabella raised an elegant eyebrow, unperturbed. "Considering recent events and the nature of Miss Wells herself, it's not impossible she'd rethink her position."

My fingers curled slightly tighter, the tips pressing hard against each other, as I struggled to maintain composure. "Harper Wells is stubbornly persistent. Quitting on a whim hardly fits her profile."

Isabella merely shrugged, leaning back slightly, her eyes glittering with barely disguised curiosity. "If you say so, Mr. Wells. Though I suspect there are layers to her you haven't yet fully uncovered."

Her subtle implication did nothing to soothe my rising frustration. Harper was a complex, infuriating enigma, and Isabella knew precisely how unsettled I felt. I resisted the impulse to growl openly, instead forcing myself into decisive action.

"Hold off on the presentation until I return," I ordered curtly, rising abruptly from my seat. Chairs creaked as executives sat up straighter, their confusion palpable as they watched me stalk toward the door.

Lucien, standing near the back of the room, shot me a questioning glance. I offered him a slight, almost imperceptible nod, silently communicating that I would handle whatever was happening personally. He returned the gesture with quiet acknowledgment.

The heavy glass doors swung shut behind me with a resonant click, cutting off renewed murmurs of speculation. Out in the corridor, silence enveloped me like a tangible weight, amplifying my anxious thoughts. With purposeful strides, I moved swiftly toward Harper's small workspace.

It was uncharacteristically empty, the neatly chaotic arrangement of coffee cups, colorful sticky notes, and overstuffed bag conspicuously absent. No lingering scent of her perfume or the sugary aroma of a half-eaten pastry. Just vacant space, mocking in its emptiness.

Frustration blossomed sharply into worry, settling cold and heavy in my chest. Without hesitation, I pulled out my phone, dialing Harper's number with impatient urgency. The soft ringing echoed through the receiver, maddeningly unanswered, until finally, her familiar voicemail greeted me with exaggerated cheerfulness.

"Dammit," I muttered under my breath, ending the call with a sharp flick of my thumb.

My pulse thrummed uncomfortably, unease growing into a palpable sense of dread. The resignation email she'd sent in the dead of night flashed through my thoughts, taunting me. She had wanted out. Had she really chosen now, of all moments, to act upon it?

Yet somehow, I doubted it. Harper was bold, impulsive, but never deliberately cruel. Her absence wasn't mere defiance; it felt wrong — dangerous. A sudden, sickening possibility twisted in my gut.

I turned sharply, nearly colliding with Lucien, who'd silently approached behind me. His dark eyes assessed my barely concealed tension, immediately understanding the situation was more severe than a mere late employee.

"Find her," I ordered quietly, the edge in my voice unmistakable. "I want Harper Wells to be located immediately. Use every resource at your disposal."

Lucien inclined his head solemnly, his expression resolute. "Consider it done."

As he strode away to mobilize our security teams, my thoughts raced wildly. Harper Wells, impulsive, stubborn, reckless, had somehow managed to slip beneath every defense I'd carefully constructed. Losing her wasn't just professionally inconvenient; it was profoundly unacceptable.

I clenched my fists tightly at my sides, refusing to acknowledge the true depth of my anxiety. Wherever Harper was, whatever trouble she'd inadvertently stumbled into—I'd find her. And God help anyone who dared to harm her.

Harper

Linda greeted me with a cautious smile when I knocked softly on her office door, awkwardly peeking around the frame as if I half-expected to find Elias lurking behind her desk, ready to pounce. Her door was open, her cozy office bathed in warm morning sunlight, offering a stark yet welcoming contrast to the sterile corporate chill outside. The walls were a gentle shade of cream, adorned with framed photos of smiling family members and motivational quotes—each one carefully chosen, radiating positivity without feeling overly cheesy. Lush green plants filled the corners, their leaves spilling gracefully from terracotta pots, adding softness and life to the room. On her cluttered but inviting desk, an assortment of colorful stationery, scattered sticky notes, and an oversized ceramic mug emblazoned with "World's Okay-est HR Manager" made the space feel effortlessly comforting, almost like stepping into a trusted friend's living room rather than an HR office.

She glanced up, eyebrows raised curiously at my frazzled appearance, concern immediately flooding her features.

"Harper, good morning," she said gently, setting aside her tablet. Her eyes took in my slightly disheveled hair and dark circles, her sympathetic gaze instantly softening. "Everything okay?"

"Oh, totally great," I joked weakly, sinking into the plush chair opposite her. "I tried to resign, Linda."

Linda's eyebrows practically shot to her hairline, eyes widening in surprise. "You resigned? I didn't see anything come through my inbox."

"Twice, actually. Apparently, Elias Blackwell doesn't accept resignations at 3 AM—or any other time, really. He literally said 'no.'

Twice. Like resignation is some kind of optional suggestion he can just reject. Is that even allowed?"

Linda's lips twitched, the corners of her mouth fighting against a knowing smile. "It's a bit of a trademark move. Usually, it works."

I groaned, pressing my palms against my eyes, suddenly feeling utterly defeated. "Well, not this time. I left the letter on his desk. He can't just ignore paper, right? That's got to be legally binding or something." "So, what now?" I asked, slumping further into the chair like a petulant teenager. "Do I chain myself to my desk until he relents, or am I supposed to stage a formal protest? Because honestly, I don't have the energy or the budget for protest signs."

She smiled softly, leaning forward with genuine sympathy now. "Harper, I can process your resignation officially, if that's truly what you want. But—and I say this carefully—if Elias isn't letting you go, it might be because he genuinely values you."

"Yeah, or he just enjoys torturing me," I muttered under my breath. But even as the words left my mouth, something traitorous fluttered in my stomach, maybe hope, or dread, or possibly hunger. Who knew at this point?

Linda smiled knowingly, tilting her head with gentle curiosity. "Is there something else going on you want to talk about?"

"Oh, nothing major," I sighed theatrically. "Just found my boss stabbed, bleeding all over his ridiculously expensive desk, yanked a knife from his chest, and I somehow managed to bandage him without fainting or vomiting. You know, normal workplace drama."

She stared at me, stunned silence hanging awkwardly between us until I let out a weak laugh, shaking my head. "Sorry, over sharing again. Ignore me. Sleep deprivation makes me…say things."

Linda softened visibly; her voice reassuringly gentle. "Harper, you're stronger than you think. But if you're serious about leaving, I can process your resignation right now."

I hesitated, suddenly aware of how final that sounded. "Can…can we hold off just a bit longer?" I finally asked, feeling utterly pathetic. "At least until I figure out what the heck Elias Blackwell is trying to prove."

Linda nodded, a knowing smile softening her features. "Of course. Take your time, Harper. Just promise you'll come talk to me if things get…weirder."

"Promise," I said, standing and giving her a grateful wave as I slipped back into the hallway, feeling both lighter and somehow even more confused.

As I headed back toward my desk to redecorate everything I'd removed, one thing became crystal clear: Elias Blackwell wasn't just difficult—he was officially impossible. And somehow, against all logic and common sense, I still hadn't run screaming in the other direction.

My stomach twisted uncomfortably, an unfamiliar mixture of nerves and warmth swirling within me. *Was Linda right? Was Elias's stubborn refusal something more meaningful than simple arrogance?* The thought simultaneously thrilled and terrified me.

Rounding the corner, I froze mid-step, nearly dropping the cardboard box I was carrying, suddenly confronted by the sight of Lucien and three imposing security guards standing near my empty desk. My heart jolted sharply, anxiety spiking as all four heads swiveled instantly in my direction.

Lucien's carefully neutral expression softened with visible relief when he saw me. "Miss Wells," he said calmly, though the slight edge to his voice revealed he'd been more worried than he wanted to admit. "We were just about to go looking for you."

I swallowed nervously, clutching my box tighter as if it were a protective shield. "Looking for me? Why? Is everything alright?"

Lucien hesitated, glancing pointedly at the cleared desk behind me. "Mr. Blackwell was…concerned when he couldn't reach you. Especially after recent events."

I glanced down awkwardly at the contents of the box—my small potted plant, a half-empty box of pens, and a picture of my parents. My cheeks flushed hotly with embarrassment. "Oh, um, I was just talking to Linda. Sorry, I didn't realize I'd cause panic. You can call off the search party."

One of the security guards chuckled softly under his breath before quickly stifling it at Lucien's sharp glance.

Lucien stepped closer, lowering his voice slightly. "Perhaps next time you decide to vanish after a violent incident, a quick message would be advisable, Harper."

"Right," I mumbled sheepishly, cheeks burning brighter. "Good advice. I'll remember that."

He gave me a small nod, dismissing the guards with a subtle gesture. As they dispersed, Lucien's eyes fell back to the box I was gripping awkwardly. He arched an eyebrow, voice gentle but probing. "And the box?"

I sighed deeply, my shoulders slumping. "I was... anticipating my resignation being accepted, I guess."

He almost smiled, shaking his head slowly. "I think you'll find Mr. Blackwell is rarely that accommodating. He's expecting you in the conference room."

My stomach twisted nervously, dread pooling heavily at his words. "Yeah, figured as much," I muttered dryly. "I suppose he's pretty upset?"

Lucien's expression remained carefully impassive, though his eyes held a glint of mild amusement. "I believe the term is 'extremely displeased.' I'd advise you to head there immediately."

"Right. Totally looking forward to that conversation," I mumbled sarcastically, setting the box back onto my desk with resignation. "Thanks for the heads up, Lucien."

He inclined his head slightly. "Good luck, Harper."

"Yeah," I said with a sigh, steeling myself as I started walking toward the conference room. "I think I'm gonna need it."

Elias

"We'll start without her," I announced firmly as I re-entered the conference room, forcing my focus back to the matter at hand. But even as I began speaking, detailing plans and strategies, a small, insistent voice whispered persistently in the back of my mind, wondering exactly where Harper was—and why her absence unsettled me so deeply.

The resignation email replayed itself stubbornly in my thoughts. Harper's defiance wasn't just an inconvenience; it was rapidly becoming a distraction—a distraction I could scarcely afford.

Marcus cleared his throat discreetly, pulling my attention back to the table. "Sir, regarding the security arrangements for the event"

"Proceed," I said curtly, masking my irritation behind a controlled façade.

He hesitated briefly, clearly reading my impatience, but continued smoothly. "We've doubled patrols and surveillance, but the invitations you've insisted on sending are still a risk."

"The event will proceed," I repeated firmly, noting the uneasy glances exchanged around the table. "The security risks are manageable."

"Sir," Isabella began, her voice cautious yet firm, "perhaps we should reconsider—"

"We reconsider nothing," I snapped, my patience fraying dangerously thin. Isabella's eyebrows rose slightly, but she wisely said nothing further, settling back into an uneasy silence. Lucien's quiet, assessing gaze flickered briefly between us, reading the tension expertly but wisely choosing to remain silent.

"Harper Wells is fairly new, Eias." Marcus interjected calmly, attempting to diffuse some of the mounting tension. "She might not fully grasp the stakes involved. Perhaps clearer expectations—"

"She understands perfectly," I interrupted sharply, my tone colder than intended. "And if she doesn't, she'll learn quickly."

"Is there a particular reason Miss Wells isn't joining us today?" Seraphina asked pointedly, her voice carefully neutral, though I caught the faint curiosity behind her gaze.

"An oversight," I replied evenly, unwilling to reveal the tension beneath my calm exterior.

Lucien gently entered the room, and his thoughtful gaze caught mine briefly, understanding clearly etched in his quiet scrutiny, though he offered no comment as he took his seat. The meeting continued uneasily, my responses clipped, each word masking deeper frustrations.

The conference room door swung open suddenly, startling everyone except me—I'd sensed her approach before the door moved. Harper stumbled in, cheeks flushed, eyes wide and apologetic, her hair slightly tousled as if she'd hurried to get here. Her gaze darted around nervously, landing finally on mine.

"I'm sorry," she blurted out immediately, waving a hand dismissively. "I had a… minor crisis involving an overly ambitious pigeon and my coffee. Long story short, the pigeon won."

A ripple of barely concealed amusement ran around the table, quickly silenced by my sharp glance. I fixed Harper with a hard stare, battling the irrational urge to smirk at her absurd yet entirely believable excuse.

"Take your seat, Miss Wells," I instructed coolly, deliberately emphasizing the formality of her name. Her eyes flickered briefly with irritation, and something else—relief, perhaps—before she moved swiftly to the empty chair beside me.

As she settled into place, I allowed myself a brief glance in her direction. Harper's presence brought an unsettling mix of relief and renewed frustration. Clearly, her resignation would require a far more detailed conversation, but for now, her presence restored a sense of normalcy—although a chaotic one—that I hadn't realized I needed.

"Now," I continued sternly, returning my attention fully to the gathered executives, "let's proceed without further distractions."

Harper

The meeting wrapped up in a strangely subdued shuffle of chairs and awkward coughs, the executives practically sprinting for the door as if the building had just caught fire. I stood too, hoping to slip away unnoticed with the wave of retreating suits, but Elias's voice caught me mid-step.

"Stay, Miss Wells."

My heart made a spectacular swan dive into my stomach, hitting every nerve on its way down. Great. This was exactly what I needed after the world's most uncomfortable morning, more alone time with Mr. Resting Murder Face himself.

I hovered awkwardly beside my chair as the last person fled the conference room, the click of the door sealing us inside together. Elias stood by the enormous window, one hand tucked in his pocket, the other broad palm braced against the glass as he stared out at the city below. Sunlight cast sharp angles across his profile, highlighting the tense lines of his jaw and the rigid set of his shoulders.

"Harper," he began, his voice deceptively calm, controlled, and annoyingly impossible to read. "We need to discuss your letter."

I swallowed nervously, clutching the back of the chair for moral support. "My resignation letter?"

He turned slowly, his golden eyes narrowed thoughtfully, assessing me like some complex puzzle he couldn't quite solve. "Did you submit another?"

"No," I admitted sheepishly, heart thudding annoyingly loud in my ears. "But considering your rather definitive answer, I thought I'd at least get creative and leave a physical copy. You know, just for dramatic effect."

His expression remained carefully neutral, though I swore I saw the faintest twitch at the corner of his mouth. "I saw it."

"Great," I muttered, suddenly very aware of how ridiculous I must look, gripping the chair like a lifeline. "So, does 'no' still stand, or should I expect a more formal rejection this time?"

Elias stepped closer, the intensity in his eyes deepening as his voice dropped lower, almost conspiratorial. "Why are you so determined to leave, Harper? Are you really that afraid of pigeons?" *His attempt at humor? What the fuck.*

Ignoring it, I huffed indignantly, folding my arms tightly across my chest, chin lifted stubbornly despite the anxiety swirling in my stomach. "Maybe I just prefer a workplace with less knife-related injuries. Call me old-fashioned."

His expression softened slightly, a shadow passing across his face...regret or something deeper, more complicated. For just a fleeting moment, the unyielding Elias Blackwell looked almost vulnerable.

"You're safer here, believe it or not," he murmured, a faint, reluctant sincerity coloring his voice.

I snorted softly, a nervous laugh escaping before I could stop it. "If this is your version of safety, Mr. Blackwell, I'd really hate to see your idea of danger."

His eyes held mine, golden and intense, unwavering beneath my attempted bravado. The silence between us stretched taut, filled with questions neither of us seemed willing—or ready—to voice aloud. Finally, Elias sighed, breaking the standoff first. He ran a hand through his hair, the gesture strangely vulnerable and human.

"Harper," he began quietly, the hard edge of command slipping briefly, replaced by something softer—something that twisted unexpectedly at my heart. "Stay."

My pulse quickened uncomfortably, betraying every logical instinct shouting at me to sprint for the nearest exit. I shifted nervously, my stubbornness warring fiercely with the unsettling warmth spreading in my chest.

"Why?" I blurted out, unable to stop myself. "Mr. Blackwell let's be real here, there are a thousand more qualified assistants who don't flinch at a bit of blood or knife-throwing assassins. I'm pretty sure your HR department has them on speed dial."

A flicker of amusement crossed his features, surprising and oddly appealing. "Because I asked nicely. Isn't that reason enough?"

I felt heat rush to my cheeks, annoyed that he'd turned my defiance into something softer, almost personal. I crossed my arms protectively, scowling at the floor. "I suppose. But next time, I'm definitely demanding hazard pay."

Elias chuckled unexpectedly, a low, rich sound that sent my heart stumbling unhelpfully against my ribs. "Hazard pay it is," he agreed quietly, eyes dancing with something suspiciously close to genuine amusement.

"Fine," I muttered grudgingly, meeting his gaze again, suddenly all too aware of how close we stood, how the space between us had shrunk without either of us seeming to move. "But just so we're clear, if another knife ends up anywhere near your chest, I reserve the right to reconsider."

Elias's mouth twitched, almost forming a real smile. "Understood."

As I turned to leave, I felt the weight of his gaze follow me, somehow both comforting and deeply unsettling. Every step away felt heavier, my heart thundering wildly, knowing I'd just made a decision I might regret but desperately hoping I wouldn't.

After surviving the epic embarrassment of having a literal search party dispatched for me—*talk about dramatic*—I trudged back to my desk, cheeks still burning fiercely. I set the cardboard box down with an exasperated sigh, eyeing its contents with mild irritation.

"So much for my big exit," I muttered sarcastically, grabbing my potted succulent and placing it defiantly back on the corner of my desk. The little plant stared back at me accusingly, as if it knew this resignation thing was never going to stick anyway.

One by one, I returned each item to its previous spot—the half-empty box of pens slid neatly into my drawer, the family picture back in its place next to my monitor. I stared briefly at the photo, my parents' warm smiles offering a small comfort amidst my current humiliation.

Just then, the soft click of heels caught my attention, and I glanced up to see Linda walking briskly past my desk, tablet tucked firmly under her arm. She slowed just enough to offer a quick, knowing glance, one eyebrow raised in silent amusement.

"Not a word, Linda," I warned playfully, feeling my cheeks flush even hotter.

"Oh, I wouldn't dare," she replied smoothly, lips curling into an understanding smile. "Good luck in there."

"Thanks," I groaned, slumping slightly into my chair. "I'm going to need every ounce of it."

Chapter 5

Chain of Events

Harper

Nearly two months later, my ill-fated resignation had become little more than an awkward memory, one I tucked away alongside other embarrassments I'd prefer never to revisit—like that unfortunate incident with my prom dress or my first attempt at parallel parking. I'd fallen into a rhythm at Blackwell Industries, navigating the controlled chaos of Elias's world with steadily increasing confidence—or at least, less outright panic.

Still, every now and then, when the office grew quiet and the late-afternoon sun slanted through the windows just so, I'd find myself replaying the strange sincerity in Elias's eyes that morning—the unsettling glimpse of vulnerability he'd allowed me.

Not that he'd ever admit it had happened, of course.

"So..." I asked brightly, holding up yet another silk tie and jacket combination—this one deep midnight-blue against crisp charcoal fabric—"are you excited for tonight?"

Elias sighed, shifting impatiently on the raised platform in the center of his expansive dressing room. Mirrors stretched endlessly around us, reflecting every angle of his imposing figure. The soft, golden glow of recessed lighting illuminated shelves of custom-tailored suits, silk ties, and polished shoes, creating an atmosphere of impeccable elegance and refined power. His expression hovered somewhere between exasperation and reluctant amusement as he glanced down at me, clearly unimpressed with my enthusiastic approach to fashion consulting.

"Excited?" he echoed dryly, meeting my eyes in the reflection with a raised eyebrow. "That's not the word I'd choose."

I rolled my eyes dramatically, stepping closer to adjust the collar of his crisp white shirt. I couldn't help but notice how the sleek fabric hugged the strong lines of his shoulders. My fingers lingered momentarily, feeling the warmth radiating subtly through the fabric, before quickly busying themselves again. "Perfect. Now, try not to scowl too much tonight, it scares the guests. They might think you're planning their demise."

Elias's lips twitched reluctantly into a half-smile. "Maybe I am."

"Well, if you are, at least pretend otherwise until after dessert. I ordered chocolate mousse, and it deserves respect." I stepped back, inspecting him with exaggerated seriousness. "And besides, a smile once in a while might actually make people think you're approachable."

He raised one brow skeptically. "We wouldn't want that now, would we?"

"Oh, heaven forbid," I quipped, stepping away to fold the unused tie carefully back into its velvet-lined drawer. "That might tarnish your reputation as a perfectly terrifying, brooding CEO."

A low chuckle rumbled softly from his chest, a sound that had grown increasingly common—and annoyingly appealing—over the last few weeks. I pretended not to notice the flutter of warmth that danced stubbornly in my chest each time it happened.

Laughing softly to cover my nervousness, I turned toward the door, feeling his gaze lingering on me as I moved.

"What are you wearing tonight?" Elias asked suddenly, his voice stopping me just as my hand reached for the polished brass doorknob.

I hesitated, glancing back over my shoulder, genuinely surprised by the question. "Oh, I wasn't actually planning on attending, Mr. Blackwell. It's not really my vibe, and I'd probably break something expensive or spill champagne on someone important. Plus, to be honest, I've got nothing remotely snazzy to wear. So, I'll sit this one out."

His brow furrowed slightly, eyes narrowing in that annoyingly determined way he had when he made up his mind about something. "Unacceptable."

"Excuse me?" I asked, eyebrows shooting upward as I turned fully to face him, leaning against the doorway with crossed arms.

"You heard me." Elias reached calmly for his phone; eyes locked on mine in a silent challenge as he began dialing. "You should know this about me by now, Miss Wells—I don't take no for an answer."

My pulse quickened inexplicably, irritation mingling with curiosity. He spoke quickly into the phone, his voice cool and commanding. "Yes, I need an evening gown delivered to Miss Wells today." He paused briefly, giving me a thoughtful once-over, his gaze slowly sweeping my frame in a way that made my cheeks grow hot. "Something sophisticated. Midnight blue—to complement my attire. Shoes to match, size seven. And have it delivered promptly."

I stared at him, speechless, my mouth opening and closing like an incredulous goldfish. "You're serious?"

Elias leaned back in the chair beside the platform, stretching out comfortably as though he'd just secured victory. A faint smirk curled at the edges of his mouth. "Always. Now you have no excuses, Miss Wells."

I narrowed my eyes at him playfully, heat still burning my cheeks. "You know, most people ask before sending unsolicited evening wear."

"Most people aren't me," Elias replied smoothly, a hint of genuine amusement brightening his usually guarded eyes. "And besides, you'll thank me later."

"Right, because forced attendance at stuffy events is always the highlight of my week," I muttered sarcastically, shaking my head in disbelief.

His expression softened just slightly, voice lowering gently, almost conspiratorially. "Come tonight. If only because I'd find it exceedingly dull without you, Miss Wells."

My heart stuttered traitorously in my chest, annoyance at my reaction melting away beneath his unexpected sincerity. I huffed lightly, pretending to consider. "Fine. But if I embarrass myself—or you—it's entirely your fault."

"Fair enough," Elias agreed with an indulgent smile, waving me off with exaggerated nonchalance.

Exiting swiftly before I changed my mind, I closed the heavy wooden door behind me, my heart still racing from frustration—and something else, something deeper, more unsettling. Elias Blackwell was infuriating, arrogant, and entirely too aware of his own charm. Yet, despite my best efforts, I found myself looking forward to the evening more than I cared to admit.

I exhaled a slow, shaky breath, wondering exactly when my professional boundaries had become so dangerously blurred—and knowing, deep down, it was probably the moment Elias had refused to let me resign.

If anyone had told me three months ago that I'd spend a random Thursday evening in my tiny Brooklyn apartment surrounded by an actual glam squad, I would have assumed they were severely overcaffeinated. Yet here I sat, perched awkwardly on a makeshift stool, watching wide-eyed as three impeccably dressed professionals fussed over me like I was prepping for the Oscars rather than an overpriced corporate gala.

"Relax your shoulders, honey," instructed the stylist—Marco, according to his engraved nameplate—as he carefully pinned my hair into an elegant, cascading style that looked deceptively effortless. He flashed me a conspiratorial wink through the mirror. "You're going to look phenomenal."

"If you say so," I muttered dubiously, eyeing the expensive midnight-blue gown hanging dramatically on the door frame. The silk fabric gleamed like liquid sapphire, undeniably gorgeous but absurdly intimidating. "I'm just praying I don't rip that thing before we even get to the venue."

Marco laughed warmly, shaking his head. "Trust me, Mr. Blackwell chose well. He knows what suits you."

Heat rose in my cheeks, and I fought the urge to roll my eyes. "Of course he does," I murmured sarcastically. "He's nothing if not thorough."

By the time they finished, I hardly recognized myself. Staring into the mirror, I felt strangely disconnected—my reflection looked polished, glamorous even, with makeup highlighting features I usually didn't bother to notice. My chest tightened with nervous excitement. Maybe Elias really did know what he was doing, after all.

A sleek black limousine waited for me outside, gleaming beneath the early evening sky. As the driver held open the polished door with practiced courtesy, I stepped inside cautiously, eyes widening at the plush leather seats and soft, moody lighting. This was definitely a few steps up from my usual Uber pool.

"Champagne, Miss Wells?" the driver asked, a slight smile flickering across his stoic features as he glanced at me through the rear-view mirror.

"Yes, please," I breathed gratefully, settling back into the sumptuous leather as he smoothly poured a bubbling flute. After a hesitant sip — then two — I finally broke the silence.

"So, how long have you been doing this? Driving, I mean?" I asked, leaning forward, desperate to fill the silence that had quickly turned awkward.

"Almost ten years," he replied evenly, amusement dancing in his eyes. "Mr. Blackwell always requests me specifically."

"Of course he does," I muttered dryly, earning another barely contained grin from my chauffeur. "Must be a real charmer to work for."

"He has his moments," the driver admitted diplomatically, guiding us expertly through evening traffic. "Though he seems particularly attentive to your comfort tonight."

"Attentive," I echoed, taking a deeper sip of champagne. "Is that what we're calling it?"

He chuckled softly, not elaborating further, leaving me to ponder exactly what he meant as we pulled up to the extravagant, historic mansion perched elegantly on the edge of Central Park. Its grand, sweeping marble staircase spilled down toward the street, warmly illuminated by hundreds of delicate, glowing lanterns. The very air seemed charged with anticipation.

My breath caught sharply. "Oh. This is…wow."

The driver smiled knowingly, opening my door with practiced ease. "Enjoy your evening, Miss Wells."

Inside, the space was already buzzing. Servers and event staff hurried gracefully through elegant rooms, carrying gleaming trays of crystal glassware and miniature gourmet appetizers. Flower arrangements towered over tables, and string quartets softly rehearsed in the grand ballroom.

"Miss Wells?" a sharply dressed woman approached, tablet in hand, her expression alert but friendly. "I'm Claire, the event manager. Nice to put face to a name. Mr. Blackwell said you'd be overseeing the final details?"

I quickly shifted into professional mode, grateful for the distraction from the fluttering nerves threatening to overwhelm me. "Yes, absolutely. Let's run through everything."

Over the next half-hour, Claire led me swiftly through the opulent halls. I adjusted table placements, confirmed music cues, and double-checked security stations, finally regaining a sense of calm amidst the controlled chaos. By the time we finished, guests had started trickling in, their excited chatter filling the air.

"You've done an exceptional job," Claire praised warmly, looking genuinely impressed. "Mr. Blackwell will be very pleased."

"Thanks," I exhaled in relief, my nerves finally settling. "I really appreciate it."

"Of course. I'll see you inside." With a parting nod, she left me alone in a quiet, ornate corridor, where I gratefully took a moment to breathe.

Through an intricately carved doorway, I noticed a secluded balcony overlooking the main ballroom. Drawn by curiosity and the urge for one last private moment, I stepped quietly onto the polished marble surface, gazing down at the breathtaking scene unfolding below. The space shimmered with candlelight, crystal chandeliers casting delicate prisms of light across the walls. Guests mingled effortlessly, their laughter echoing softly upwards like music.

And then, as though sensing my presence, Elias turned suddenly from his conversation below, his gaze locking unerringly onto mine. Standing there, framed by the luxurious surroundings and impeccably dressed guests, he looked effortlessly powerful—a king surveying his domain. Yet, as our eyes met, the intensity in his gaze softened into something far more complicated, more intimate.

My pulse quickened traitorously, heat rushing to my cheeks as I held his stare. Elias's expression was unreadable—except for the faintest, almost imperceptible lift at the corner of his lips, as if my presence alone had shifted something within him.

My breath caught sharply in my chest. Damn him, he knew exactly what he was doing.

Gathering my scattered courage, I raised one eyebrow challengingly and offered him a subtle, defiant smirk of my own. Elias's gaze deepened, eyes glinting with approval—or possibly amusement—before finally, reluctantly, he returned his attention to his guests.

As I slowly started my way down the elegant stairway, my fingers brushed gently against the polished banister, each step resonating softly against the gleaming marble beneath my feet. My heart thundered in my chest, nerves and excitement blending into a dizzying rush. I felt his eyes lift toward me, appreciative murmurs mingling with the gentle hum of conversation.

In that moment, with Elias's gaze subtly tracking my every move from across the ballroom, a surge of pride filled my lungs. Tonight wasn't just about being his assistant, running errands and dodging his icy stares. Tonight, I stood on my own, embraced by an unfamiliar confidence—part of something larger, something extraordinary.

Maybe, just maybe, I belonged here after all.

Elias

The afternoon passed in a whirlwind of meticulous preparation, each detail requiring my sharpest attention—security protocols, guest arrivals, and carefully coordinated escape strategies. Lucien stood steadfast beside me, his calm, methodical presence grounding my restless energy as we moved through the grand ballroom. The usually empty hall had been utterly transformed; glittering crystal chandeliers bathed the room in soft golden light, their reflections shimmering across the polished marble floors. Elegantly draped tables lined the edges, the subtle floral arrangements casting delicate splashes of color and fragrance through the expansive space.

"Surveillance is in place," Lucien reported, his eyes never straying from his tablet as he moved smoothly at my side. "We've doubled perimeter patrols, and all entry and exit points are secured."

"Excellent." My gaze traveled critically across the decorated hall, assessing each corner, each shadow. "And the surrounding buildings?"

"All secured. Our men are strategically positioned. Nothing will slip past us tonight."

"Don't underestimate Ambrose," Isabella warned sharply, her heels clicking rhythmically against the marble as she approached. She wore a sleek black gown, her hair pulled into a tight, elegant bun, every line of her posture radiating authority and vigilance. "If he's involved, he'll exploit even the smallest crack in our defenses."

Marcus joined us calmly, his large frame exuding a quiet strength, a steady counterbalance to Isabella's fiery temperament. "We've coordinated with Seraphina to ensure the surveillance network has no blind spots. Ambrose won't find any weaknesses tonight."

Seraphina moved toward us gracefully, her soft steps nearly silent, her emerald gown flowing like water around her slender figure. "I've also secured escape routes. We have backup teams positioned discreetly nearby if needed."

I felt a sudden surge of gratitude for my pack, the powerful bonds of trust and loyalty connecting us in ways deeper than mere words could express. "Stay vigilant," I said firmly, meeting each of their eyes in turn. "Tonight is crucial. We cannot afford mistakes."

"We understand the stakes, Elias," Isabella responded, her tone softening just a fraction. "No one will catch us unaware."

"Good," I affirmed quietly, allowing a small measure of relief to settle my tension. But beneath my composed exterior, a nagging anxiety persisted—Harper's safety had become an unforeseen priority, complicating matters in ways I still struggled to comprehend.

The murmur of arriving guests stirred me from my introspection, prompting me to adjust my cuff links and straighten my posture. Turning to greet the early arrivals, I froze, the breath stolen abruptly from my lungs.

Harper stood framed in the grand doorway, bathed in the soft glow of evening light, utterly transformed. She wore the midnight blue gown, the rich fabric molding beautifully to her curves before falling elegantly to the floor. A daring slit revealed a hint of smooth, toned leg with every careful step she took down the stairway. The gown's neckline dipped enticingly, highlighting her delicate collarbones, and the off-shoulder sleeves drew attention to the luminous softness of her skin.

My heart thudded uncomfortably in my chest, warmth rushing through my veins, every nerve ending suddenly, acutely aware of her presence. Her hair was styled loosely at her nape, a few rebellious tendrils framing her face, accentuating the innocent yet bold expression she wore. For one unsettling moment, my carefully maintained control threatened to unravel entirely.

Lucien cleared his throat subtly, pulling me from my trance. "Everything all right, sir?"

"Yes," I managed tightly, forcing myself to look away, though my voice betrayed more strain than intended. "Perfectly."

Isabella's gaze flickered knowingly between Harper and me, amusement dancing in her eyes. "Oh, clearly," she murmured dryly, only loud enough for Lucien and me to hear. "Not distracted in the slightest."

I shot her a sharp glare, which only seemed to fuel her quiet laughter. Lucien, ever discreet, maintained his neutral expression, though his slight shift in stance betrayed that he too was keenly aware of my discomfort.

Harper approached, her smile bright and mischievous, confidence and lingering uncertainty mingling irresistibly in her gaze. She paused, smoothing her dress self-consciously. "I gotta say, I clean up kinda nice, right?"

I struggled momentarily, her nearness wreaking havoc on my carefully cultivated composure. "Indeed, you do, Miss Wells," I murmured, my voice rougher than I intended. "Exceptionally well."

Her eyes widened briefly, cheeks flushing with warmth at my admission. But rather than retreat, she stepped even closer, reaching up with surprising boldness to straighten my tie. Her fingers brushed my chest lightly, sending a jolt of electricity cascading through my nerves, igniting an ache deep within me.

"Thanks boss," she whispered, glancing upward through her lashes, voice suddenly intimate, conspiratorial. "Just so you know, though, you're totally rocking the Resting Murder Face right now. Maybe throw in a smile tonight—at least pretend you're enjoying yourself."

A startled laugh escaped me, strangled and incredulous. Lucien's low chuckle and Isabella's barely suppressed snort heightened my embarrassment, though neither dared openly tease.

I cleared my throat, regaining some measure of dignity. "Noted," I replied dryly, arching an eyebrow, though my pulse refused to slow.

She grinned triumphantly, clearly pleased at having once again disrupted my equilibrium. With a graceful pivot, she walked away, the tantalizing glimpse of her exposed leg leaving my throat parched and thoughts scattered.

Lucien discreetly leaned toward me, voice low enough for only my ears. "Careful, sir. Your scent is becoming increasingly difficult to mask."

I stiffened subtly, embarrassment and frustration surging. Isabella, ever observant, inhaled delicately and leaned closer with exaggerated subtlety, eyes gleaming with amusement. "Indeed, brother. She certainly has your...attention."

"Careful, Isabella," I warned quietly, jaw tight, "Curiosity doesn't suit you."

Her soft laughter grated on my nerves. "Oh, please. Any wolf within a mile can sense your reaction. You're fooling no one."

Lucien interjected calmly, a note of warning in his voice, though amusement lingered beneath. "Perhaps we should focus on our guests."

"Yes," I agreed sharply, attempting to force my attention back to the event. But Harper's image stubbornly lingered in my mind—the scent of her skin, the warmth of her touch, the defiance in her eyes. She'd slipped beneath my defenses effortlessly, embedding herself deeply into my consciousness.

Harper Wells had become far more than a distraction.

Harper

"How long have you worked for Elias?" I glanced up, mid-bite into the flaky pastry I'd impulsively snagged from the dessert table. It was sweet, gooey, and I had absolutely no clue what it was—only that it tasted like heaven wrapped in carbs. Around us, soft laughter mingled with piano melodies, crystal chandeliers scattering glittering reflections across polished marble floors.

The woman staring down at me, however, seemed less impressed by my choice in snacks. Her gaze was sharp, inquisitive, borderline intense, matching her statuesque figure perfectly. Seriously, did everyone Elias associated with look like they just stepped out of a luxury fragrance ad?

I swallowed quickly, clearing my throat. "Um, about three months?" My words came out muffled as I awkwardly wiped crumbs from the corner of my mouth. "Or maybe three eternities. I haven't decided yet."

She tilted her head slightly, assessing me with eyes the color of midnight, her dark hair cascading elegantly over one shoulder. Her expression was unreadable, hovering somewhere between amused curiosity and polite judgment.

"Hmm. That's longer than most." Her voice was smooth, melodic—yet there was an undercurrent of something sharp, like steel hidden beneath velvet. "Elias isn't known for keeping assistants around very long."

"Yeah, I've noticed," I said, swallowing hard and glancing nervously toward where Elias stood, effortlessly commanding attention across the room. "Honestly, I'm still waiting for the day he realizes I have no idea what I'm doing and kicks me to the curb."

To my surprise, the mysterious woman laughed—a genuine sound that somehow made her both less intimidating and more fascinating. "I doubt that will happen," she said conspiratorially, leaning in closer. "If anything, it looks like you've caught his attention far more than most. I haven't seen him this… unsettled in decades."

I choked on the pastry, coughing inelegantly as heat flamed my cheeks. "Oh no, it's definitely annoyance. I promise."

She merely smiled again, a knowing glint sparkling mischievously in her eyes. "If you say so, Harper. But take my advice—be careful. Elias Blackwell's attention isn't always the safest place to be."

With that cryptic warning lingering heavily between us, she gave a graceful nod and drifted away, leaving me clutching my pastry and wondering exactly what I'd gotten myself into this time.

As soon as she departed, a wonderfully distracting replacement was at my heels.

"Hi, Harper. I'm Damian."

His voice, low and rich as warm honey, sent chills cascading down my spine, igniting parts of me that had been dormant for far too long. Over a year, to be exact—not that anyone was counting.

Slowly, I turned, blinking up at yet another unfairly attractive man who seemed to have emerged straight from a secret fantasy. Damian's dark curls brushed just above his collar, stormy gray eyes dancing with barely concealed amusement. When he adjusted his cuffs, the intricate tattoos caught my eye again—sharp black lines weaving in mysterious patterns that hinted at stories far darker than his charming smile suggested.

He extended his hand, his warmth instantly making my pulse quicken. "Harper Wells," I managed softly, voice embarrassingly breathless. I cleared my throat, attempting a more dignified tone. "Nice to meet you."

His smile deepened, showing a flash of perfect teeth. "Believe me, the pleasure is entirely mine."

I laughed awkwardly, immediately regretting it as my cheeks heated, certain they were a telltale shade of crimson by now. "I highly doubt that."

"Oh, don't sell yourself short," Damian murmured, stepping just a fraction closer, his voice dropping low enough to send a fresh wave of shivers down my spine. "You've been the main topic of conversation tonight."

"Great," I muttered, heart hammering uncontrollably. "That's not terrifying at all."

Damian chuckled softly, eyes glittering as he reached to casually adjust his sleeve cuffs, drawing my attention to the intricate tattoos snaking over his wrists. "Relax, Harper. I promise we're mostly harmless."

"Mostly?" I echoed faintly.

He leaned forward, lowering his voice conspiratorially. "Well, I might bite. But I don't mean anything by it…usually."

I stared up at him, heart racing as my mind scrambled uselessly for words. Damian radiated a magnetism that was both exhilarating and terrifying. My thoughts felt suddenly fuzzy, tangled with an impulsive, reckless longing I'd thought long buried. A small voice whispered warnings in the back of my mind, but they faded rapidly beneath the power of his gaze.

"So," he continued, straightening up, eyes glinting playfully, "care to save me from the boredom of corporate small talk?"

I hesitated only a heartbeat before nodding, curiosity outweighing caution. "Absolutely. Lead the way."

He took a slow step closer, his presence warm, magnetic, almost overwhelming as his eyes locked onto mine, a teasing smile playing across his lips. I inhaled sharply, suddenly dizzy from whatever impossibly delicious scent seemed to swirl around him, filling my senses and clouding every rational thought. He smelled earthy, rich, and dangerously alluring—like a midnight forest after rain.

"You like it?" Damian asked softly, his voice a low hum that vibrated deep into my chest. His gaze flickered between me and the tranquil, moonlit waters, a playful smile curling the corners of his mouth.

"It's…perfect," I murmured breathlessly, unable to tear my eyes away from him even long enough to appreciate the view. "Honestly, I didn't even know this was back here, and I booked the freaking venue!"

He laughed softly, warm and deep, the sound curling pleasantly around me, soothing nerves I didn't realize were frayed. "Then I'm glad to be the one showing you hidden secrets," he said, stepping closer still.

Suddenly, I was acutely aware of his proximity, the warmth radiating from his body mingling intoxicatingly with that scent. My heart quickened, a fluttering pulse betraying every rational thought.

Damian reached up, fingers lightly brushing away a stray tendril of hair from my cheek, lingering just a moment too long. "You seem nervous," he teased gently, eyes glittering in the faint starlight.

"You noticed that, huh?" I laughed weakly, feeling a heat rush into my cheeks. "I mean—you're…you know, kind of ridiculously beautiful. And very tall."

His laughter was warm, genuine, and deep, vibrating pleasantly in the air between us. "And you, Harper Wells, are refreshingly honest."

I swallowed, looking up into his dark, mesmerizing eyes. "It's a curse," I said quietly, unable to look away. "I over share, trip over nothing, and apparently forget to finish sentences around men who smell like…" I hesitated, flustered. "I don't even know how to describe it, but it's really, really good."

He leaned closer, eyes dancing with amusement and something deeper, more primal. "Good," he murmured softly. "That's exactly how I want you to feel."

My breath caught, heart pounding as Damian leaned ever closer, completely and utterly capturing me in his orbit.

Damian's lips brushed softly against mine, gentle yet commanding, erasing every coherent thought from my mind in an instant. My heart skipped, tripped, and then proceeded to completely malfunction as warmth flooded my entire body. A delicious shiver rolled down my spine, and every nerve ending lit up like tiny fireworks beneath my skin.

I pulled back slightly, dazed and blinking up at him, suddenly breathless. "Um—hi. Hello. Sorry. I don't normally kiss complete strangers. Or, well, anyone. Honestly, it's been a while. Clearly."

He chuckled lowly, his breath ghosting softly over my cheek. "Then I'm honored to be the exception, Harper."

I laughed nervously, trying—and failing—to sound casual. "You're dangerously charming, you know that? It's probably illegal somewhere."

Damian's lips curved into a slow, playful grin, his eyes darkening with mischief. "I'll risk it."

His face dipped lower again, his mouth brushing mine gently, teasingly, and for a heartbeat, I surrendered completely to the intoxicating pull between us. But somewhere in the hazy back corner of my mind, alarm bells began softly chiming, whispering urgently that this was madness—dangerous, reckless madness.

"You know," I murmured shakily, pulling back again, though every instinct in me protested, "as amazing as this is—and it really is, believe me—I think I should probably get back. My boss kind of scares me, and I don't think I can afford to be fired tonight. Or ever."

He chuckled warmly, stepping back just enough to give me space, though his eyes held promises that made my knees weak. "Then we should continue this later."

"I'd like that," I admitted softly, smiling helplessly. "A lot, actually."

He offered his arm, guiding me gently back toward the bustling event inside, leaving me to wonder just how I'd manage to function normally with the taste of Damian still lingering on my lips.

The event hall was alive with the gentle murmur of conversation, soft laughter mingling effortlessly with the delicate melody of a nearby piano. Crystal chandeliers overhead cast gentle, glittering reflections across the polished marble floors. Every time Damian leaned in to speak, the subtle scent of his cologne mixed seductively with the crisp, floral notes from the nearby bouquets, making my head spin even more.

Elias

The grand ballroom shimmered under the glow of a thousand crystal chandeliers, their light refracting through the amber liquid in my glass like shards of captured sunlight. The hum of conversation and the faint strains of a string quartet filled the air, a symphony of wealth and power that I had long since grown accustomed to. Yet tonight, the opulence felt hollow, the noise grating against my nerves like sandpaper. My gaze swept over the sea of tailored suits and glittering gowns, searching for the one person who could anchor me in this sea of pretense.

Harper.

She had been gone too long, her absence a gnawing ache in my chest. The city officials and corporate executives who hovered near me were nothing more than background noise, their words blending into a monotonous drone. I nodded absently at Councilman Grayson, his pudgy face flushed with the effort of ingratiating himself.

"Yes, Councilman," I murmured, my voice smooth and practiced, though a faint undercurrent of disgust tightened my jaw as I met his gaze. His eyes, a shade too pale, glinted with a cold, calculating light that belied his warm smile. The faint scent of decay clung to him, masked poorly by the heavy cologne he wore—a futile attempt to hide what he truly was. A vampire. One of the many parasites who had infiltrated the city's power structures, feeding on its resources and its people while hiding behind a veneer of respectability.

"I understand your concerns," I continued, my tone carefully neutral, "but Blackwell Industries has always prioritized the city's needs. You have my assurances the project will benefit everyone involved."

The councilman's smile widened, revealing teeth that were just a little too sharp, a little too white. "Of course, Mr. Blackwell," he said, his voice slick and ingratiating. "Your reputation speaks for itself. I have no doubt you'll deliver on your promises."

I forced a tight smile, my stomach churning at the way his gaze lingered on me, predatory and assessing. He was testing me, probing for weakness, as his kind always did. But I had long since mastered the art of hiding my revulsion. To him, I was nothing more than a useful tool, a means to an end. And to me, he was a necessary evil, a stepping stone in a game I had no choice but to play.

"Your confidence is appreciated, Councilman," I replied, my voice cool and measured. "I'll ensure the details are handled with the utmost care."

He nodded eagerly; his relief palpable as he clutched his champagne flute like a lifeline. The faintest hint of red stained the rim of the glass, and I fought the urge to recoil. How many lives had he drained to maintain his position? How many more would he destroy if given the chance?

As he turned to leave, I allowed myself a moment to exhale, the tension in my shoulders easing slightly. But the taste of bile lingered in the back of my throat, a bitter reminder of the world I navigated—a world where monsters wore suits and smiles, and the line between ally and enemy was razor-thin.

My gaze drifted back to the crowd, searching once more for Harper. She was the only light in this darkness, the only thing that kept me grounded. And I would do whatever it took to protect her from the predators who lurked in the shadows—even if it meant playing nice with the likes of Councilman Grayson.

And then, there she was.

Harper reappeared through the glass doors that led from the terrace, her cheeks flushed from the cool night air. My pulse quickened at the sight of her, only to sour abruptly as I noticed the man at her side. He was tall, with broad shoulders and a confident stride, his hand resting lightly on the small of her back as he leaned in to whisper something in her ear. Harper laughed softly, the sound like music, her eyes sparkling with a warmth that sent a surge of possessive fury coursing through me.

The room seemed to shrink, the air thickening with the cloying scent of perfumes and colognes. My vision narrowed, zeroing in on the pair as they moved through the crowd. The man's smile was too wide, his posture too familiar, and the way Harper's gaze lingered on him made my jaw tighten.

As though sensing my gaze, Harper glanced up, her eyes meeting mine for a brief moment before she quickly looked away. Her laughter faded, replaced by an awkward silence that only fueled my irritation. Good. She should feel the weight of my displeasure.

I set my glass down with more force than necessary, the delicate crystal trembling on the table. Lucien materialized at my side like a shadow, his sharp eyes following my gaze to Harper and her companion.

"Is there a problem, Elias?" he asked, his voice low and measured.

"There might be," I growled, my tone dark and edged with a possessiveness I couldn't conceal. "Find out exactly who that man is. I want every detail."

Lucien inclined his head subtly, his expression unreadable. "Consider it done."

Without another word, I straightened my shoulders and moved through the crowd with purposeful strides. The guests parted before me, their conversations faltering as they sensed the storm brewing beneath my calm exterior. Harper was mine to protect, mine to claim, and I would not tolerate another man's intrusion.

I closed the distance between us in an instant, my fingers curling around Harper's arm as I let out a low growl aimed at this stranger. I pulled Harper into the seclusion of a small, dimly lit side room. She gasped softly, her eyes wide with surprise as I pressed her gently but firmly against the closed door. The scent of another man on her skin was maddening, sharp and intrusive, triggering something raw and territorial deep within me.

"Who was he?" My voice was low, dangerous, edged with an intensity that I didn't bother to conceal.

Harper blinked rapidly; her confusion evident. "What? Who?"

"The man you were with on the terrace," I growled, leaning in closer, my voice a low, dangerous rumble that vibrated between us. My hands, still gripping her arms, slid down to her wrists, pinning them gently but firmly against the door. Harper's breath hitched, her chest rising and falling rapidly as she stared up at me, her wide eyes searching mine for answers I wasn't ready to give. Her hands twitched beneath my grasp, not struggling but not yielding either, as if she were caught between pushing me away and pulling me closer.

My gaze dropped to the pulse racing erratically in her throat, the delicate flutter of her heartbeat betraying her nerves. Before I could stop myself, I dipped my head toward her, inhaling deeply along the curve of her neck, her jaw, her face. Her scent flooded my senses, sweet and intoxicating—like wildflowers and sunlight, a stark contrast to the cold, calculating world I inhabited. Yet threaded through it was the undeniable scent of another man, aggressive and unwelcome, a violation of something I hadn't realized I'd claimed as mine.

A low, possessive sound escaped me, unbidden, as my hands tightened slightly on her wrists. My body pressed closer, almost of its own accord, the heat of her skin searing through the thin fabric of her dress. I could feel the rapid rise and fall of her chest against mine, her breath warm and uneven against my cheek. The combination of her proximity and the lingering scent of the stranger was maddening, a volatile mix that sent a surge of conflicting emotions coursing through me—anger, yes, but something else, too. Something darker, that tightened my gut and sent a dangerous heat pooling low in my abdomen.

Harper's hands flexed beneath mine, her fingers curling slightly as if she were considering reaching for me. Instead, she tilted her head back, exposing more of her throat in a way that made my pulse spike. Her lips parted, a soft, breathless sound escaping her, and for a moment, I forgot why I was angry. All I could think about was how easy it would be to close the distance between us, to claim her mouth with mine and erase the scent of anyone else who dared to touch her.

But then she spoke, her voice trembling but defiant, snapping me back to reality. Mr. Blackwell," she whispered, her tone equal parts confusion and arousal. "What are you doing?"

Her words were like a splash of cold water, pulling me back from the edge of whatever precipice I'd been teetering on. I exhaled sharply, forcing myself to loosen my grip on her wrists, though every instinct screamed to hold on tighter. My hands slid away reluctantly, coming to rest on either side of her head, caging her in without touching her. I leaned back just enough to meet her gaze, my own eyes dark and stormy with emotions I couldn't—or wouldn't—name.

A possessive growl vibrated deep in my chest, surprising even me.

"Who was he, Harper?" I demanded again, my voice low and dangerous. "Did he touch you?"

She trembled slightly beneath my gaze, her breath hitching as my lips brushed dangerously close to her skin. "I—I don't know," she stammered, her voice breathless. "Dammit, Elias, what's gotten into you?"

I forced myself to step back slightly, though my gaze never left hers.

"Be careful who you trust," I warned quietly, my tone dark and edged with frustration I couldn't fully conceal. "Not everyone here is who they seem."

Harper's eyes narrowed, her arms folding defensively across her chest. "Yeah…uh, I'm kind of getting that vibe," she replied, her voice trembling slightly despite her attempt at bravado. "What the hell, Mr. Blackwell? Have you had too much to drink or something?"

I exhaled sharply, running a hand through my hair. "Quite the opposite," I muttered darkly, my eyes narrowing. "I'm painfully sober, Harper, and perhaps seeing things clearer than ever."

She blinked up at me, uncertainty and frustration mingling openly on her face. Her chin tilted stubbornly upward, her defiance both irritating and irresistibly endearing. "Then explain, because I'm officially confused," she insisted, her voice sharper now, demanding clarity. "You're acting like—like some jealous boyfriend. Which, spoiler alert, you're not."

Her words hit harder than I'd expected, a sudden surge of possessive anger flashing dangerously through me. I narrowed my eyes slightly, taking another slow, controlled breath, regaining the composure that had momentarily slipped.

"You're correct, Miss Wells," I said finally, my voice tightly controlled, colder than I intended. "I'm not. But I am responsible for your safety. This event—these people—it's more dangerous than you realize. Be cautious. Do you understand?"

She stared back at me for a long moment, visibly processing my warning. Her eyes softened slightly, confusion giving way to cautious understanding. Finally, she nodded slowly.

"Fine," she murmured, more subdued this time. "But if there's danger, maybe give me a heads-up next time before the creepy manhandling?"

Despite the tension, I felt a reluctant smile tug at my lips, softening the harsh edges of my frustration. "Noted, Miss Wells."

She rolled her eyes, visibly relaxing as the tension between us slowly began to ease. "Good. Glad we're on the same page. Can I go now, or do you have more cryptic warnings to impart?"

I hesitated for a brief moment before nodding reluctantly. "Go. But stay in sight."

She smirked slightly, already stepping toward the door. "Yeah, wouldn't wanna miss any more drama."

As she left, the lingering scent of another man's touch still clung stubbornly to my senses, an irritating reminder of a threat I couldn't yet name—and a possessiveness I wasn't yet ready to face. The ballroom seemed colder now, the glittering facade of wealth and power stripped away to reveal the dangerous undercurrents that flowed beneath. Harper was a beacon in this darkness, a light I couldn't afford to lose. And I would do whatever it took to keep her safe—even if it meant confronting the shadows within myself.

Harper

I practically fled from Elias, my heels clicking rapidly across the polished marble floors as I escaped the intensity of whatever the *heck* had just happened. My heart hammered in my chest, loud enough that I was convinced the entire party could hear it. Heat scorched my cheeks, and every step I took felt slightly unsteady, like my legs had suddenly forgotten how to function. The ballroom blurred around me, a kaleidoscope of glittering gowns, clinking glasses, and murmured conversations that felt miles away. All I could focus on was the memory of Elias's hands on me, his voice low and dangerous, his scent wrapping around me like a trap I didn't want to escape.

My breath still came in shallow, ragged gulps, and I instinctively touched my arm where he'd held me, the skin still tingling, imprinted by the heat of his touch. It had been possessive—almost feral—and far more intense than I'd ever expected from him. And that *scent*. God, his scent had wrapped around me like smoke, woodsy and rich, intoxicating enough to blur the edges of rational thought. When he leaned into me, breathing me in, it felt as if my entire body was tethered to him by some invisible thread. I could still feel the heat of his breath, the electric hum of his anger mixed with something else, something raw and hungry and unmistakably dangerous.

"Harper?" A voice cut through the haze, sharp and concerned. I blinked, realizing I'd stopped in the middle of the hallway, one hand braced against the wall for balance. Turning, I saw Claire, one of the event coordinators, staring at me with wide eyes. "Are you okay? You look like you've seen a ghost."

I forced a laugh, though it came out shaky and unconvincing. "Yeah, I'm fine. Just… too much champagne, I think. Need some air."

Claire frowned, her gaze flicking over my face like she didn't believe me. "You sure? You're pale as a sheet. Do you want me to get you some water?"

"No, no, I'm good," I said quickly, waving her off. "Really. Just need a minute."

She hesitated, then nodded reluctantly. "Okay, but if you need anything, let me know."

"Thanks," I murmured, already turning away. The last thing I needed was someone hovering over me, asking questions I couldn't answer. Questions I didn't even know the answers to myself.

I leaned against the wall, trying desperately to regain control of my racing pulse. My cheeks burned, my breath uneven as I closed my eyes, the memory of Elias's warmth and scent lingering stubbornly. My fingers still tingled from touching him, and I curled them tightly into fists, willing myself to get a grip.

"What the hell was that?" I muttered under my breath, my voice trembling. My mind was spinning. Elias Blackwell, the cold, calculating CEO who made grown men quake, had *lost control* because another man had touched me—or smelled like he'd touched me, anyway. His grip on my arm had been firm, unyielding, but not painful—just possessive enough to send a wave of heat rippling through my body, pooling embarrassingly low in my stomach. For a second there, I'd felt him—*felt him*, close enough that I could sense the tension in every muscle, the strength coiled beneath the tailored fabric of his suit, the barely contained power that radiated from his body like a storm threatening to break.

God, had he felt it too? That electric pull, that undeniable connection that made my skin prickle and my breath catch? Or was I just imagining things, projecting my own stupid, lustful feelings onto him?

"You are so screwed, Harper," I whispered shakily, opening my eyes and exhaling a trembling breath. "So incredibly, irreversibly screwed."

Yet even as the words left my lips, I couldn't help the tiny, traitorous thrill that ran down my spine at the thought of just how dangerously *right* that might be. Because despite the chaos, despite the fear and confusion and the sheer absurdity of it all, there was a part of me—a reckless, stupid part—that wanted to go back. That wanted to step into the storm and see what happened when it broke.

But even as I said it, I knew it was a lie. Because the truth was, Elias Blackwell had already thrown me off my game. And the worst part? I wasn't sure I wanted to get it back.

I didn't wait for the party to wind down. The moment I felt steady enough to move, I pushed off the wall, smoothing my hands over my dress in a futile attempt to calm my nerves. The ballroom loomed ahead, its golden light spilling into the hallway like a siren's call. I could hear the faint strains of the string quartet, the murmur of voices, the clink of glasses. Normalcy. Safety. But it felt like a world away, like I'd stepped into some alternate reality where nothing made sense and everything was too bright, too loud, too *much*.

"Get it together, Harper," I muttered, squaring my shoulders. "You're not some damsel in distress. You're not going to let him—or anyone—throw you off your game."

I made my way to the coat check, my heels clicking sharply against the marble floor. The attendant handed me my wrap and clutch with a polite smile, and I muttered a quick "thank you" before heading toward the grand entrance of the venue. The cool night air hit me like a balm as I stepped outside, the chaos of the ballroom fading behind me.

"Harper."

His voice stopped me in my tracks, low and urgent, cutting through the quiet hum of the valet station. I didn't need to turn around to know it was Elias. His presence was like a gravitational pull, impossible to ignore. I clenched my jaw, forcing myself to keep walking, but his footsteps followed, quick and determined.

"Harper, wait." He caught up to me, his hand brushing my arm before I jerked away. I turned to face him, my expression carefully neutral, though my heart was pounding all over again. He looked… disheveled, for lack of a better word. His tie was slightly loosened, his hair ruffled as if he'd run his hands through it in frustration. His eyes, though—those piercing, golden eyes—were as intense as ever, locked on mine with an urgency that made my stomach twist.

"Don't," I said sharply, holding up a hand to stop him before he could say more. "Whatever you're about to say, save it. I'm not in the mood for another cryptic warning or… or whatever *that* was back there."

He flinched, just barely, but it was enough to make me feel a flicker of satisfaction. Good. Let him feel off-balance for once. Let him feel as unmoored as I did.

"I'm sorry," he said, his voice low and rough, like the words were being dragged out of him. "I didn't mean to—I shouldn't have—" He broke off, running a hand through his hair again, and I noticed the faint tremor in his fingers. "Just… don't leave. Not like this. Let me explain."

I stared at him, my chest tightening with a mix of anger and something else I refused to name. "Explain what, exactly?" I asked, my voice colder than I intended. "Why you manhandled me in front of half the city's elite? Why you acted like some kind of… of possessive lunatic over a guy I barely even know? Or maybe you'd like to explain why you think you have any right to tell me who I can and can't talk to?"

His jaw tightened, a muscle flickering in his cheek as he struggled to keep his composure. "It's not that simple," he said finally, his voice strained. "There are things you don't understand—things I can't explain right now. But you need to trust me."

"Trust you?" I let out a bitter laugh, shaking my head. "You've done nothing to earn my trust, Mr. Blackwell. If anything, you've done the opposite."

He stepped closer, his presence overwhelming, and I had to fight the urge to step back. "Harper," he said, his voice dropping to a near-whisper, "please. Just… don't go. Not yet."

For a moment, I almost wavered. There was something in his voice—something raw and vulnerable—that made my resolve falter. But then I remembered the way he'd looked at me, the way he'd touched me, like I was something to be claimed rather than a person with my own agency. And that was a line I couldn't let him cross.

"I'll see you at the office, Mr. Blackwell," I said coolly, turning away before he could respond. My car pulled up just then, the valet holding the door open for me. I slid into the backseat without looking back, though I could feel Elias's gaze burning into me as the door closed.

"Home, please," I told the driver, my voice steadier than I felt. As the car pulled away, I finally let myself exhale, my shoulders slumping as the tension began to drain from my body. But the moment of relief was short-lived. The memory of Elias's hands on me, his breath against my skin, his scent wrapping around me like a vice—it all came rushing back, flooding my senses and sending a shiver down my spine.

I leaned my head against the window, the cool glass doing little to calm the heat simmering beneath my skin. My fingers brushed over the spot on my arm where he'd held me, the skin still tingling as if his touch had left a permanent mark. My breath hitched as I replayed the moment in my mind—the way he'd pressed me against the door, the way his voice had dropped to that low, dangerous growl, the way his eyes had darkened with something I couldn't quite name but felt in every fiber of my being.

God, what was wrong with me? Why was I letting him get under my skin like this? He was my boss, for crying out loud. A man who thrived on control, who played games I didn't even understand. And yet, here I was, my body betraying me with every traitorous thought, every lingering sensation.

I closed my eyes, trying to push the memories away, but they only grew sharper, more vivid. The way his chest had felt against mine, solid and unyielding, the heat of him searing through the thin fabric of my dress. The way his breath had warmed my neck, sending shivers cascading down my spine. But it was the feel of his beard—rough and tantalizing—against my jaw, my neck, my collarbone that lingered most vividly in my mind. The scrape of it against my sensitive skin had been electric, a contrast to the softness of his lips as they brushed dangerously close, teasing but not quite touching.

I could still feel the ghost of his mouth hovering near my pulse point, the warmth of his breath sending a flush of heat through me. His lips had been so close, so achingly close, that I'd almost arched into him, almost begged him to close the distance. The memory of it made my breath hitch, my fingers tightening around the edge of the seat as a flush spread through me, warm and undeniable.

"Get a grip, Harper," I muttered under my breath, though the words did little to calm the storm raging inside me. Because the truth was, I didn't want to get a grip. Not entirely. A part of me—a reckless, stupid part—wanted to see where this dangerous game would lead. Wanted to know what would happen if I stopped running and let him catch me.

But that was a thought for another time. For now, I just needed to get home, to put as much distance between myself and Elias Blackwell as possible. Even if I knew, deep down, that no amount of distance would ever be enough.

Elias

The venue lights glittered mockingly as I turned my back on Harper's retreating transport. Each step I took back toward the revelry felt weighted, leaden, pulling against an invisible tether drawing me back to her. My jaw clenched, matching the turmoil boiling beneath my composed exterior. Her scent still lingered, haunting my senses, a whispering ghost I couldn't banish.

Inside, laughter still bubbled through the grand hall, glasses chiming like tiny bells of celebration. But the joy felt alien to me now, grating and artificial. My gaze skimmed over faces blurred by alcohol and pretense, and my chest tightened further, claustrophobic.

"Elias?"

I stiffened slightly at the sound of Lucian's voice behind me, his tone carefully measured, cautious. Turning slowly, I met his eyes briefly, noting the crease between his brows—a silent plea for honesty.

"Everything all right?" he asked, watching me closely, his voice gentle but edged with unease.

"Fine," I snapped, regretting it instantly. My jaw tightened painfully. "Just keep things under control. I'll handle the rest."

He hesitated, lips parting as though he might press further, then wisely reconsidered. With a brief nod, he withdrew, leaving me alone in the sea of revelers whose joy felt oppressive and wrong.

Harper.

Her name echoed in my mind with a painful persistence, haunting and sweet. The defiance in her eyes had stirred something dark and powerful in me, a yearning I could neither deny nor fully understand. I recalled the precise tremor in her breath as I leaned closer, how her heart had thrummed beneath my fingertips, rapid and enticing. And her scent—a heady fragrance of warmth and innocence—still lingered, branding my skin like a searing mark.

Unable to endure the charade any longer, I slipped away, ducking into an empty corridor where shadows draped the walls in velvet darkness. My phone felt heavy in my palm as I retrieved it, the screen glaringly bright against the dim lighting. I typed quickly, fingers moving without conscious thought:

Harper, please, talk to me.

I stared at the words, vulnerable and open, before my thumb hovered over the send button. Taking a shaky breath, I tapped it and waited, my heart heavy with anticipation and dread.

Seconds stretched into agonizing minutes. The screen stayed silent, devoid of even the faintest glimmer of a reply. No dots dancing, no signs of acknowledgment. Frustration surged through me, and I thrust the phone into my pocket, a harsh sigh escaping my lips.

Of course she wouldn't answer. I'd frightened her, let her glimpse the beast that simmered beneath my carefully cultivated surface. Perhaps that was what hurt most—not that she'd seen me, but that I'd confirmed what she likely already feared.

When I could no longer stand the suffocating tension inside, I slipped away, leaving the noise and lights behind for the darkness of solitude. My driver awaited me, wordlessly opening the car door. Inside the vehicle, I pressed my forehead against the glass, watching the city slip past in blurred streaks of neon and shadow.

Home offered no refuge. The silence was deafening, a hollow mockery of the storm raging inside me. Every empty room amplified my turmoil, the walls pressing in, suffocating me with memories I couldn't escape. I needed to drown them out—burn them away.

The shower hissed to life, steam rising in thick, swirling clouds as I stepped under the scalding spray. The water lashed at my skin, near-painful in its heat, but it did nothing to purge the images seared into my mind. Instead, each droplet was a cruel reminder—sharpening my hunger, stoking the fire in my blood.

Harper.

Her name was a curse, a prayer, an obsession.

"Damn it," I snarled, my voice raw, echoing off the slick tiles. My palm slid down my chest, fingers twitching with restless need. There was no stopping it—no fighting the pull of memory. Behind my clenched eyelids, she materialized: Harper, with her dark, knowing eyes, lips parted just enough to tease. The phantom sensation of her skin against mine, the way her breath hitched when I dragged my mouth along her throat—it all crashed over me, relentless, intoxicating.

My hand wrapped around my hardening length, already hard, aching. A rough groan tore from my throat as I stroked myself, slow at first, then faster, desperate. The water beat down, scalding and slick, but I barely felt it—not when my mind was filled with her. The way she'd look up at me through her lashes, the sinful curve of her mouth as she whispered my name. The imagined weight of her breasts in my hands, the tight clutch of her body around me—

Fuck.

My breath came in ragged bursts, my grip tightening, strokes turning punishing. My other hand braced against the wall, fingers digging into the tile hard enough to ache. The steam thickened, the air too hot, too heavy, but I didn't care. I was lost in the fantasy—her nails raking down my back, her teeth grazing my shoulder, her moans hot against my ear.

"Harper—" Her name was a broken sound, torn from my lips as pleasure coiled tight in my gut. My hips jerked, chasing the release that hovered just out of reach. Every muscle tensed, every nerve alight, until—

A sharp, guttural cry escaped me as I came, my release spilling over my fist in hot, pulsing waves. For a second, the world blurred—nothing but white-hot ecstasy and the ghost of her touch.

Then, just as quickly, it was over.

I slumped against the wall, chest heaving, water sluicing over my trembling body. The emptiness rushed back in, sharper than before. No amount of pleasure could erase her. No amount of pain could make me forget.

And that was the worst torment of all.

For a moment, I just stood there, my forehead pressed against the tile, my breath slowly returning to normal. But the emptiness that followed was worse than the ache had been. The steam faded around me, leaving only a chill that penetrated my bones. I stepped out, numb and hollow, and wrapped a towel around my waist.

I grabbed my phone again, foolishly hopeful for a reply, but the screen was blank, silent, mocking. Of course, Harper hadn't responded. I didn't deserve her reply. Didn't deserve her forgiveness.

Exhausted, drained, I leaned against the bathroom sink, staring into the fogged mirror, knowing without needing to see it clearly—the hunger, the desperation, the raw need etched into my face.

"Who am I fooling?" I whispered bitterly, wiping condensation from the glass, revealing tired eyes that had witnessed centuries of pain yet were still haunted by one woman's gaze.

Harper saw my mask past tonight. And now, I feared, she was gone forever.

Chapter 6

The Aftermath

Harper

Stepping into the sleek lobby of Blackwell Industries on Friday morning felt suspiciously like stepping into the lion's den after poking the lion. Or wolf. Whatever metaphor Elias was. Either way, it was nerve-wracking.

The clicking of my heels on the marble floors echoed painfully loud, announcing my presence more dramatically than I'd ever intended. I tugged nervously at the hem of my skirt—a flirty, curve-hugging pencil skirt that I'd convinced myself was a good idea this morning but was now second-guessing with every step. Paired with a silky blouse that dipped just low enough to be suggestive without crossing the line, the outfit had seemed empowering when I'd put it on. Now, it felt like a neon sign flashing *"Look at me!"* in bold letters.

I still couldn't wrap my head around what had happened at the party—the sharp edge in his voice, the possessiveness in his grip, and that look in his eyes, a mix of anger and something else I'd never seen from him before. It had been exhilarating and terrifying, leaving me restless and jittery, like I'd just downed four espressos back-to-back. And then there were the texts. Three of them, sent late last night, each one more terse than the last. I hadn't responded. Not because I didn't want to, but because I didn't know what to say. How do you reply to your boss—your infuriatingly attractive, impossibly complicated boss— after he practically growls at you for talking to another man?

As I approached my desk, I glanced cautiously toward Elias's office door, half-expecting him to burst out and demand an explanation for why I smelled like some mysterious stranger's cologne. But the door remained firmly closed, silent and intimidating, betraying no hint of the chaos that had occurred just hours before.

"Hey, Harper," Linda called out softly, stepping from her own office and eyeing me curiously. "You're early."

"Yeah, well, sleep and I broke up last night," I joked awkwardly, offering a sheepish shrug. "Figured I'd just come in and try not to break anything today."

Linda chuckled warmly, shaking her head. "Well, let's hope that holds true. Elias has already been asking if you arrived yet."

My stomach dropped instantly, heart racing anew. "Is he broody?"

Linda raised a careful eyebrow, a knowing smile flickering on her lips. "More like…agitated."

"Great," I muttered dryly, sinking into my chair with a sigh. "My boss thinks I'm a walking hazard, and he's definitely not wrong."

Linda laughed again as she moved away, leaving me alone at my desk, my gaze stubbornly drifting back toward Elias's office. Anxiety twisted in my gut, tinged with an excitement I refused to examine too closely.

"I am in way over my head," I whispered to myself, burying my face in my hands. "So, so over my head."

I knocked softly on Elias's door, half-hoping he wouldn't answer. My heart hammered wildly in my chest as the silence stretched on, just long enough to give me a flicker of hope that maybe he wasn't there.

But then, his voice sliced through the wood, deep and commanding as ever. "Enter."

Great.

Pushing open the heavy door, I stepped hesitantly inside, my eyes immediately finding him seated behind his desk, the morning sunlight filtering gently across his strong profile. He was leaning back, shirt sleeves rolled up just enough to reveal the intricate ink sprawled across his forearms. The memory of his tattoos—and the heat of his skin beneath my fingers—sent warmth flooding into my cheeks, turning them an embarrassingly obvious shade of red.

"Good morning," I said weakly, plastering on a smile that I sincerely hoped appeared more confident than the jittery mess I actually felt. "Thought I'd check in—since yesterday was, um, eventful."

Elias leaned back slowly in his leather chair, the tattoos on his chest just barely visible through the unbuttoned collar of his shirt. His long fingers steepled thoughtfully beneath his chin, the intensity in his golden eyes sending a nervous flutter straight to my stomach. He looked annoyingly composed, despite the chaos of yesterday, while I felt about as put-together as wet cardboard.

"Eventful is certainly one way of putting it," he drawled slowly, eyes narrowing slightly as they held mine captive. "But not inaccurate."

"Right. So, uh, look," I started awkwardly, shifting my weight from one foot to the other like a kid caught in detention. "I figured I should check in. You know just in case you were planning to fire me today. If that's the plan, can we just get it over with quickly? I have a pint of ice cream in the freezer, waiting to soothe my inevitable breakdown."

His eyebrow lifted fractionally, and I caught the faint twitch at the corner of his mouth—almost a smile before it vanished behind his usual cool mask. "I'm not firing you, Harper."

"Oh," I breathed, a rush of relief washing over me as I visibly relaxed, shoulders sagging slightly. "Good. Because honestly, grocery shopping was way overdue, and losing my job right now would totally ruin my plans for anything fancier than dollar-menu ramen."

A quiet laugh escaped him, more of a reluctant exhale than actual amusement, but his gaze remained sharp and assessing. "But there is still yesterday's matter to address."

I tensed immediately, heart speeding up again as he stood slowly from his chair, his movements smooth and controlled, each step bringing him closer until he was standing directly before me. Close enough that his scent—warm, dark, with a hint of spice and something dangerously inviting—washed over me, making my breath hitch. A flush rushing through me, heat flooding my cheeks as I suddenly became hyper-aware of how short my skirt was, how low my blouse dipped.

A flicker of something dark and predatory crossed his expression, his golden eyes narrowing slightly as they held mine captive. My pulse spiked, a traitorous thrill racing down my spine as I struggled to maintain my composure.

"The man you were with last night," he began carefully, his voice low, threaded with a note of barely concealed arousal. "Who was he?"

"Is there something else, Harper?" he asked, his voice low and rough, the faintest hint of amusement threading through the words.

I swallowed hard, forcing myself to meet his gaze despite the heat still burning in my cheeks. "Honestly? I don't really know. Damian something, I think? Tall, dark, smelled ridiculously good. Like, distractingly good—" my voice coming out higher than I intended.

Elias's jaw tightened sharply, his eyes darkening to a deeper shade of gold, something dangerous flickering just beneath the surface. "And you were with him willingly?"

"Well, yeah. It's not like he kidnapped me," I joked weakly, regretting it immediately when I saw the anger flare in his eyes.

He took a slow breath, clearly wrestling to control something deep inside himself. "You need to be more careful."

"Okay, sure," I muttered, rolling my eyes slightly, "but if you're worried I'll embarrass the company, don't be. He was perfectly nice— right up until he ghosted me like a bad Tinder date."

Elias's gaze sharpened further, his voice a low growl that made my pulse jump uncomfortably. "Did he touch you?"

I blinked, startled by the rawness of the question, the possessive edge beneath his carefully maintained composure. "He kissed…we ki…we kissed," I admitted clumsily, watching his reaction closely. "If that matters."

"Kissed," he repeated, voice dangerously quiet. He exhaled slowly, a tight, controlled breath betraying an unsettling hint of jealousy. "Stay away from him."

My eyebrows shot up. "Are you okay? Did you, like, hit your head last night? You're being weird, even for you. Maybe ease off the bourbon a little?"

He gave me an incredulous stare before shaking his head slightly, irritation blending with resignation. "Just trust me. He's trouble you don't need."

I tilted my head, meeting his eyes with open curiosity. "Noted. Anything else?"

He hesitated for a long, uncomfortable moment, as though debating whether to say something more, before shaking his head firmly. "No, that's all."

"Right. Good talk." I nodded awkwardly, stepping back toward the door. "If you need me, I'll be at my desk, pretending this conversation wasn't super weird."

Elias said nothing, but the intensity of his gaze lingered, following me all the way out the door. My pulse thundered wildly, and I closed my eyes briefly, leaning against the wall outside his office, still trying to catch my breath.

Elias

The office door shut softly behind Harper, its quiet click echoing louder than it had any right to. I stood rigidly beside my desk, fists clenched tightly, heart pounding with a rhythm born of possessiveness and barely restrained fury. My breath rasped in my throat as my mind relentlessly conjured vivid images—images far more explicit than Harper's innocent explanation had implied.

Damian.

His name was a growl inside my head, an arrogant interloper whose touch had branded Harper in ways that twisted at something deep inside me. A carnal instinct raged beneath my skin, fueling my imagination with cruel clarity: his hands—hands that had no right— sliding along Harper's slender waist, brushing her smooth, exposed shoulders, drawing soft gasps from lips that belonged only to—

A low, involuntary growl escaped my chest, echoing through the oppressive silence of my office.

I paced restlessly, muscles coiled tight, each step doing nothing to calm the storm raging within me. The vision sharpened, torturing me further—Damian's lips pressed against hers, tasting her sweetness, feeling the way her body yielded willingly. Her hands clinging to his shirt, nails tracing paths down his neck, sighing his name in breathless surrender—

"Damnit!"

Before rational thought could intervene, my hand shot out, seizing the porcelain vase perched on the corner of my desk. With a furious snarl, I hurled it violently against the opposite wall. It shattered spectacularly, shards scattering like sharp fragments of ice across the polished floor. Chest heaving, I stared blindly at the wreckage, trying desperately to reclaim control.

The silence that followed was suffocating, broken only by the harsh rasp of my breathing. Jealousy — a brutal, consuming force I had never experienced in such intensity — left me raw, exposed, vulnerable.

I had underestimated Harper's effect on me. Somehow, without permission or warning, she'd slipped beneath layers of ancient armor, embedding herself so deeply I couldn't tear her out, even if I wanted to.

A hesitant knock broke through the deafening quiet, followed immediately by the cautious opening of the door. I turned sharply, every muscle tense, heart racing again as Harper stepped carefully into the room. Her wide eyes flickered from the shattered vase to my rigid stance, confusion and concern dancing openly across her features.

"Everything okay, boss?" Her voice was gentle, tentative, as though she sensed she was approaching a dangerous animal — which wasn't far from the truth at this moment.

"I'm fine," I replied roughly, voice harsher than intended. Forcing myself to draw a deep, calming breath, I attempted to soften my tone. "Just... an accident."

She raised an eyebrow skeptically, clearly unconvinced as she carefully picked her way through the fragments toward me. As she approached, the full impact of her appearance struck me again — harder this time, without the distraction of our earlier confrontation.

Her outfit was sinful. The skirt hugged her hips and curves perfectly, the silky blouse teasingly low, drawing my eyes helplessly down the delicate lines of her throat to the tantalizing hint of cleavage below. Desire surged sharply through me, overwhelming my already compromised senses.

"You look anything but fine," she murmured, stopping mere inches from me, her scent filling every breath I took. Her brows knitted together with stubborn determination. "Did something happen?"

I shook my head sharply, trying desperately to ignore the warmth pooling low in my gut. She was close enough now that I could clearly see the fluttering pulse at the base of her throat, tempting me unbearably. My body reacted instantly and painfully, the growing hardness between my legs becoming impossible to hide.

Harper's gaze flickered downward, and I cursed silently as her cheeks flared an immediate, enticing shade of pink. Her eyes widened, surprise mingling with something darker, something curious and thrillingly unafraid.

"Harper…" My voice came out rougher, lower than intended, edged with warning and an undeniable heat.

She swallowed visibly, gathering her composure with impressive speed, then offered a small, teasing smirk. "Did I… catch you at a bad time?"

Her bravery drew an involuntary chuckle from deep within my chest, momentarily easing the tension, though it did little to diminish the ache she'd awakened. "You have impeccable timing."

She tilted her head slightly, studying me carefully, humor fading into genuine concern. "Seriously though—are you sure everything's okay? It's not every day you shatter a priceless artifact."

I hesitated, the words nearly tumbling free—words of jealousy, possessiveness, and longing. Instead, I clenched my jaw and forced myself to hold back. "It's nothing you need to worry about," I said stiffly, turning away toward the window. "Go home, Harper. Take the day off."

She didn't move. Instead, her voice softened further, a gentle persistence I was quickly learning was dangerously effective. "I'm not leaving until you tell me what's wrong."

I spun back, unable to hide the intensity burning in my eyes, unable to mask the desperation edging into my voice. "Why were you with him?"

She blinked, startled by my sudden directness. "Damian?"

"Yes," I growled, stepping closer until barely an inch separated us, my pulse thundering violently in my ears. "He doesn't deserve to touch you. No one does."

She looked up at me, her breath hitching slightly, the heat in her cheeks intensifying. Yet her gaze didn't waver. Instead, she searched my eyes, seeking answers I wasn't ready to give—even though every fiber of me was screaming to close the distance, claim her mouth, and erase Damian's memory forever.

"Mr. Blackwell...Elias" she whispered softly, the sound of my name on her lips nearly breaking the fragile hold I had left on my self-control.

"You have no idea how close I am to losing control," I murmured, voice shaking dangerously, the ache in my body nearly unbearable. "Go home, Harper. Please."

Her eyes widened again, understanding dawning alongside something deeper—recognition, excitement, fear perhaps—all mingled together in that vulnerable expression.

"Okay," she finally relented softly, stepping back slowly, never breaking eye contact until she reached the door. She paused briefly, offering a hesitant smile tinged with a gentle humor that twisted painfully in my chest. "But just for the record, next time you decide to shatter expensive antiques in a rage, give me a heads-up. We're running out of replacements."

Despite myself, I felt my lips twitch into a reluctant, genuine smile. "Noted. Enjoy your day off, Miss Wells."

Her eyes sparkled with warmth as she quietly closed the door behind her, leaving me alone in a room that felt emptier, colder without her presence.

Collapsing into my chair, I buried my face in my hands, struggling to regain control. Harper had seen through me—seen through the careful masks and walls I'd built around myself for centuries. And she hadn't run. Instead, she had stayed, faced the intensity head-on with bravery that left me utterly disarmed.

Harper

The office door clicked shut behind me, the sound unnaturally loud in the quiet hallway. My heart was still racing from the intensity of the moment with Elias. His eyes, dark and burning, had been impossible to read, yet they'd pinned me in place, leaving me breathless. I could still feel the weight of his gaze, the way it had lingered on me, as if he were trying to unravel something deep inside me. And that vase—shattered into pieces against the wall—what had that been about? I shook my head, trying to clear the image, but it clung to me like a shadow.

I gathered my things from my desk, my hands trembling slightly as I stuffed papers into my bag. Elias's voice echoed in my mind, low and rough, edged with something I couldn't quite name. *"Why were you with him?"* The question had been a growl, possessive and raw, and it had sent a shiver down my spine. Damian. He'd been talking about Damian. But why did it matter so much to him? Why did *I* matter so much to him?

I slung my bag over my shoulder and headed for the elevator, my thoughts a tangled mess. The way Elias had looked at me—like he was barely holding himself back—it had been thrilling and terrifying all at once. I'd never seen him like that, so unguarded, so... human. And yet, there was something dangerous in that vulnerability, something that made me want to step closer even as my instincts warned me to run.

The elevator doors slid open, and I stepped inside, leaning against the cool metal wall as it descended. My reflection stared back at me, cheeks flushed, eyes wide. I looked like someone who'd just stepped out of a storm. Maybe I had. Elias had that effect on me—like a force of nature, unpredictable and overwhelming.

The lobby was quiet when I stepped out, the midday sun streaming through the glass doors. I pushed them open, the warm air hitting my face as I walked down the steps. My stomach growled, reminding me I hadn't eaten. I decided to stop for lunch at the little café a few blocks away. It was one of my favorite spots, cozy and familiar, and right now, I needed something to ground me.

The café was bustling when I walked in, the smell of coffee and fresh bread wrapping around me like a hug. I found a table by the window and ordered a sandwich and an iced tea, my mind still replaying the scene in Elias's office. The way he'd stepped closer, his voice trembling with barely restrained emotion—*"You have no idea how close I am to losing control."* What would have happened if I hadn't left? If I'd stayed, if I'd pushed him just a little further? The thought sent a jolt of heat through me, and I quickly took a sip of my tea, trying to cool down.

I was halfway through my sandwich when the bell above the door chimed, and I glanced up out of habit. My breath caught in my throat. Damian. He stood in the doorway, his sharp features lighting up with a smile as soon as he saw me. He looked as effortlessly polished as always, his dark hair perfectly styled, his tailored suit fitting him like a second skin. He made his way over to my table, his confidence drawing the attention of nearly everyone in the room.

"Harper," he said, his voice smooth and warm. "Fancy running into you here."

I forced a smile, my mind racing. Of all the people to run into right now, it had to be him. "Damian. Hi."

He slid into the seat across from me without waiting for an invitation, his eyes scanning my face with that familiar intensity. "You look... distracted. Everything okay?"

I hesitated, unsure how much to say. "Just a long morning," I said finally, picking at the crust of my sandwich. "Work stuff."

He nodded, leaning back in his chair. "Ah, the joys of corporate life. Though I have to say, you're looking as stunning as ever, even if you are a little frazzled."

I rolled my eyes, but a small laugh escaped me. "Thanks, I think."

He grinned, that charming, slightly cocky smile that had probably won over half the city. "So, what are you doing here all by yourself? No Elias Blackwell to keep you company?"

The mention of Elias's name made my stomach twist. "He's... busy," I said carefully, avoiding Damian's gaze. "I just needed a break."

Damian studied me for a moment, his expression unreadable. Then he leaned forward, his voice dropping slightly. "You know, Harper, if you ever need a break from all that intensity, I'm always here. No strings attached."

I looked up at him, surprised by the sincerity in his tone. For all his charm and confidence, there was something genuine in the way he said it, something that made me wonder if maybe I'd misjudged him. But before I could respond, the bell above the door chimed again, and my eyes flicked toward it instinctively.

"Let me offer a distraction," Damian said, his voice smooth and teasing as he reached over and plucked a piece of my sandwich crust from my plate. He popped it into his mouth, his eyes never leaving mine. "Just for a few hours."

I blinked at him, caught off guard by the boldness of the gesture. "A distraction?" I repeated, my voice tinged with skepticism. "What kind of distraction?"

He leaned back in his chair, that confident smirk playing on his lips. "The fun kind. No work, no stress, no..." He paused. "No complications."

I swallowed hard, my mind racing as I tried to think of something to say. "Thank you" I said finally, my voice barely above a whisper. "I think that would be nice."

Elias

The day dragged on interminably, as if I'd been trapped in a cruel, endless loop. Each minute ticked past with agonizing slowness, every moment replaying vividly behind my eyes—Harper's soft voice, her laughter, and the faint, tantalizing scent of her lingering in my memory. Hours had crawled by, the staff and cleaning crews long since vanished, leaving the office cloaked in silence and oppressive solitude.

I stood by the floor-to-ceiling window, staring out at the city skyline, the lights blurred into distant points of gold against a backdrop of heavy clouds. The room was bathed in muted shadows, the lamplight casting fractured patterns across the rich mahogany of my desk. With a sigh of restless agitation, I reached for the crystal decanter of scotch, pouring a generous measure into the heavy glass. The amber liquid gleamed richly, catching the faint glow of light as it slid against the glass walls.

Lucien stood near the doorway, his posture rigid, military-straight, hands clasped behind his back. It was a stance I recognized immediately—one signaling bad news. His normally implacable expression held traces of hesitation, deepening the uneasy coil twisting inside me.

"Speak, Lucien," I commanded quietly, sharper than intended, swirling the scotch absently. The ice clinked softly, punctuating the tense silence.

Lucien shifted slightly, producing a thin folder from inside his tailored jacket. "I had surveillance track Miss Wells today. As you know, she took a personal day."

"Yes," I snapped impatiently, the muscles in my jaw flexing tightly.

"And?"

He stepped forward, silently placing several glossy photographs on my desk. My chest tightened painfully as my gaze settled on the images—each one like a razor across exposed nerves. My hand clenched involuntarily around the glass, knuckles whitening.

The first photograph showed Harper smiling softly up at Damian, sunlight catching the copper highlights in her hair, her eyes bright and trusting. Another depicted the two standing at the edge of a pier, the ocean behind them glittering innocently in the background. Damian's posture was deceptively casual, his fingers resting intimately at the small of her back. My teeth ground together sharply, jealousy flaring dangerously beneath my skin.

But the last photograph—it cut deepest of all. Harper's face was tilted upward, eyes closed in a moment of vulnerability, her lips parted as Damian claimed them possessively in a kiss. Rage surged hot and visceral, a dark, violent force I struggled desperately to contain.

"You had her followed," I managed, voice low and lethal.

"Given recent events," Lucien replied cautiously, carefully maintaining his composure, "it seemed prudent."

"Explain," I demanded coldly, my voice trembling slightly beneath the tightly controlled surface.

Lucien cleared his throat uncomfortably. "Damian Shaw is a hired mercenary. He belongs to the Greystone Coven—one of the oldest, most dangerous witch lineages known for precision, ruthlessness, and manipulation."

He paused, holding my gaze steadily. "Damian possesses a unique and powerful form of magical persuasion. Through touch, proximity, even his voice, he can influence thoughts, emotions—desires."

I stilled instantly, my grip tightening further around the glass, pulse spiking dangerously. "You believe Harper's attraction to him isn't genuine?"

Lucien nodded slowly, eyes serious. "Precisely. Damian exploits vulnerabilities. He finds weaknesses, manipulates his target's feelings until they're entirely under his control. Harper, with her openness and trust, is an ideal victim. Her actions today might not be entirely voluntary."

My chest constricted sharply, anger and protectiveness warring violently within me. The thought of Harper being manipulated, her innocence twisted and exploited—it ignited a possessive fury I'd never experienced so intensely. The image of Damian's lips touching hers was torture, each imagined detail fueling my rage further.

"She's vulnerable," Lucien added quietly, sensing the dangerous direction of my thoughts. "She has no idea the true danger she's courting."

I stared at the photographs again, Harper's face smiling naively up at Damian, utterly unaware of the predator beside her. I felt an ache deep in my chest, unfamiliar and agonizing, mixed dangerously with jealousy and territoriality.

"Did she look harmed? Upset? Forced?" I asked, almost desperately, needing reassurance that her free will hadn't been completely compromised.

Lucien hesitated, choosing his words carefully. "Not harmed, no. But there was something...unfocused in her demeanor. Damian's persuasion is subtle but potent. Harper likely isn't even aware she's being influenced."

I exhaled sharply, tension tightening my shoulders. "How do we counter it?"

"Bring her closer," Lucien advised softly, his voice cutting through the storm of my thoughts. "Keep her within your sphere of influence, away from Damian's reach. Your presence, your proximity, is the best defense she has against his manipulation." He paused, his gaze steady and probing, as if he could see the turmoil raging beneath my carefully constructed facade. "But Elias, your protectiveness of her, the rage—it speaks to something deeper. You understand this, right?"

I stiffened, my grip tightening on the glass of scotch I still held. The amber liquid sloshed dangerously close to the rim, but I didn't care. Lucien's words struck a nerve, one I had been desperately trying to ignore. "I don't know what you're implying," I said coldly, though the lie tasted bitter on my tongue.

Lucien raised an eyebrow, unimpressed by my deflection. "Don't you? You've always been a man of control, Elias. Calculated, precise, untouchable. But Harper... she's unraveling you."

I turned away, unable to meet his gaze. The truth in his words was undeniable, and it infuriated me. Harper had slipped past my defenses, embedding herself in my thoughts, my desires, my very being. She was a distraction I couldn't afford, a weakness I couldn't afford. And yet, the thought of her in danger, of Damian's hands on her, of his influence twisting her mind—it ignited a fury in me that was almost impossible to contain.

"She's an employee. A liability. And I'll deal with her—and Damian—as such."

Lucien sighed, the sound heavy with unspoken reproach. "You can lie to yourself, Elias, but don't lie to me. I've known you too long. I've seen the way you look at her, the way you react when she's near. This isn't just about protecting her from Damian. This is about you. About your wolf.

I slammed the glass down on the desk, the sound sharp and final. "Enough, Lucien," I snapped, my voice low and dangerous. "I don't need a lecture on my feelings—or lack thereof. What I need is a solution. A way to neutralize Damian and keep Harper safe. That's all."

Lucien studied me for a long moment, his expression unreadable. Then he nodded, accepting the boundary I had drawn—for now. "Very well. But know this, Elias: the longer you deny what's happening, the harder it will be to control. And when it finally breaks free, it won't be pretty."

I didn't respond, my jaw clenched so tightly it ached. Lucien's words echoed in my mind, a relentless reminder of the truth I was trying so hard to avoid. Harper wasn't just an employee. She wasn't just a liability. She was something more—something I couldn't define, couldn't quantify, couldn't control.

And that terrified me.

Lucien turned to leave, his footsteps echoing softly in the cavernous office. But before he reached the door, he paused, glancing back at me over his shoulder. "Bring her closer, Elias. Not just to protect her. But because you need her, whether you're ready to admit it or not."

The door clicked shut behind him, leaving me alone with my thoughts—and the photographs still scattered across my desk. I stared at them, at Harper's smiling face, at the way Damian's hand rested so possessively on her back. The rage that had simmered beneath the surface flared anew, hot and consuming.

I pressed my fingertips to the bridge of my nose, releasing a ragged breath. I had known Harper Wells was dangerous from the start, but I had underestimated just how deeply she'd embedded herself within me. This jealous rage was foreign, unsettling, leaving me dangerously exposed and vulnerable.

With frustration, I shoved away from my desk, pacing restlessly toward the window. Rain now splattered gently against the glass, droplets sliding downward in erratic paths, mirroring my own internal chaos.

I finished the Whiskey in my glass and refilled it, one after another. The amber liquid burned its way down my throat, a temporary balm for the storm raging inside me. The bottle was nearly empty now, its contents no match for the chaos in my mind. I stared at the photographs on my desk, Harper's face haunting me with every sip. Her smile, her innocence, her trust—all of it felt like a cruel joke, a reminder of how dangerously close I was to losing control.

Harper

Sleep was impossible again.

I lay sprawled across my bed, staring up at the cracked plaster ceiling, tracing the shadows cast by passing headlights from the street below. The faint hum of the city filtered through my thin apartment walls, a distant reminder of the world outside. But inside, my mind was a whirlwind, replaying the events of the day on an endless loop—especially those moments on the pier with Damian.

His soft laughter echoed in my ears, a sound that was both comforting and unsettling. I could still feel the warmth of his breath ghosting over my skin, sending shivers down my spine even now. I rolled onto my side, pressing my fingertips to my lips, still feeling the phantom imprint of his kiss. It had been gentle at first, almost tentative, but then it deepened, and for a moment, I had let myself get lost in it.

Everything about today had felt surreal, like a dream I wasn't sure I wanted to wake up from. It had started innocently enough—Damian appearing beside me at the coffee shop with that easy, charming smile of his.

"Mind some company?" he'd asked casually, sliding into the seat opposite me without waiting for a response.

"Uh, sure," I had replied awkwardly, nearly spilling my coffee in surprise. "Not like I've got anywhere better to be."

He'd laughed then, a soft, rich sound that made his eyes sparkle mischievously in the sunlight. It was easy with Damian—effortless, really, like we'd known each other forever rather than mere days. Before I knew it, we'd walked to the pier, his fingertips brushing lightly against my lower back, sending small sparks of awareness along my skin.

The lake had stretched out before us, glittering beneath the late-afternoon sun. Damian had leaned casually against the wooden railing, the wind gently ruffling his dark hair. His eyes—warm, inviting, and deceptively safe—had studied me intently.

"Do you always follow strange men to romantic piers, Harper?" he'd teased, one corner of his mouth lifting in a playful smirk.

"Only the mysterious ones with killer smiles and annoyingly irresistible cologne," I'd teased back, feeling bold and reckless.

He laughed—a rich, inviting sound that rolled effortlessly from his chest. "Flattery will get you everywhere, Miss Wells."

I had felt myself blush deeply, dropping my gaze to the worn wooden planks at our feet. "I wasn't aware I was trying to get anywhere."

His hand had lifted gently to my chin, tilting my face upward to meet his eyes, and I'd suddenly found myself unable—or unwilling—to move. His gaze searched mine deeply, his voice dropping into a low murmur, edged with unexpected sincerity.

"You have no idea how enchanting you are, do you?"

Before I could reply, his lips had brushed against mine, gentle at first, then deepening slowly until my thoughts dissolved entirely, replaced only by the heat of his touch and the dizzying sensation that this was both profoundly right and absolutely crazy.

Now, alone in my apartment, the memory made my cheeks burn and my pulse flutter with an intensity I couldn't deny. Elias's harsh words about Damian echoed stubbornly in my mind, warnings mingling annoyingly with the lingering warmth of that kiss. Was Damian really as dangerous as Elias claimed? It was impossible to reconcile the easy warmth of his touch with the idea that he posed some kind of threat.

I rolled my eyes in the darkness. "Dangerous," I muttered sarcastically to the ceiling. "Please. Elias clearly needs to relax."

Damian had been nothing but kind—maybe a bit forward, sure, but dangerous? I couldn't picture it. Not when his touch had been so gentle, his laughter genuine, and his smile so…warm.

I groaned softly, dragging a pillow over my face. "Great, Harper," I mumbled sarcastically to myself. "Way to complicate an already complicated life."

Life was officially complicated.

Yet despite Elias's warnings—and despite every ounce of common sense screaming at me—I couldn't shake the feeling that Damian wasn't the villain Elias claimed him to be.

Maybe I was being naive. Maybe I was just tired. Or maybe, a traitorous little voice whispered stubbornly in my mind, Elias was jealous.

I rolled over with another frustrated sigh. One thing was certain: sleep wasn't happening anytime soon, and this mess wasn't about to resolve itself.

A rude, obnoxiously loud knock shattered whatever happy little daydream I'd been foolish enough to let myself get lost in. I shot up, heart hammering in my chest, glancing frantically at the clock glowing accusingly on my bedside table.

One AM. Seriously?

I knew better than to answer the door at this ridiculous hour—especially given the questionable reputation of my neighborhood—but apparently, whoever stood on the other side didn't care. Another knock echoed through the apartment, louder this time, practically rattling the walls.

"Okay, okay, hold your horses," I grumbled, hastily yanking a tank top over my bare body as I stumbled toward the door, the thin fabric barely concealing my sleep-rumpled state. My heart hammered in my chest, adrenaline kicking into full force as I tiptoed to the peephole, mentally preparing a stern lecture on common decency and late-night disturbances.

One quick glance froze me in place, my heart immediately launching into a frantic sprint. Elias stood there, illuminated harshly beneath the flickering hallway light, his jaw set in a hard, tense line, golden eyes narrowed dangerously as he stared directly at the door—as though he could sense my presence through the solid wood.

"Shit," I whispered, pressing my forehead briefly against the cool door as my stomach lurched uncomfortably. "What the hell?"

Another sharp knock echoed, even more impatient this time, rattling the flimsy wood frame and sending fresh waves of anxiety through me.

Taking a steadying breath, I finally unlocked the door, opening it just a crack—painfully conscious of my lack of proper clothing, and peering cautiously out at him. My pulse thundered in my ears, drowning out rational thought.

"Mr. Blackwell?" I tried—and spectacularly failed—to sound casual, as if my boss appearing unannounced at my apartment door at one in the morning was totally normal. "Is everything okay?"

He stared down at me, silent and unmoving. Every muscle of his body appeared tensed, coiled tightly as if holding himself back from something—though whether that was anger or something else entirely, I couldn't quite tell. The sight of him stole my breath entirely: he was utterly out of character, completely out of uniform. He wore a simple black tank, snug against the muscular planes of his torso, highlighting intricate tattoos that covered every inch of skin on his powerful arms and sculpted chest. Dark jeans hung loosely from his hips, emphasizing his commanding frame. In this raw, casual attire, he looked dangerously, distractingly beautiful—an unsettling reminder of just how little separated us.

"May I come in?" he asked finally, his voice low and deceptively calm, yet threaded with something deeper—something raw and dangerously intense. The quietness of his tone did nothing to hide the undercurrent of urgency, sending a shiver racing down my spine.

"I…um…" I swallowed thickly, heart pounding even harder as his eyes drifted slowly downward, lingering briefly on my barely dressed body, his jaw clenching even tighter as something flickered behind his gaze—something unmistakably possessive.

He met my eyes again, lifting a single eyebrow in challenge, his voice dropping to a husky whisper. "Please, Harper."

Against every instinct telling me this was a terrible, reckless idea, I stepped back, pulling the door open wider with trembling fingers.

"Sure," I managed faintly, acutely aware of the sudden heat pooling low in my belly. "Just—just try not to get blood on the carpet, okay? That stuff's a bitch to clean."

He strode inside without hesitation, his presence immediately overwhelming the tiny space of my apartment, filling every corner and crevice with tension so thick it was nearly suffocating. The door clicked shut softly behind him, sealing us into a space that suddenly felt charged, electric—dangerous, somehow.

Before I could turn or ask what the hell he thought he was doing here at one in the morning, Elias was already moving. In a blur, he closed the distance between us, spinning me around, pinning my back hard against the wall beside the door. My breath hitched sharply as I stared up at him, wide-eyed and stunned into silence.

"Mr. Blackwell—" I started, my voice embarrassingly weak.

He didn't respond—not verbally, at least. Instead, his eyes darkened, dilating into pools of raw intensity as his gaze roamed slowly, hungrily, over my face. He leaned in closer, pressing one palm flat against the wall beside my head. My pulse fluttered wildly beneath my skin, awareness of him exploding through every nerve ending in my body. I felt heat radiating from him, scorching me through our clothes, melting the little resolve I had left.

He moved closer still, nose brushing softly along the side of my neck, inhaling deeply. I shivered involuntarily, my eyes fluttering shut at the intimacy of it, heart hammering wildly. Whatever scent he found there seemed to awaken something untamed in him, because the low, rumbling growl that followed didn't sound human—it was animalistic, raw, vibrating through his chest and into mine.

My breathing quickened, pulse hammering as adrenaline flooded my veins. His hands gripped my hips firmly, the heat of his palms searing into my bare skin. With effortless strength, he lifted me off the ground, pinning me higher against the wall. My legs instinctively wrapped around his waist, anchoring me to him, drawing him even closer until our bodies pressed impossibly tight. The air between us thickened, electrified by an undeniable tension, an urgency I had never felt before.

Elias growled again, the sound deep, bestial, and unmistakably animalistic. My pulse jumped wildly, desire flooding my system, igniting every cell until rational thought dissolved into pure instinct. His fingers dug into my thighs possessively, sending a shudder of want through my entire body. I could feel his hardness pressing insistently between us, and it ignited something reckless and wild within me.

"Fuck…Harper," he growled against my skin, his voice raw and dark, infused with a hunger so deep it felt ravenous .

I gasped softly, threading my fingers through his thick, dark hair, gripping desperately as if he might vanish if I let go. My pulse thundered in my ears, a wild, erratic rhythm that drowned out everything else—the faint hum of the city outside, the creak of the old apartment walls, even the voice of reason in my head that screamed this was a terrible idea. But reason had no place here, not when Elias's lips brushed against the curve of my neck, his breath hot and uneven, sending shivers cascading down my spine like sparks from a live wire.

The rough stubble of his jaw grazed my collarbone, the sensation both tender and raw, and I arched into him instinctively, my body betraying every ounce of restraint I thought I had. My hands tightened in his hair, pulling him closer, craving more of his touch, more of the fire he was stoking inside me. It was a fire that burned away every doubt, every warning, every memory of Damian's kiss that had lingered on my lips just hours before. This was different. This was all consuming, and utterly inescapable.

Elias growled low in his throat, the sound vibrating through me, and his hands slid up my shirt to grip my breasts, his fingers digging into my skin with a possessiveness that should have terrified me but instead sent a thrill of heat pooling low in my stomach. He pressed me harder against the wall, his body pinning me in place, and I could feel the rapid rise and fall of his chest against mine, the way his heart pounded in time with mine.

"Harper," he murmured against my skin, his voice rough and strained, like he was fighting to hold himself back. But the way his lips trailed up my neck, the way his teeth grazed the sensitive spot just below my ear, told me he was losing that fight. And I didn't want him to win.

My name on his lips was a plea and a warning all at once, but I didn't care. I didn't care about the consequences, about the lines we were crossing, about the storm that would inevitably follow this moment. All I cared about was the way he made me feel—alive, wanted, *needed*.

But before I could catch my breath or even fully process what was happening, Elias suddenly pulled back, breaking contact with an abruptness that left me reeling. My feet hit the floor roughly, knees nearly buckling beneath me as I stared in shock, trying desperately to understand what just happened. Elias stood a step away, breathing raggedly, eyes dark and fierce, his entire body rigid with barely restrained tension.

The cool air of the apartment rushed over my exposed skin, a stark contrast to the heat of his body that had just been pressed against mine. My tank top clung to me, damp with sweat, and I suddenly felt painfully aware of how little I was wearing. My bare legs trembled, and I crossed my arms over my chest, not out of modesty but out of a desperate need to hold myself together.

Elias's gaze raked over me, lingering for a moment on the way my tank top had ridden up, exposing the curve of my waist, the arch of my thighs. His jaw tightened, and I saw the struggle in his eyes—the battle between whatever had driven him to my door and whatever was forcing him to pull away now.

"Elias," I whispered, my voice trembling, "what are you doing, what's happening?"

He didn't answer. Instead, he took a step back, then another, his chest rising and falling with the effort of controlling his breathing. His hands clenched into fists at his sides, and I could see the tension coiled in every muscle of his body, like a predator ready to pounce.

"I shouldn't have come here," he said finally, his voice low and rough, edged with something that sounded like regret—or maybe frustration.

"Then why did you?" I asked, my voice barely above a whisper. My heart was still racing, my body still humming with the aftershocks of his touch.

He hesitated, his eyes flickering to mine for a brief moment before he looked away. "Because I couldn't stay away," he admitted, the words torn from him as if it pained him to say them.

The admission hung in the air between us, heavy and charged. I wanted to reach for him, to close the distance he had put between us, but something in his expression stopped me. There was a darkness there, a warning, and I wasn't sure if it was directed at me or at himself.

Without another word, he turned abruptly, storming back through the doorway, practically sprinting into the hallway beyond. The door slammed shut behind him, leaving me trembling, gasping, and utterly bewildered.

The room spun around me as I sagged weakly against the wall, still breathless, heart pounding painfully. What the hell had just happened?

My mind raced chaotically, emotions spinning wildly between confusion, desire, fear, and frustration. My body ached painfully for him, yet I had no idea what had just driven him to behave like that—or why he'd fled so suddenly, leaving me flushed, trembling, and completely alone.

I stood there, breathless and bewildered, the ghost of his touch still burning against my skin. The cool night air seeped through the cracks in the windows, raising goosebumps on my bare arms and legs. I shivered, but it wasn't from the cold. It was from the memory of his hands on me, his lips against my skin, the way he had looked at me like

I was the only thing in the world that mattered.
Sleep was now utterly impossible.

Elias

The car ride to Harper's apartment was a blur. The city lights streaked past the tinted windows, their glow muted and distant, like stars obscured by a storm. I sat in the backseat, my fingers gripping the edge of the leather seat, my jaw clenched so tightly it ached. The scotch I'd consumed earlier still burned in my veins, dulling the edges of my thoughts but doing nothing to quiet the storm raging inside me.

Lucien's words echoed in my mind, a relentless reminder of the danger Harper was in. Damian. The name alone was enough to make my blood boil. The images Lucien had shown me—Harper smiling at him, laughing with him, kissing him—played on a loop in my head, each one fueling the possessive fury that had driven me to this reckless decision.

"Faster," I snapped at the driver, my voice low and sharp. He nodded, pressing harder on the accelerator, but the car still felt like it was moving too slowly. Every second that passed was another second Damian had to sink his claws deeper into her. Another second I had to sit here, trapped in this suffocating limbo, fighting the urge to tear the world apart to get to her.

The alcohol had made me reckless, but it had also made me honest. Too honest. It had stripped away the layers of control I'd spent centuries building, leaving me raw and exposed. And now, as the car sped through the empty streets, I could feel that control slipping further and further away.

When we reached her building, the SUV had barely come to a stop before I was out of the car, striding toward her door, my pulse pounding in my ears. The night air was cool against my skin, but it did nothing to calm the fire burning inside me.

I knocked on her door, the sound sharp and impatient. When she finally opened it after my third round of knocking, her eyes wide with surprise and confusion, I felt something inside me snap. She was standing there, her hair tousled, her cheeks flushed, wearing nothing but a thin tank top that left far too much of her bare skin exposed, though she tried to keep the door barely cracked to retain some semblance of modesty. The sight of her—vulnerable, beautiful, and utterly unaware of the danger she was in—ignited something carnal in me.

"Mr. Blackwell?" she asked, her voice trembling slightly. "Is everything okay?"

"May I come in?" I asked, my voice low and strained. She didn't answer immediately, startled by my presence at her home at this hour. "Please, Harper," I added, the plea slipping out before I could stop it.

She hesitated for a moment, then opened the door wider, stepping aside to let me in. The apartment was small, cramped, and filled with the scent of her—sweet and warm and intoxicating. It wrapped around me, pulling me closer, and before I could stop myself, I had her pinned against the wall.

Her breath hitched, her eyes wide and startled, but she didn't push me away. "Mr. Blackwell…" Her voice was barely a whisper, trembling with a mix of fear and something else—something that made my blood burn hotter.

I leaned in closer, pressing a palm flat against the wall. She was beautiful, looking up at me through her lashes, her breath heavy, her chest rising and falling with each ragged inhale. The thin fabric of her tank top did little to hide the way her body responded to me, and the sight of her—flushed and trembling—nearly undid me.

Her aroused scent reached my nose, and I ran my face along her neck, inhaling deeply. She was my drug, my weakness, my undoing. But then I caught it—the faint trace of him. Damian. His scent lingered on her, a subtle but unmistakable reminder of his presence. A low growl rumbled in my chest, raw and animalistic, as I lifted her off the ground, pressing her harder against the wall. Her legs wrapped around my waist, anchoring her to me, and I could feel the heat of her, the way her body trembled with the same desperate need that was consuming me.

"Fuck…Harper," I growled against her skin, my voice rough and dark, infused with a hunger so deep it felt ravenous. I wanted her — needed her — in a way I hadn't needed anything in centuries. My hands roamed over her body, her stomach, her breasts, each touch igniting a fire that threatened to consume us both.

But even as I lost myself in her, the rational part of my mind screamed at me to stop. This wasn't right. She didn't know what I was, what I was capable of. She didn't know the darkness that lived inside me, the monster I kept chained and hidden. And if I didn't stop now, I would hurt her. I would ruin her.

"Harper…" I pleaded, my voice breaking as I pulled back abruptly, setting her down roughly. My chest heaved as I fought to regain control, the storm inside me raging against the chains I'd tried so hard to keep intact.

She stared at me, her eyes wide and confused, her arms wrapped around her chest. "Elias," she whispered, her voice trembling, "What are you doing? What's happening?"

I didn't answer. I couldn't. Instead, I took a step back, then another, putting as much distance between us as I could. My hands clenched into fists at my sides, my nails digging into my palms as I fought to keep myself from reaching for her again.

"I shouldn't have come here," I said finally, my voice low and rough, edged with regret. The alcohol had worn off completely now, leaving me cold and clear-headed — and horrified by what I'd almost done.

"Then why did you?" she asked, her voice barely above a whisper. Her eyes searched mine, filled with a mix of confusion and hurt that made my chest ache.

"Because I couldn't stay away," I admitted, the words torn from me as if it pained me to say them. It was the truth, but it wasn't enough. It would never be enough.

Without another word, I turned and walked out the door, leaving her standing there, trembling and bewildered. The cool night air hit me like a slap, but it did nothing to ease the guilt and frustration burning inside me. I climbed back into the car, my hands shaking, my mind racing.

"Drive," I said sharply, and the car pulled away from the curb, leaving Harper and the mess I'd made behind.

As we sped through the empty streets, I leaned my head back against the seat and closed my eyes. The storm inside me had quieted, but it hadn't gone away. It was still there, simmering beneath the surface, waiting for the next time I let my guard down.

And I knew, with a sinking certainty, that there would be a next time. Because no matter how hard I tried, I couldn't stay away from her.

Harper

The door clicked shut behind him, the sound final and deafening in the sudden silence of my apartment. I stood frozen, my back pressed against the wall, my heart pounding so hard I could feel it in my throat. The air still felt charged, electric, as if the room itself was holding its breath, waiting for something—anything—to happen. But Elias was gone, and all that remained was the ghost of his touch and the ache of his absence.

I slid down the wall until I was sitting on the floor, my legs trembling too much to hold me up. My fingers brushed against my lips, still tingling from the heat of his kiss, and I let out a shaky breath. *What the hell had just happened?* One minute, he was there, his body pressed against mine, his hands on my skin claiming me in a way that left no room for doubt or hesitation. And the next... he was gone. Just like that.

I wrapped my arms around my knees, pulling them to my chest, and rested my forehead against them. My mind was a whirlwind of emotions—confusion, frustration, desire, and something deeper, something I couldn't quite name. Elias had always been a mystery, a man of contradictions. Cold and distant one moment, intense and overwhelming the next. But this... this was something else entirely. This was raw, unfiltered, and it had left me reeling.

I replayed the moment in my head, the way his hands had gripped my hips, the way his lips had trailed up my neck, the way he'd growled my name like it was the only word he knew. It had been possessive, feral, and yet there had been something tender in it too, something that made my chest ache in a way I couldn't explain. He had wanted me—

that much was clear—but he had stopped himself. Why? What was he so afraid of?

I lifted my head, staring at the door as if it might give me answers. But it was just a door, silent and unyielding, and Elias was on the other side of it, gone as quickly as he'd come. I thought about chasing after him, demanding an explanation, but something held me back. Maybe it was the look in his eyes when he'd pulled away, the way he'd looked at me like I was both the answer and the problem. Or maybe it was the fear that if I went after him, I'd only make things worse.

I groaned softly, burying my face in my hands. "What is wrong with you, Harper?" I muttered to myself, my voice muffled. "Why can't you just leave well enough alone?"

But I knew the answer to that. It was the same reason I couldn't stop thinking about Damian, couldn't stop replaying the moments on the pier, couldn't stop wondering if Elias was right about him. It was the same reason I'd let Elias pin me against the wall, let him touch me like he was starving and I was the only thing that could satisfy him. I was drawn to them both, to their darkness, their intensity, their secrets. And it was going to get me into trouble—if it hadn't already.

I pushed myself to my feet, my legs still unsteady, and walked to the window. The city stretched out before me, a sea of lights and shadows, and I leaned my forehead against the cool glass, trying to calm the storm inside me. Outside, the world kept turning, oblivious to the chaos in my head. But inside, everything felt upside down, like the ground had shifted beneath my feet and I was still trying to find my balance.

I thought about Elias's warning, the way he'd looked at me when he'd said Damian was dangerous. Was he right? Was I being naive, letting myself get caught up in Damian's charm, his easy smiles, his warm laughter? Or was Elias the one I should be wary of? He was the one who had shown up at my door in the middle of the night, the one who had kissed me like he was claiming me, the one who had walked away without an explanation.

I sighed, running a hand through my hair. There were no easy answers, no clear path forward. All I knew was that I couldn't keep doing this—couldn't keep letting myself get pulled in two different directions, couldn't keep pretending I wasn't in over my head.

But as I stood there, staring out at the city, I couldn't shake the feeling that whatever was happening between me and Elias, between me and

Damian, was only just beginning. And no matter how hard I tried to convince myself otherwise, I knew I wasn't ready for what was coming.

The Council

Elias

My hands were shaking—actually trembling—as I slammed the door of the car and strode swiftly across the dark driveway toward the house. I could still feel the ghost of Harper's skin against mine, the lingering heat of her body, the scent of her clinging to my clothes. My chest tightened painfully, fear and frustration battling fiercely within me. I'd lost control—completely. I'd allowed instinct, raw and predatory, to rule me entirely. The moment replayed over and over in my mind, each loop more vivid and unsettling than the last.

The house stood before me, shadowed in the late-night gloom, lit only by soft, golden light filtering through windows on the first floor. As I approached the heavy wooden doors, they swung open before I could reach them, revealing Lucien standing rigidly on the threshold, his dark eyes studying me closely, concern etched deeply into the lines of his face.

"Elias," he said quietly, stepping aside to let me pass. "We felt it—your shift in energy. The pack is gathered inside. Everyone's waiting."

I exhaled sharply, forcing myself past him without a word, the pressure of the pack's collective presence already thickening the air. As I entered the large, softly lit drawing room, I felt their eyes on me immediately—Isabella, Marcus, Seraphina—all watching carefully, silently, their collective tension radiating outward like heat waves.

Marcus was the first to break the silence, his voice steady but gentle. "What happened tonight, Elias?"

"I lost control," I admitted sharply, my voice rough and raw with humiliation. The confession burned like acid in my throat, a stark reminder of weakness I hadn't shown in centuries. "With Harper. I went to her apartment, and I—" I cut myself off, fists clenching at my sides. "I let the wolf take hold."

Isabella exhaled quietly, concern flickering across her normally impassive features. "Is she unharmed?"

"Yes." I nodded shortly, rubbing my hand roughly over my face. "But only because I managed to leave before—before anything worse happened."

The pack exchanged uneasy glances, their worry palpable. Seraphina moved forward, her delicate expression soft with empathy, eyes wide with understanding. "Elias, your bond with Harper is deeper than we realized. If your wolf is surfacing this intensely…it's a warning, a sign."

"A sign?" I echoed bitterly, shaking my head. "It felt like madness, Seraphina. It felt like chaos. I've had mates before, long ago, but this— this is something entirely different. It was like I wasn't even myself."

"Perhaps because you haven't fully acknowledged what it truly is," Lucien interjected carefully, stepping closer. His voice was measured, calm, and unshakably sure—yet there was a cautious gentleness to it, one he only used when guiding me to truths I'd rather not see. "It may be time to seek answers beyond our usual sources, Elias."

I frowned, my jaw tightening slightly. "What are you suggesting?"

Lucien hesitated only briefly, glancing toward Isabella for a moment before continuing, his tone reverent. "I think you need to go and speak with Elowen."

At her name, an immediate hush settled across the room. Elowen— the Oracle, the Elder, the Pack Sage—had become a shadowed legend among our kind. Respected, revered, and endlessly wise, she rarely left the seclusion of her remote sanctuary deep in the woods. The thought of visiting her—of facing the truths she might reveal—filled me with equal parts dread and reluctant hope.

Isabella nodded slowly in agreement, eyes serious. "Lucien's right, Elias. Elowen has guided this pack through centuries of uncertainty. If anyone can help you understand the complexity of your bond to Harper, it's her."

Marcus placed a reassuring hand on my shoulder, his voice firm with conviction. "You don't have to face this alone. You have us—all of us."

I glanced at Lucien, recognizing the unwavering certainty in his gaze, and exhaled slowly, reluctantly releasing my resistance. "Fine," I murmured, resignation mingling with a desperate need for clarity. "Then it's decided. I'll seek out Elowen."

Lucien's mouth curved faintly, relieved. "I'll make arrangements immediately."

I turned to stare out the broad window overlooking the moonlit gardens beyond. Harper's face lingered stubbornly in my mind—her wide-eyed confusion, the breathless way she'd stared up at me when I pinned her against that wall. Even now, the memory of her scent stirred something fiercely possessive inside me. I closed my eyes briefly, inhaling sharply.

I needed answers. I needed control. Because the truth was becoming dangerously clear:

I wasn't just losing control to my wolf—I was losing myself to Harper. And unless I understood why, I risked destroying everything, including her.

Elowen, wise keeper of our lore, might hold the key I desperately needed. I could only hope that I was prepared to face whatever truths she would reveal.

The journey to Elowen's sanctuary began at dawn, the forest cloaked in a heavy mist that clung to the trees like a shroud. I moved swiftly, my wolf close to the surface, my senses heightened as I navigated the winding trails that led deeper into the woods. The air was thick with the scent of pine and damp earth, and the only sounds were the crunch of leaves beneath my boots and the distant calls of birds greeting the morning.

The further I ventured, the more the forest seemed to change. The trees grew taller, their branches intertwining to form a canopy that filtered the sunlight into a soft, golden glow. The underbrush thinned, replaced by a carpet of moss and ferns, and the air grew cooler, carrying with it a faint, almost electric hum of energy. I could feel it in my bones, a subtle vibration that grew stronger with every step. This was no ordinary forest—it was a place of power, a place where the veil between worlds was thin.

By midday, I reached the edge of a clearing, and there it was: Elowen's sanctuary. A small, ancient cabin stood at the center, its wooden walls weathered and worn but still standing strong. Smoke curled from the chimney, and the scent of herbs and incense wafted through the air. Surrounding the cabin was a garden filled with wildflowers and medicinal plants, their colors vibrant even in the muted light.

I hesitated at the edge of the clearing, my heart pounding in my chest. The weight of what I was about to do settled heavily on my shoulders. Elowen was not just a wise woman—she was a seer, a keeper of secrets, and her words had the power to change everything. Taking a deep breath, I stepped into the clearing and approached the cabin.

Before I could knock, the door creaked open, and there she was. Elowen stood in the doorway, her presence filling the space like a quiet storm. She was neither young nor old, her agelessness defying time itself. Her silver hair cascaded down her back in waves that seemed to shimmer faintly, as if touched by moonlight even in the dim glow of the cabin. It wasn't just hair—it was a cascade of starlight, each strand alive with a subtle, almost imperceptible glow.

Her eyes were her most striking feature, a piercing, otherworldly blue that seemed to hold the depth of centuries. They were not merely eyes but windows—windows into a world I could not begin to understand, filled with knowledge and secrets that stretched far beyond my comprehension. When her gaze met mine, it felt as though she could see straight through me, past the walls I had built, past the mask I wore as alpha, straight into the raw, unguarded core of who I was. It was unnerving, yet there was a gentleness there too, a quiet understanding that made me feel both exposed and strangely comforted.

She was tall, her posture regal and effortless, as if the weight of the world rested lightly on her shoulders. Her movements were fluid, unhurried, each step deliberate and graceful, like a dancer gliding across a stage. She wore a simple robe of deep indigo, its fabric flowing around her as though it were alive, catching the faint light and reflecting it in subtle, shifting patterns. Around her neck hung a pendant—a single, smooth stone that seemed to pulse faintly, as if in rhythm with her heartbeat.

Her skin was pale, almost luminous, with a faint, silvery sheen that made her seem as though she were not entirely of this world. There were no lines or marks to suggest age, yet her face carried the weight of wisdom, each feature etched with a quiet authority that commanded respect without demanding it. Her lips curved into a faint, knowing smile, one that suggested she had already seen the questions in my mind before I could voice them.

The air around her seemed to hum with energy, a soft, electric vibration that made the hairs on the back of my neck stand on end. It wasn't just her appearance—it was her presence, an aura that felt ancient and timeless, as if she were a living embodiment of the forest itself. She was not beautiful in the conventional sense, nor was she meant to be. She was something far more—something ethereal, something transcendent.

I felt a pang of something akin to reverence as I met her gaze, a deep, instinctual recognition of her power and wisdom. This was no ordinary woman. This was Elowen, the Oracle, the Elder, the keeper of secrets and the guide of souls. And in that moment, I understood why the pack spoke of her with such awe, why her name carried the weight of legend.

"Elias," she said, her voice soft but carrying the weight of centuries. "I've been expecting you."

I frowned, my brow furrowing. "You have?"

She smiled faintly, a hint of amusement in her eyes. "The threads of fate are not so easily ignored, Alpha. Especially when they involve a bond as powerful as yours."

I stiffened, my heart pounding. "What do you mean?"

Elowen stepped closer, her movements fluid and unhurried. "You know what I mean. The bond between you and the human. It is not something you can run from, no matter how hard you try."

I shook my head, my frustration bubbling to the surface. "I don't understand. I've lived for centuries without a mate. Why now? Why her?"

Elowen's gaze softened, and she reached out, placing a hand on my arm. Her touch was warm, grounding, and for a moment, the storm inside me stilled.

"The bond chooses us, Alpha, not the other way around," she said gently. "And it is not something to be feared. It is a gift, a connection that transcends time and reason. But it is also a responsibility—one that requires you to confront the parts of yourself you have long buried."

I looked away, my jaw tightening. "I don't know if I can."

Elowen's hand tightened on my arm, her voice firm but kind. "You must. For her. For yourself. For your pack. These bonds are a thread woven into the fabric of destinies, Alpha. To deny it is to deny who you are."

Her words hung in the air, heavy with truth, and I felt the weight of them settle deep in my chest. I had spent centuries running from my past, from the pain of loss, from the vulnerability of connection. But Harper… she had broken through my defenses, and now there was no going back.

"What do I do?" I asked, my voice barely above a whisper.

Elowen smiled, her eyes filled with a quiet wisdom. "You face it. You embrace it. And you trust that the bond will guide you, even when the path is uncertain."

I nodded slowly, the tension in my chest easing slightly. For the first time in centuries, I felt a glimmer of hope—a fragile, tentative thing, but hope nonetheless. Yet, as I turned to leave, Elowen's voice stopped me.

"Wait," she said, her tone firm but gentle. "Your journey here is not yet complete."

I paused, glancing back at her. "What do you mean?"

She stepped closer, her gaze piercing yet kind. "You came seeking answers, Alpha, but answers alone will not be enough. To truly understand the bond, you must confront the part of yourself that resists it—the part that fears it. Your wolf."

I stiffened, my jaw tightening. "My wolf is not the problem. It's my control that's failing."

Elowen's smile was knowing, almost sad. "Your wolf is not separate from you, Alpha. It is you. And until you reconcile with it, the bond will remain a source of conflict, not strength."

Before I could protest, she gestured toward the center of the clearing. The air seemed to shift, the mist thickening and swirling around us. The ground beneath my feet felt alive, pulsing with a low, resonant energy. I watched as the mossy earth parted, revealing a circle of ancient stones etched with runes that glowed faintly in the dim light.

"Step into the circle," Elowen instructed, her voice carrying the weight of command. "This is not just a ritual of understanding, Alpha. It is a reckoning."

I hesitated, my instincts screaming at me to refuse. But something in her gaze—something ancient and unyielding—compelled me forward. I stepped into the circle, the air growing heavier with each step. The runes flared brighter, their light casting eerie shadows on the trees around us.

As soon as my feet crossed the threshold, the ritual began.

A surge of energy shot through me, sharp and electric, and I fell to my knees as my wolf surged to the surface. My limbs stiffened, my bones cracking under unseen pressure, forcing me to the ground. I gasped, the pain searing through me like fire, and I clawed at the earth, trying to anchor myself against the onslaught.

Elowen's voice echoed in my mind, steady and unyielding. "Face it. Do not fight it. Embrace it."

But the wolf was relentless, its presence overwhelming, its voice a growl in my mind. You deny me. You fear me. But I am you.

The voice wasn't just a voice—it was a chorus, an echo of every version of myself over the centuries, forcing me to confront who I had been and what I had done.

I am the hunter in the dark, it snarled, its voice twisting inside me, something ancient, something hungry. The beast in the blood. The shadow that never fades. And yet, you bury me?

I clenched my fists, my nails digging into my palms as I struggled to maintain control. But the wolf was relentless, its rage a searing force that threatened to rip me apart.

You deny me. You fear me, it growled, its voice a snarl. But I am you. And I will take what you refuse to give.

I felt my limbs tremble, my bones shifting against my will. My vision blurred—I saw myself, standing in the circle, but it wasn't me. It was a creature with blackened veins, its mouth curled in a savage grin.

My wolf. Unbound.

It stepped forward, stalking me, its voice a growl in my ears. You are afraid. Afraid of losing control. Afraid of losing her.

The words struck like a blade, cutting deep into the part of me I had tried to bury.

I was afraid.

For centuries, I had ruled with precision, power, and control. But Harper—she unraveled me. And if I accepted the bond, if I let myself feel it—what would become of me?

The wolf lunged, and I did not step back.

I met its charge head-on, my body wracked with the pain of the shift. My muscles screamed, my bones cracked, and my vision blurred as the wolf's presence surged against my mind, its rage a searing force that threatened to rip me apart.

No more.

I reached for the beast—not to destroy it, but to pull it into myself, to force it to acknowledge me as its master.

Pain. Heat. A violent collision of wills.

And then—silence.

When I opened my eyes, the world was different. The circle was still glowing faintly, the runes etched into the stones pulsing with a soft, steady light. But the weight on my mind had changed. The wolf was no longer something separate, no longer a force I had to fight or suppress. It was there, beneath my skin, watching—but for the first time, it did not fight me.

I blinked, my vision blurry, my body heavy and stiff. The air was cool against my skin, the scent of pine and earth sharp and familiar. I tried to sit up, but my muscles protested, aching as though they had been pushed to their limits and beyond.

"Careful," a soft voice said, and I turned my head to see Elowen sitting nearby, her silver hair shimmering in the dim light. Her expression was calm, her eyes filled with that same quiet wisdom that had drawn me to her in the first place. "You've been through much."

"How long?" I croaked, my voice rough and unfamiliar.

"Three days," she replied, her tone matter of fact. "The ritual was…intense, Alpha. Your body needed time to heal, to adjust."

I stared at her, my mind struggling to process the words. Three days. I had been unconscious for three days. The thought should have alarmed me, but instead, I felt a strange sense of calm, as if the storm inside me had finally settled.

I looked down at my hands, flexing my fingers slowly. They felt the same, and yet…different. There was a new awareness in me, a quiet strength that hadn't been there before. The wolf was still there, its presence a low hum in the back of my mind, but it was no longer a threat. It was a part of me, as it had always been meant to be.

Elowen's voice broke through my thoughts, soft but firm. "Now, you understand. But Alpha, the moon rises full tonight. Its light will reveal what shadows hide. You must prepare wisely."

I exhaled slowly, my chest rising and falling with something that felt dangerously close to peace. Not submission. Not defeat. Balance.

For the first time in centuries, I felt whole.

As I left the sanctuary and began the journey back, the forest seemed different—brighter, more alive. The weight of Elowen's words stayed with me, a quiet reassurance that I was not alone in this. The bond with Harper was not a curse or a weakness—it was a gift, a chance to heal, to grow, to become more than I had ever been.

And for the first time, I felt ready to face it.

Harper

I woke up gasping, my heart hammering against my chest as though I'd just been ripped from a nightmare. The dim glow of the clock—5:47 a.m.—blurred before my eyes as memories surged through me: Elias at my door, his hands tight around my wrists, pressing me against the wall, the fire blazing in his eyes. Then the abrupt, inexplicable way he'd pulled away and vanished into the night.

"What the hell was that?" My voice cracked in the darkness, swallowed by the silence of my bedroom.

I lay there, wide-eyed and restless, the sheets tangled around my body, every nerve ending buzzing with unresolved tension. Sleep refused to return, chased away by relentless questions swirling like a hurricane through my mind.

When the first rays of dawn finally broke through the curtains, I grabbed my phone, dialing Sophie's number without a second thought. She answered on the third ring, her voice muffled by sleep. "Harper? It's barely six. What's wrong?"

"Soph," I whispered urgently, pacing my apartment barefoot. "Something happened. I really need to talk."

She hesitated briefly before responding, "Alright. Our usual place, twenty minutes?"

"Yes. Please."

We met at our usual café, it was warm, the scent of fresh espresso and cinnamon pastries thick in the air, but even its familiar comfort couldn't calm the chaos spinning inside me. Sophie slid into the seat across from mine, hair pulled back hastily into a ponytail, her eyes alert. She took one look at me and raised an eyebrow. "Okay, spill. What's going on? You look like you haven't slept in a week."

I slumped into a chair, clutching my coffee like a lifeline. "It's Elias," I said, my voice low. "He showed up at my apartment last night. In the middle of the night. And he just… he just…"

Sophie leaned forward, her eyes wide. "He just what? Did something happen?" I hesitated, my cheeks flushing as the memory came rushing back—his body pressing me against the wall, his breath hot on my skin, the way his eyes had burned into mine. "I don't even know, Soph," I said, running a hand through my hair. "He was acting so weird. Like, intense. And then he just left. I don't know what to think."

Sophie frowned, sipping her coffee thoughtfully. "Okay, let's break this down. What exactly did he do?"

I bit my lip, my face heating up even more. "He… pinned me against the wall. Like, full-on pinned me. His hands were on my wrists, my body…everywhere and he was just… looking at me. Like he was trying to figure something out. And then he left. Just like that."

Sophie's eyebrows shot up. "He pinned you? Like, romantically? Or…?"

"I don't know!" I said, throwing my hands up. "It wasn't romantic. It was… God, Soph, it was so intense. Like, he was so close, and I could feel his breath on my neck, and his body was pressed against me. And his eyes—they were so dark, like he was fighting with himself or something. And then he just walked out. I don't know what to do. I don't even know what to feel."

Sophie's eyes widened, and she leaned in closer, her voice dropping to a whisper. "Okay, wait. Back up. He pinned you against the wall, and you could feel his breath on your neck? Harper, that's not just intense. That's… kind of hot."

I groaned, burying my face in my hands. "Don't say that. It wasn't hot. It was… I don't know. It was terrifying and confusing and… okay, fine, maybe a little hot. But that's not the point!"

Sophie smirked, clearly enjoying this way too much. "Oh, it's definitely the point. So, what happened after he pinned you? Did he say anything? Did you say anything?"

I shook my head, my face still burning. "He said he shouldn't have come to my place. I asked him why he did. Soph, he said because he couldn't stay away. And then he walked out. Just like that. No explanation, no nothing."

Sophie's smirk faded, replaced by a more serious expression. "Okay, that's… weird. And kind of messed up. But let's be real, Harp. If anyone else had done that, I'd be telling you to call the cops. But it's Elias. And let's be honest—you've been low-key obsessed with him since day one."

"I'm not obsessed," I said quickly, though the way my voice cracked probably didn't help my case. "He's just… different. There's something about him, Soph. Something I can't explain."

Sophie sighed, leaning back in her chair. "Look, I get it. He's mysterious, he's intense, and yeah, he's ridiculously hot. But that doesn't give him the right to mess with your head like this. You deserve better."

I nodded, but the knot in my stomach didn't loosen. "I know. But it's not just about how he looks or how he acts. It's… I don't know. It's like there's this pull between us, something I can't ignore. And last night when he was that close… I felt it even more. Like, my whole body was on fire, and I couldn't think straight. And then he just left, and now I'm sitting here wondering if I did something wrong or if he's just… I don't know, losing it."

Sophie reached across the table, squeezing my hand. "You didn't do anything wrong. If anything, he's the one who owes you an explanation. Showing up at your place in the middle of the night? Pinning you against a wall? That's not okay, Harp. You know that, right?"

"You're right," I said softly, determination creeping into my voice. "I have to confront him. I need answers."

I spent the rest of the weekend spring cleaning the apartment, then spring cleaning it again. I scrubbed every surface until it gleamed, rearranged furniture until my back ached, and even tackled the junk drawer I'd been avoiding for months. I blared my music loud enough to drown out my thoughts—playlists of upbeat pop songs and angry rock anthems that made me feel like I could power through anything. But no matter how hard I scrubbed or how loud I turned up the volume, Elias's face kept creeping back into my mind.

I tried calling him again on Saturday afternoon, my fingers trembling as I dialed his number. It went straight to voicemail, just like the last five times. "Hey, it's Harper," I said, my voice wavering slightly. "I just… I need to talk to you. Call me back, okay?"

I hung up and stared at my phone, half hoping it would ring immediately. It didn't.

By Sunday, I was a mess. I'd cleaned the apartment so thoroughly that there was nothing left to do, and my music playlist had looped three times. I sat on the couch, staring at my phone, willing it to buzz with a message from him. But the screen stayed dark, and the silence in the apartment felt heavier than ever.

I grabbed my keys and headed out for a walk, hoping the fresh air would clear my head. The streets were quiet, the kind of peaceful that only comes on a lazy Sunday afternoon. But even the sunshine and the chirping birds couldn't shake the knot of frustration and worry in my chest.

I stopped by the park and sat on a bench, watching a group of kids play on the swings. Their laughter was infectious, and for a moment, I felt a little lighter. But then my phone buzzed in my pocket, and my heart leapt—only to sink again when I saw it was just a text from Sophie.

Sophie: *Hey, how are you holding up?*

I sighed and typed back. **Harper:** *I'm fine. Just trying to keep busy.*

Sophie: *You're not fine. You're obsessing. Have you heard from him yet?*

Harper: *No. And I'm not obsessing. I'm just… concerned.*

Sophie: *Uh-huh. Concerned. Sure. Look, if he's ghosting you, he's not worth your time. You deserve better.*

I didn't reply. I knew Sophie was just trying to help, but her words didn't make me feel any better. Because deep down, I knew Elias wasn't ghosting me. Something was wrong—I could feel it. And until I knew what it was, I couldn't let it go.

That night, I lay in bed, staring at the ceiling, my mind racing. Tomorrow was Monday, and that meant Elias would be at the office. I'd see him again, face-to-face, for the first time since he'd shown up at my apartment and left without a word. The thought made my stomach churn.

I tossed and turned, the sheets tangling around my legs as I tried to find a comfortable position. But no matter how I lay, I couldn't quiet my thoughts. What would I say to him? What would *he* say to me? Would he act like nothing had happened? Or would he finally explain why he'd been so… intense?

I groaned, flipping onto my side and punching my pillow into a more comfortable shape. "Get it together, Harper," I muttered to myself. "It's just Elias. You've dealt with him before. You can handle this."

But the truth was, I wasn't sure I could. The memory of that night was burned into my brain—his body pressing me against the wall, his breath hot on my skin, the way his eyes had burned into mine. It had been terrifying and exhilarating all at once, and I didn't know how to feel about it. About him.

I glanced at the clock on my nightstand: 1:23 a.m. I groaned again, rolling onto my back. Sleep was clearly not happening. I grabbed my phone and scrolled through my messages, hoping for some kind of distraction. But there was nothing new—just a few texts from Sophie and a reminder about a meeting tomorrow.

I opened my contacts and hovered over Elias's name, my thumb trembling slightly. I wanted to call him, to demand an explanation, to hear his voice and know that he was okay. But I couldn't bring myself to do it. What if he didn't answer? What if he did, and he sounded cold and distant, like none of it had mattered to him?

I tossed my phone onto the nightstand and buried my face in my pillow. "Why does this have to be so complicated?" I muttered, my voice muffled.

The hours dragged on, the minutes ticking by with agonizing slowness. I tried counting sheep, listening to calming music, even reading a boring article about tax reforms—anything to quiet my mind. But nothing worked. Every time I closed my eyes, I saw Elias's face, his dark eyes staring into mine, his expression unreadable.

By the time the first rays of sunlight peeked through my curtains, I was exhausted but no closer to sleep. I dragged myself out of bed and into the shower, the hot water doing little to ease the tension in my shoulders. As I got ready for work, I caught a glimpse of myself in the mirror—dark circles under my eyes, my hair a mess, my expression tense. I looked like I hadn't slept in days. Because I hadn't.

I grabbed my bag and headed out the door, my stomach in knots. Whatever happened today, I told myself, I'd handle it. I had to. But as I walked to the office, my heart pounding with every step, I couldn't shake the feeling that I was walking into a storm.

Chapter 8

We Need To Talk

Elias

"You look much better, brother," Isabella greeted me at the door with a tight, unusual hug. Her arms wrapped around me with a fierceness that surprised me, and for a moment, I let myself lean into it. She smelled like lavender and pine, her presence a comforting anchor after the chaos of the past few days. Her embrace was warm, grounding, and for the first time since I'd left Elowen's sanctuary, I felt like I could breathe.

Lucien stood a few steps behind her, his arms crossed and his expression unreadable as usual. But I could see the faint flicker of relief in his eyes as he took me in. "You're alive," he said dryly. "That's an improvement."

I rolled my eyes, pulling away from Isabella. "Thanks for the vote of confidence."

Isabella took a step back, her nose wrinkling as she gave me a once-over. "But wow…" she said, her tone teasing but her eyes serious. "Do you smell."

I frowned, lifting my arm to sniff myself. "What are you talking about?"

"You smell like the forest," she said, her lips curving into a smirk. "And sweat. And… something else. Something wild. What the hell happened to you?"

I hesitated, not sure how much to share. The ritual with Elowen had left me raw, my body and mind still adjusting to the balance I'd found with my wolf. The trek home had only made it worse—every step had felt like a battle, my muscles aching, my bones heavy, as if the forest itself had been trying to hold me back. But Isabella and Lucien were my pack, my family. They deserved the truth.

"I saw her. Elowen," I said finally, my voice low. "She… helped me."

Isabella's smirk faded, replaced by a look of concern. "I am so jealous. What did she do?"

"She forced me to confront my wolf," I said, running a hand through my hair. "To really face it. And it wasn't… easy."

Lucien raised an eyebrow. "Understatement of the century, I'm sure."

I shot him a glare, but there was no real heat behind it. "It was necessary. I couldn't keep fighting it. Not if I want to understand it all."

Isabella's eyes softened, and she reached out to squeeze my arm. "We're proud of you, Elias. It takes strength to face something like that."

I nodded, her words easing some of the tension in my chest. "Thanks. But I'm not out of the woods yet. Elowen seemed to be warning me about the full moon tonight. She said to prepare wisely."

Lucien stepped forward, his expression calm but resolute. "We're prepared, Elias. We have the lock-up ready for all of us. Reinforced walls, extra chains, and enough space to keep everyone contained if things get… intense."

I glanced at him, surprised. "You've already set it up?"

"Of course," Lucien said, his tone matter-of-fact. "We knew the full moon was coming, and after everything that's happened, we figured it was better to be over prepared than caught off guard."

Isabella nodded, her arms crossed as she leaned against the door frame. "We've got it covered, Elias. You don't have to worry about us. Just focus on yourself tonight."

I felt a flicker of gratitude, but it was quickly overshadowed by a gnawing sense of unease. The lock-up was a necessary precaution—a secure, reinforced space deep downstairs where the pack could ride out the full moon without risking harm to themselves or others. But Elowen's warning hadn't been about the pack. It had been about *me*.

"It's not just about the lock-up," I said slowly, my voice low. "Elowen wasn't just talking about the moon's pull. She said to prepare wisely. There's something else coming tonight. Something I'm not ready for."

Lucien's brow furrowed, and he exchanged a glance with Isabella. "What do you mean?"

I shook my head, frustration bubbling up inside me. "I don't know.

She didn't explain. But I can feel it—something's different this time. The moon… it's not just a challenge. It's a test."

Isabella stepped closer, her expression softening. "Then we'll face it together. You're not alone in this, Elias. Whatever's coming, we'll handle it as a pack."

I wanted to believe her, to let their confidence ease the weight on my shoulders. But Elowen's words echoed in my mind, a quiet, insistent warning I couldn't ignore. *Prepare wisely.*

"I appreciate that," I said finally, my voice rough.

As I walked further into the house, the weight of the past few days settled heavily on my shoulders. My body ached, every muscle protesting as I moved. The ritual had taken more out of me than I'd realized, and the journey home had only made it worse. The forest had been alive, the trees whispering secrets I couldn't understand, the shadows shifting in ways that made my skin crawl. By the time I'd reached the house, I'd been exhausted, my body and mind pushed to their limits.

But there was no time to rest. The full moon was tonight, and Elowen's warning echoed in my mind. *Prepare wisely.* I didn't know what that meant, but I knew one thing for certain—whatever was coming, I had to be ready.

Sitting on the edge of my bed, feeling the weight of the night to come on my shoulders, I dared to look at my phone for the first time since leaving Harper's apartment. The screen lit up, and my stomach dropped as I saw the notifications—several texts and missed calls from her, each one more intense than the last. My thumb hovered over the screen, hesitating. I didn't want to open them. I didn't want to see the hurt and confusion in her words, the questions I couldn't answer. But I couldn't ignore them either.

The first text was simple, sent just a few hours after I'd left her apartment:

Harper: *Hey, it's Harper. I just… I need to talk to you. Call me back, okay?*

The next one came later that night:

Harper: *Elias, I'm really worried. Please just let me know you're okay.*

By the next day, her tone had shifted, the worry giving way to frustration:

Harper: *This isn't fair. You can't just show up like that and then disappear. I deserve an explanation.*

The most recent message, sent just a few hours ago, made my chest tighten:

Harper: *Elias, I don't know what's going on, but I need to hear from you. We need to talk.*

I stared at the screen, my jaw clenched. Harper's words were a mirror, reflecting back everything I'd been trying to avoid—my own fear, my own guilt, my own inability to face what was happening between us. I wanted to call her, to explain, to tell her everything. But how could I? How could I explain something I didn't even fully understand myself?

"Elias?" Isabella's voice broke through my thoughts, and I looked up to see her standing in the doorway, her expression concerned. "Everything okay?"

I shook my head, slipping my phone back into my pocket. "No. Not really."

She stepped closer, her arms crossed. "Is it Harper?"

I didn't answer, but the look on my face must have said enough. Isabella sighed, her tone softening. "You can't keep avoiding her, you know. She's not going to just let this go."

"I know," I said, my voice rough. "But what am I supposed to tell her? That I'm losing control? That I'm not sure I can protect her from myself? From my wolf?"

Isabella's eyes softened, and she reached out to squeeze my arm. "You tell her the truth. She deserves that much. And maybe… maybe she can handle more than you think."

I wanted to believe her, but the doubt gnawed at me. Harper was strong, yes. But this wasn't just about strength. This was about the bond, about the pull between us that I couldn't explain, couldn't control. And now, with the full moon rising tonight, I wasn't sure I could keep her safe—from me, or from whatever was coming.

"I'll figure it out," I said finally, though the words felt hollow. "But right now, I need to focus on the pack. On the moon."

Isabella nodded and walked away, though her expression was still worried.

I made the final preparations to the lock-up, taking in the scene with a critical eye. The reinforced walls stood solid and unyielding, the chains and restraints carefully arranged to keep the pack contained during the full moon. The space was familiar, a necessary evil we'd all come to accept, but tonight it felt different. The air was charged, heavy with the anticipation of what was to come. The full moon was rising, and with it, the wild, untamed energy that always threatened to consume us.

I double-checked the locks, the chains, the barriers—anything to keep my mind off what was coming. But no matter how much I busied myself, I couldn't shake the unease that had settled deep in my chest. It wasn't just the moon. It was Harper.

I wasn't sure what unnerved me more—the full moon or seeing her again.

After the lock-up was secured, I headed back upstairs and quickly showered, the hot water doing little to ease the tension in my muscles. I dressed in my usual suit, the crisp lines and tailored fit a stark contrast to the chaos churning inside me. The Alpha had to look the part, even if I felt anything but in control.

As I made my way to the office, my mind raced. Harper's texts were still burning a hole in my pocket, her words echoing in my head. She was coming to the office today. She wanted answers. And I had no idea what to tell her.

The drive was a blur, the city streets passing by in a haze of gray and steel. By the time I pulled into the parking garage, my hands were gripping the steering wheel so tightly my knuckles were white. I took a deep breath, trying to steady myself, but it did little to calm the storm inside.

The elevator ride up to the office felt like an eternity. Every second stretched, every heartbeat a reminder of what was waiting for me. When the doors finally slid open, I stepped out into the familiar space, the hum of activity a stark contrast to the chaos in my mind.

And then I saw her.

Harper was standing by her desk, her back to me as she sorted through a stack of files. She looked the same as always—her hair pulled into a loose ponytail, her blouse neatly tucked into her skirt, her posture straight and professional. But there was something different about her today, something in the way she moved, the way she held herself. She was tense, her movements sharp and deliberate, as if she was bracing herself for something.

I hesitated, my feet rooted to the spot. For a moment, I considered turning around, walking away, avoiding this confrontation altogether. But then she turned, her eyes meeting mine, and I knew there was no escaping this.

Her expression was unreadable, but I could see the questions in her eyes, the hurt, the frustration. She crossed her arms, her gaze steady as she took a step toward me. "Mr. Blackwell," she said, her voice calm but firm. "We need to talk."

I nodded, my throat tight. "I know."

Harper

Elias watched me closely as I entered his office first, his gaze piercing and unsettlingly intense. He walked behind me with a forced calmness, shoulders squared, arms crossed tightly against his broad chest as if holding himself back from something dangerous.

The office was dimly lit, shadows clinging possessively to the corners, soft sunlight filtering through the window and casting an eerie glow across Elias's already intimidating features. The faint tick of the antique clock on his desk punctuated each tense moment between us.

I swallowed nervously, shifting from foot to foot as his silence stretched out painfully, softly closing the office door.

"Listen," I began, forcing confidence I didn't feel into my voice. "About Friday night... I mean, I'm flattered, or confused—or honestly, both—but can we maybe rewind and pretend you didn't show up at my apartment smelling like the world's hottest whiskey commercial?"

He raised one eyebrow slightly, and my traitorous cheeks flushed immediately. Way to stay smooth, Harper.

"You want to pretend it didn't happen? I thought you'd want to talk about it, get answers?" His voice was quiet, dangerously calm.

I blinked, warmth flooding my face. "I mean, that's not exactly—I just—" I stopped, exhaling sharply. "I just want things to go back to normal. Yes, I want to pretend it didn't happen."

"Harper," Elias sighed, running a hand through his hair—a gesture that was growing more and more disheveled, more desperate. His voice was low, edged with a frustration he couldn't quite hide. "Do you want to pretend it didn't happen, or pretend you didn't enjoy it?"

I was floored. *What?*

My mouth opened, but no words came out. For a moment, I just stared at him, my mind scrambling to process what he'd just said. Did he really just ask me that? After everything? After showing up at my apartment, pinning me against the wall, and then disappearing for days without a word? Now he had the nerve to stand here and act like *I* was the one pretending?

"Excuse me?" I finally managed, my voice sharp and incredulous. My arms crossed tightly over my chest, as if the gesture could shield me from the sting of his words. "You're kind of making this difficult."

Elias took a slow step forward, closing the distance between us with deliberate ease. His presence overwhelmed my senses—rich, masculine. I swallowed nervously, tilting my chin stubbornly upward to maintain eye contact, even as every cell in my body seemed to be screaming contradictory instructions: stay, run, kiss him, flee—maybe all at once.

"Did you want to kiss Damian, Friday?" he asked suddenly, his voice rougher, more raw than I'd ever heard it before. His golden eyes darkened, flickering with something dangerously close to possessiveness.

My mouth opened, then closed, struggling for words. "How do you even know about that?"

He scoffed softly, shaking his head in frustration. "You're not exactly subtle, Harper. And neither is he."

I felt heat rising furiously in my cheeks, embarrassment blending swiftly with irritation. "Not that it's your business, but it wasn't exactly planned. It just...happened."

Elias stepped even closer, towering over me, his voice dropping to a husky whisper. "Do you want it to happen again?"

I stared up at him, stunned, my heart racing uncontrollably. "Excuse me?"

"I know you were with him Friday, Harper," Elias growled softly, the rough timbre of his voice sending involuntary shivers down my spine. "At the pier."

"You had me followed?" I asked, incredulous anger briefly overpowering my confusion. "Seriously?"

"I protect what's mine," he said firmly, his gaze unwavering. The possessiveness in his voice both terrified and thrilled me, twisting my stomach into knots.

"I'm not yours," I replied stubbornly, trying desperately to reclaim some small measure of control. But even as I spoke the words, my heart betrayed me, racing wildly beneath his unrelenting gaze.

Elias's lips curled faintly, eyes softening just enough to disarm me completely. He leaned closer still, voice dropping to a rough whisper that danced maddeningly over my skin.

"Aren't you?"

I stared up at Elias, speechless, my heart hammering painfully in my chest. The way he looked at me—intense, possessive, almost wild—sent chills skittering down my spine, setting my nerves on edge even as warmth pooled dangerously in my stomach. I drew a shaky breath, trying desperately to reclaim a shred of control.

"I—I'm pretty sure we never had that conversation," I finally managed, my voice a breathy whisper, betraying my struggle to remain composed. "In fact, I distinctly remember resigning, which you conveniently ignored."

His eyes softened slightly, the fierce intensity flickering momentarily into something more vulnerable, almost regretful. He exhaled sharply, running a frustrated hand through his dark hair, the tattoos on his arm flexing with the movement. My gaze lingered helplessly, tracing the intricate lines and symbols that disappeared beneath the crisp sleeve of his shirt.

"I wasn't exactly thinking clearly last night," he admitted roughly, jaw clenched. "Showing up at your apartment—drunk and out of control—that was irresponsible. And entirely out of character."

My breath hitched slightly at the rare confession, but I forced my composure back, arms folding stubbornly across my chest. "Then why did you come?"

His golden eyes locked onto mine again, the tension between us crackling, electric. "Because I can't stop thinking about you."

The honesty in his voice shocked me into silence, leaving me gaping at him like a fool. Heat blossomed through my body, setting my cheeks aflame and turning my legs to jelly. Elias took a tentative step closer, his voice dropping to a low, velvet murmur.

"Harper, Damian isn't who you think he is. He's dangerous, manipulative—someone who'll use you to get to me."

I shook my head stubbornly, despite the sudden unease creeping through me. "He hasn't given me any reason to doubt him. And honestly, you're not exactly the poster boy for trustworthiness right now, *Elias. What is the problem?"* I demanded, frustration finally breaking through my trembling voice. "You don't get to storm into my apartment, act possessive, and then vanish like I imagined it all. I deserve an explanation—more than just cryptic warnings."

His jaw tightened, a flicker of pain crossing his expression, quickly hidden behind his controlled façade. "He's dangerous, Harper. Trust me."

"Funny, he said the same about you," I countered sharply, holding my ground despite the tremor in my voice.

"Then he wasn't lying entirely," Elias replied quietly, stepping even closer until mere inches separated us. His voice softened to a murmur, low and intimate, sending heat surging through my veins. "I am dangerous. Far more dangerous than you realize. But not to you."

"Why?" I asked softly, desperately searching his gaze for answers to questions I couldn't even articulate. "Why am I different?"

He reached up slowly, his fingers brushing my cheek in a gentle caress that made my breath catch painfully. "Because you are mine, Harper. Whether you acknowledge it or not."

My pulse skittered uncontrollably at his words, heart betraying my resolve, hammering furiously beneath the surface. I pulled away abruptly, backing toward the door, needing distance from the intensity of his gaze and the heat of his touch.

"You can't just decide that, Elias," I whispered shakily, my hand trembling slightly on the doorknob. "People aren't possessions."

He didn't move, but his eyes stayed fixed on mine, burning with quiet certainty. "Perhaps not," he conceded softly. "But that doesn't change how I feel, Harper."

I hesitated, my heart aching, torn between fleeing and staying, terrified by both possibilities.

"Please just be careful," Elias added softly, the warning and the plea unmistakably entwined in his voice. "He's not what you think."

I didn't respond, simply opened the door and stepped through, closing it softly behind me. Yet even as I walked away, Elias's words echoed stubbornly in my mind, my heart twisted painfully with confusion.

And worse, despite everything, I knew I believed him.

Elias

I stood in silence, my entire body tense as Harper's lingering scent filled the empty office, mocking my crumbling self-control. She had barely closed the door behind her, but already I felt her absence keenly, like a physical ache deep inside my chest. I clenched my fists tightly at my sides, forcing myself not to turn around and slam them into something, anything, to relieve the pressure building inside me.

What the hell was happening to me?

I'd survived countless battles, endured centuries of loneliness and rage, but this feeling—this raw, overwhelming jealousy—was entirely new. It consumed me, pushing my thoughts into dark, dangerous territory.

Lucien quietly stepped into the office, his footsteps careful, his expression cautious as he took in my rigid posture. He didn't say anything right away, but I felt his eyes on me, patiently waiting for me to acknowledge him.

"What?" I snapped, sharper than I'd intended. I immediately regretted my tone but was too far gone to soften it.

He paused a moment, carefully choosing his words. "Elias, the full moon rises tonight. Your instincts are amplified, emotions heightened. You're starting to lose your grip."

I closed my eyes briefly, exhaling sharply. The cool glass of the window pressed firmly against my palm was little comfort, but at least it provided something solid to cling to. "Trust me, Lucien, I know." My voice sounded tired, drained. "This feels worse—far worse than it ever has. Maybe this is what Elowen warned me about. I need to prepare."

He studied me with quiet sympathy, something rare and unsettling. "It's not just the moon, and you know it. It's Harper. Your wolf chose her. Fighting it is making everything harder."

I shook my head stubbornly, eyes still fixed on the city beyond the window—quiet, peaceful, oblivious to the turmoil tearing me apart. "She's human," I reminded him bitterly. "Fragile. Temporary. Pulling her into this madness isn't fair."

Lucien stepped closer, his voice gentler now, coaxing rather than confronting. "The bond isn't something you can argue with. Elowen warned you—fighting it won't change the truth. You're torturing yourself and putting everyone else on edge. Make a decision, Elias. Claim her fully or let her go—but you can't stay stuck like this."

I thought of Harper's kiss with Damian, and jealousy coiled tighter in my gut. The thought of another man touching her, tasting her lips, holding her—my muscles flexed involuntarily, tension radiating through me like electricity.

"She kissed him," I said through gritted teeth, the words feeling like poison on my tongue. "Knowing he touched her—"

Lucien interrupted firmly. "Then make sure it never happens again. Do something. Standing here tormenting yourself won't fix anything." He softened, stepping closer, lowering his voice further. "You always ask the pack to face tough decisions and stay strong. Now it's your turn. Remember what Elowen said: denying the bond only leads to pain."

I closed my eyes again, forcing myself to absorb his words. Lucien was right, damn him. Harper had slipped past all my defenses effortlessly, becoming a part of me so quickly I barely recognized my own heart. "I hate that you've all seen me like this," I admitted softly, unable to hide the crack in my voice. "It makes me feel weak."

Lucien placed a comforting hand briefly on my shoulder, a gesture he rarely showed. "Then maybe it's time to stop pretending you have everything under control. You don't have to carry it all alone. Let yourself accept this—it might finally bring you peace."

He left quietly after that, leaving me to confront my thoughts in solitude. I stared at the closed door, where Harper had vanished moments before, feeling utterly helpless. Every part of me screamed to go after her, to make her mine. But how could I risk bringing her into this mess?

As night fell, dread coiled tighter within me, sharp and unyielding. I descended swiftly to the lower chambers beneath my estate, each step echoing ominously in the silence. The reinforced steel door of my personal holding cell stood ready, its cold metallic surface scarred deeply with claw marks, a harsh reminder of the many nights I'd spent locked away, battling the monster I'd long tried to bury.

My hands trembled slightly as I secured the final lock from inside, sealing myself into solitude. I stripped quickly, skin prickling beneath the chill air, every nerve raw with anticipation. Moonlight crept steadily through the narrow, barred window, inching along the floor like liquid silver. The pain began subtly—a slow ache deep in my bones—but I knew from experience it was merely the calm before the storm.

Pain shot through my body suddenly, sharp and brutal. I sank heavily to my knees, muscles already trembling, my breath ragged.

Suddenly, footsteps echoed beyond the door, sharp and deliberate. I tensed immediately, heart pounding, instincts screaming that something was horribly wrong.

The heavy lock clicked loudly, and the steel door swung open with an agonizing creak. My vision blurred, but through the haze of pain I saw a hooded figure.

"Who are you?" I snarled, voice distorted as agony surged through me. My control frayed completely, rage boiling into every pore. "Get. Out."

The intruder said nothing, merely observed with detached curiosity as I fought against my shifting bones, my muscles rippling violently beneath my skin and slowly walked away.

Elowen's quiet voice echoed clearly in my memory, her cryptic prophecy ringing painfully true:

"Prepare wisely."

My bones cracked brutal finality, the wolf tearing free with an unbearable, savage cry that echoed off the cell's walls.

Clarity vanished beneath the vicious force of the transformation, and all rational thought was obliterated by the overpowering instinct, but beneath it all lingered one final coherent thought:

Harper.

Then the darkness took over completely.

Chapter 9

Boundaries

Harper

Stepping into the office this morning felt less like a regular Tuesday and more like entering the Thunder Dome. Seriously, I was about five seconds away from flipping a coin each morning to decide which Elias I'd encounter: the hot blooded boss with a nasty habit of leaving blood on the floor, or the smoldering enigma who leaned in way too close, whispering things that made my brain malfunction and my body betray me completely.

Both options were a disaster waiting to happen.

Today, as I strode through the glass doors of Blackwell Industries, my heels echoed obnoxiously loud against the marble floors, as if the universe itself was determined to announce my arrival in the most dramatic fashion possible. I tugged nervously at the hem of my skirt—a flirty, curve hugging pencil skirt that had felt incredibly confident back in my bedroom mirror but now screamed, "Look, Elias, I'm trying way too hard!" My silky blouse dipped just low enough to tempt without breaking any professional codes, though apparently it broke every code of self-preservation I had left.

"Morning, Harper," Marcus greeted warmly, giving me a once-over that clearly signaled surprise at my newfound fashion confidence. "Looking sharp today. Special occasion?"

"Just trying to boost morale around here," I joked weakly, already feeling my cheeks flush. "Figured someone needed to make an effort besides Lucien's ties."

Marcus chuckled, shaking his head. "Mission accomplished,

Harper."

"Thanks," I murmured awkwardly, ducking my head. "I think."

As I settled at my desk, powering up my computer and desperately avoiding eye contact with Elias's ominously closed office door, I noticed Lucien standing rigidly near Elias's office. He had his signature calm-but-intense look nailed down—complete with the crossed-arms-and-furrowed-brow combo. It wasn't exactly comforting.

"Hey, Lucien," I called, doing my best impression of casual. "You haven't seen Elias yet today, have you?"

Lucien turned sharply, his dark eyes widening briefly before settling into a carefully practiced calm. "Miss Wells, good morning. And no, actually—I haven't."

"Huh." I chewed my lip nervously, anxiety beginning to coil in my stomach. "He's usually annoyingly punctual."

"Yes, he is," Lucien admitted, a crease deepening between his brows. He glanced quickly at Elias's empty office, something unreadable crossing his features. "Perhaps he was delayed by traffic."

I stared at him incredulously, eyebrows raised. "Lucien, you don't even believe that. Elias could probably part traffic like the Red Sea just by glaring at it. Seriously, should we be worried?"

He hesitated, his eyes narrowing briefly before finally sighing. "I don't know yet. But I'll find out soon. In the meantime, if he contacts you—"

"You'll be my first call, trust me," I finished dryly, nodding. Lucien gave me a strained smile and disappeared back down the hallway, shoulders set rigidly. Something was clearly off, and Lucien wasn't even bothering to hide it anymore.

I swiveled back to my computer, attempting—and failing—to dive into my inbox. But my eyes kept flicking back to Elias's vacant office. Every unanswered message, every second of silence made my stomach churn tighter. He wasn't exactly Mr. Warm-and-Fuzzy, but Elias was predictable, at least when it came to his schedule. His absence was a crack in the carefully maintained armor of Blackwell Industries, and everyone felt it.

By mid-morning, whispers had started up like a storm cloud brewing quietly in the distance.

"Elias, seriously, where the hell are you?" I murmured quietly, frustration laced with genuine concern.

My heart twisted uncomfortably. His absence had thrown the whole office off balance. And I realized, with an uneasy jolt, that my worry wasn't just professional. It was personal, in a way I didn't quite understand yet—but desperately wanted to ignore.

"Lucien, seriously, where the hell is Elias, he's normally here by now?" I demanded, pacing anxiously back and forth in front of his desk, my nerves strung tighter than piano wire. It was nearly noon several hours silence since Elias had disappeared without a word, since that unsettling conversation in his office that still left my head spinning.

Lucien glanced up from his work with an expression that hovered between amused patience and mild irritation, as if dealing with an over-eager puppy. "Miss Wells, as I've already told you several times, Mr. Blackwell is handling a personal matter. He'll return later today when he's able."

I stopped pacing, planting both hands firmly on Lucien's polished mahogany desk, leaning forward and leveling a look at him. "Seriously? You're not even a tiny bit worried? He vanished, Lucien. Gone. Radio silence. Poof!"

Lucien sighed, setting his pen down carefully, clearly weighing how much he could say—or wanted to say. He regarded me for a long moment, a hint of genuine sympathy breaking through his usually unflappable composure. "Harper, I assure you, Elias is fine. This isn't the first time he's needed to…take a few days."

"That's helpful," I muttered, irritation mingling with the lingering unease gnawing relentlessly at the pit of my stomach. "He could've at least texted. Or called. Or sent a carrier pigeon—hell, smoke signals would've been appreciated."

Lucien's mouth twitched slightly at the corner, a reluctant smile threatening to escape his careful restraint. "He's safe, Harper. You have my word."

I pushed out a frustrated breath, pacing restlessly across his office once more, ignoring Lucien's curious gaze as I muttered mostly to myself, "Well, as long as I have your super-reassuring word…"

"Harper," Lucien said, his voice softening with unexpected sincerity. "Elias is complicated. But he knows what he's doing."

"Great. Complicated. Got it." I crossed my arms tightly, deflating a little as I met his steady, unreadable stare. "Just… promise me if something was seriously wrong, you'd tell me?"

Lucien hesitated a moment, then nodded slowly. "You'd know."

I exhaled, defeated. "Fine. I'll just go back to my desk and, you know, keep refreshing my inbox like a psycho stalker until he magically reappears."

He chuckled softly, returning to his paperwork, clearly considering our conversation over. As I turned away, my mind immediately flooded with images of Elias—dark eyes burning into mine, tattoos rippling over broad shoulders, and the raw, dangerous vulnerability he'd shown the last time I'd seen him.

Yeah. Complicated didn't even begin to cover it.

I froze mid-step, my heart racing when Lucien's voice rose sharply—something I'd never once heard before. The sound was so out of character, so alarming, that goosebumps prickled across my skin.

When my nerves had finally calmed, Lucian slammed Elias' office door open, racing down the corridor without even noticing me. Panic fluttered like a trapped bird in my chest as I hesitated only a moment before making a split-second decision. Without even thinking twice, I grabbed my coat from my chair and hurried after him.

Keeping just enough distance to remain unnoticed, I watched Lucien slide swiftly into a sleek black sedan, barking instructions into his phone before speeding off. My pulse thundered frantically as I hailed the nearest cab, heart pounding a frantic rhythm against my ribs.

"Follow that car," I practically shouted, my voice shaky and urgent. The driver glanced back skeptically, but one look at my anxious face convinced him to floor it.

We wound through traffic, the city lights blurring past my window as I fought to steady my breathing and my racing thoughts. Images flashed through my mind, each scenario worse than the last. Something was wrong. Something had happened to Elias. The realization made my throat tighten painfully, an unfamiliar fear clawing its way into my chest.

The sedan eventually pulled up to a sprawling, secluded estate I'd never seen before, hidden deep within a thick corpse of towering trees. I had the cab stop a safe distance back, handing him more cash than necessary as I jumped out and crept closer, staying hidden behind dense bushes.

Lucien stood talking to Seraphina outside the gates, their voices too low to make out clearly. But even from a distance, their tense postures were unmistakable. Whatever had happened, it wasn't good.

The car pulled up abruptly, tires crunching against the gravel driveway as dust settled around it. My breath caught sharply in my throat as Marcus stepped out first, his face grim and set like stone. Isabella emerged next, her usual sharp confidence shaken, replaced by an anxious tension I'd never seen before.

And then I saw him.

Elias stumbled out last, his body battered and barely covered, blood smeared across his bare chest. Dark tattoos sprawled intricately over his skin, interwoven with cuts and bruises that marred his usually flawless appearance. My pulse spiked, adrenaline surging through me as fear and worry tangled painfully in my chest.

"Elias," I whispered helplessly, frozen in place as I watched him sway unsteadily on his feet. His torso was covered in bruises, blood drying along the jagged edges of a fresh wound near his shoulder, and for the first time, he looked human—painfully, unsettlingly human.

Lucien appeared at his side instantly, supporting Elias's weight with quiet, practiced efficiency. Elias raised his head slowly, eyes glazed and unfocused, exhaustion written clearly across every inch of his battered body. Even beaten, he radiated an intensity that gripped me like a physical force.

"Get him inside," Isabella ordered sharply, eyes flashing toward me momentarily, her gaze unreadable yet piercing. Marcus looped an arm under Elias's shoulders, carefully steadying him as they moved toward the entrance.

As they passed me, Elias turned slightly, his gaze finding mine through his daze. Something flickered briefly in his expression— recognition, surprise, then anger—as if my presence here was somehow both expected and completely unacceptable.

"Harper," he rasped roughly, voice thick with exhaustion and pain. The sound of my name on his lips made my chest tighten painfully. "You shouldn't—"

"Not now," Lucien interrupted firmly, casting a stern look between us. His expression softened fractionally when he turned to me. "Harper, stay here. I'll be back shortly."

I nodded numbly, watching helplessly as they led Elias away. The front door swung shut, echoing with a heavy, final sound that rattled through my bones, leaving me alone on the driveway.

The sudden silence seemed deafening, broken only by the erratic rhythm of my heartbeat. My mind raced desperately, the memory of Elias' battered body etched painfully into my consciousness. Fear and confusion tightened their hold on me, and as the quiet returned, I realized just how deeply Elias had somehow woven himself into my life—and how utterly lost I felt seeing him in pain.

Lucien reappeared what felt like an eternity later, his typically composed face drawn and weary, dark circles shadowing the intensity of his gaze. He moved toward me quickly, blocking my view of the house with his broad shoulders.

"You need to go home now, Harper," he said firmly, his voice gentle but allowing no argument. "Elias will be in touch."

I bristled instantly, planting my feet stubbornly, folding my arms across my chest. My pulse pounded loudly in my ears, an anger and protectiveness I didn't fully understand rising swiftly in my chest.

"You're absolutely mad if you think I'm leaving here without seeing him, Lucien," I shot back defiantly. "Did you see him? He was bleeding. And limping—and he was practically naked, for crying out loud! What the hell is going on?"

Lucien sighed deeply, clearly exhausted, his normally unshakable composure fraying around the edges. His dark eyes regarded me carefully, measuring the resolve in my expression. He hesitated, clearly debating how much to share.

"Harper, listen to me—Elias is in no condition to see anyone right now. Least of all you," he said firmly, but gently. "Trust me when I say that giving him space tonight is the best thing you could possibly do."

I shook my head sharply, frustration mingling with an ache of worry I couldn't quite hide. "No, Lucien, that's not good enough. He was covered in blood. He looked like he just crawled out of a car wreck! You can't honestly expect me to just go home and pretend everything's fine."

Lucien took a careful breath, his expression softening just slightly as he stepped closer. "Elias is stubborn, Harper. And proud. He wouldn't want you to see him like this."

My voice wavered despite my effort to sound steady. "He doesn't always get what he wants. He should know that by now."

Lucien returned several minutes later, looking resigned but unsurprised to see me still rooted stubbornly in the same spot.

"He won't like it," Lucien warned, though his tone was soft enough that I knew he wasn't truly trying to stop me. "But come on. Just don't say I didn't warn you."

I followed him through the dimly lit halls, the echo of my footsteps suddenly too loud against the polished marble floor. My heart was racing so loudly I was convinced Lucien could hear it, the anxious rhythm of it matching every hurried step. As we approached a partially opened door at the end of the corridor, an unmistakable sound reached my ears—a deep, tortured groan that instantly turned my blood cold.

I hesitated, heart jumping into my throat as I paused in the doorway. Elias sat on the edge of a large bed, stripped down to nothing but a thin pair of form fitting boxer shorts, revealing more than I'd ever anticipated. His powerful torso, now fully visible, was marked by a stunning array of dark tattoos etched over his muscular chest and shoulders and legs, stark against skin glistening with sweat. His jaw was clenched tight, tendons visibly straining with each painful breath he took.

Beside him stood an older woman—her white hair piled loosely atop her head, eyes sharp yet compassionate—applying a pungent green paste mixed with crushed herbs and leaves to the worst of his injuries. Elias hissed loudly as her fingers pressed firmly into a wound on his chest, muscles tensing violently beneath her touch.

"Hold still," she murmured gently, her voice soothing yet authoritative. "Almost done."

Another harsh, involuntary sound of pain ripped from Elias's throat, his fists clenched tightly at his sides, knuckles white from the effort of holding back. Sweat glistened across his broad chest, highlighting intricate tattoos that spiraled beautifully over taut muscles—a mesmerizing blend of dark, swirling lines and ancient symbols that I couldn't even begin to decipher.

"Is—is this normal?" I whispered anxiously to Lucien, feeling both horrified and mesmerized by the surreal scene unfolding before me.

Lucien nodded solemnly, eyes focused forward. "Unfortunately, yes."

Elias suddenly groaned louder, startling me back to attention. His eyes flashed open, blazing fiercely golden, pupils narrowed sharply with pain and irritation as he looked up and found me standing there, frozen in the doorway. For a heartbeat, everything went utterly still, my presence registering slowly in his gaze. His expression darkened with irritation, embarrassment, and something else I couldn't quite name.

"Harper," he growled through gritted teeth, the word laced with undeniable frustration. "Why are you here?"

I swallowed nervously, my throat dry, pulse racing at his obvious distress. "I—I just wanted to make sure you were okay," I replied awkwardly, wincing internally at how small my voice sounded.

His eyes flashed dangerously, muscles rippling as he gripped the edge of the mattress. "Does it look like I'm okay?"

The healer shot me a quick, sympathetic glance, offering a reassuring nod before returning to her painful ministrations. Elias groaned again, muscles tightening visibly as another wave of pain washed over him, his breath ragged and harsh.

I took a cautious step forward, helplessness washing over me. "Can I help?"

"No," Elias snapped sharply, eyes blazing as his control visibly frayed. "You can leave, Miss Wells."

His harsh tone startled me, stinging despite my understanding of his pain. But beneath the anger, I could hear vulnerability—one that he desperately wanted to conceal. I hesitated again, glancing toward Lucien, who shook his head subtly, warning me silently not to push further.

"Fine," I murmured softly, voice barely audible above Elias's labored breathing. "I'll go—but if you need anything…"

Elias turned away sharply, eyes closing tightly, shutting me out completely. I retreated reluctantly, glancing back once more before stepping silently into the hallway.

Lucien quietly closed the door behind us, expression unreadable. "He'll be fine, Harper. He just needs time."

I nodded numbly, but as we moved down the silent corridor, my heart twisted painfully. Elias's tortured groans echoed stubbornly in my mind, refusing to fade, leaving behind an aching, helpless feeling I couldn't begin to shake.

I jumped slightly as Lucien gently placing a hand on my shoulder. His voice, always calm and steady, felt strangely reassuring as he leaned in to speak softly.

"You don't have to go, Harper," he said quietly. "In fact, maybe it's better if you stay."

I swallowed nervously, heart pounding, turning to face him. "Are you insane, Lucien? Elias just made it very clear I'm the last person he wants here right now."

Lucien shook his head, offering me a faint, knowing smile. "You're wrong. You're exactly what he needs—even if he won't admit it." His gaze softened slightly, his voice gentle but firm. "Stay here tonight. I'll send someone to fetch a few things from your apartment. Trust me, Harper. He's struggling, and your presence…it might anchor him."

I hesitated, torn between my instinct to run and an unexpected, stubborn desire to stay. Another muffled groan came from Elias's room, deep, raw, and undeniably pained. Lucien watched me closely, reading every flicker of emotion crossing my face.

"Please," he added gently. "Trust me."

Reluctantly, I nodded, exhaling sharply as Lucien gave me a reassuring pat before stepping away. My gaze drifted back through the doorway, heart aching at the sight of Elias—strong, powerful, usually invincible Elias—so visibly broken. I sank slowly onto a plush bench in the hallway, gripping the edge tightly, deciding that if my stubborn presence could offer even the smallest comfort, then I'd willingly endure his anger tomorrow.

Tonight, Elias Blackwell wouldn't have to suffer alone—even if he didn't realize I was here.

Elias

Hours had dragged by since Gloria left, the lingering scent of sage and lavender from her healing rituals still clinging stubbornly to my skin. My body ached less now, though the deeper wounds—the invisible ones to my pride—remained stubbornly raw. Gloria had worked her miracles as always, knitting broken flesh and bruised bones back together, but even her ancient magic couldn't erase the bitter humiliation of vulnerability.

I sat up slowly, muscles protesting at every subtle movement, feeling the bandages pull tightly against freshly healed skin. My shirt lay discarded nearby, streaked with blood and torn fabric—a stark reminder of tonight's near-fatal mistake. Leaning forward, I rested my elbows heavily on my knees, head bowed in exhaustion, the muscles in my back tightening as frustration and fury simmered beneath my skin.

It was happening again. I could feel it—the creeping loss of control that accompanied every approaching full moon. A vicious aggression coiled tightly inside me, razor-sharp and barely contained, fraying at the carefully constructed edges of my composure. It was reckless, dangerous, and entirely unwelcome.

The door opened quietly, breaking my introspection, and Lucien stepped cautiously into the room, his gaze wary but determined.

"What is it?" I growled, unable to hide the sharpness in my voice. I didn't have patience left for diplomacy.

"The family is waiting for you, we need to discuss last night." Lucien started. "And she's still here," Lucien replied evenly, not flinching from my irritation. "I asked Harper to stay."

A sharp pang shot through my chest at the sound of her name, frustration mixing bitterly with something softer—something I refused to acknowledge. I straightened carefully, ignoring the ache that still lingered in my ribs.

"You let her stay?" I asked incredulously, my voice dangerously low.

Lucien's calm gaze held steady. "I thought her presence might...benefit you."

"Benefit me?" I snapped bitterly, running an irritated hand through my disheveled hair. "You allowed a human—my assistant, no less—to stay here, after what she's already seen tonight? Have you lost your mind, Lucien?"

He regarded me silently for a moment, his face calm but resolute. "You're losing control, Elias. And we both know it's not just the moon. Harper steadies you—whether you admit it or not."

"I don't need her," I growled fiercely, standing abruptly and pacing restlessly across the room, my body still aching with every strained step. "I don't need anyone."

Lucien didn't argue, though his silence spoke volumes. He knew me too well—knew the internal war I was fighting, battling instincts that urged me to seek Harper out, to lose myself entirely in the scent and softness of her presence. She was a vulnerability I couldn't afford, a risk I couldn't take, and yet the thought of sending her away was physically painful.

"I'll handle it," I finally murmured, my voice weary and rough-edged. "Just keep her away from this. All of it, Lucien."

Lucien nodded slowly, understanding perfectly what I couldn't fully articulate, and turned to leave. Pausing briefly at the doorway, he glanced back, his expression softened with quiet understanding.

"Perhaps, Elias, she's exactly what you need. She's in the East Wing."

The door clicked softly shut behind him, leaving me alone in the darkened room, my fists clenched tightly against the restless ache inside my chest. Harper Wells was trouble—beautiful, maddening trouble—and my desire for her was a complication I neither expected nor wanted.

Each step felt heavier than the last as I slowly climbed the staircase toward the drawing room, pain still rippling through my muscles like lingering echoes of a distant storm. I gripped the polished wooden railing, knuckles turning white, my body screaming a reminder of the harshness of the night before.

Muted voices drifted through the hallway, a gentle hum broken only by occasional sharp notes of tension. I paused at the threshold, inhaling deeply, forcing composure onto my features. This was my pack, my family—the ones I was supposed to protect.

I pushed open the heavy oak doors, the familiar groan echoing softly in the expansive room. Lucien stood abruptly at my arrival, tension easing slightly from his rigid posture, though his expression remained deeply troubled. Isabella sat poised on the edge of her seat, arms folded tightly across her chest, her sharp gaze fixed upon Seraphina, whose delicate frame seemed smaller than usual, shoulders hunched, eyes lowered to the floor in shame. Marcus hovered silently near the fireplace, his expression stoic but watchful, ready to intervene at any moment.

"Elias," Lucien spoke first, voice gentle but firm as he stepped forward to steady me, placing a steady hand on my elbow. The quiet concern in his eyes told me exactly how fragile I must have appeared. "Thank you for coming down. I wouldn't have called for you unless it was important."

I offered him a curt nod, ignoring the ache still burning beneath my skin, the stubborn remnants of my injuries. "Tell me what happened," I said sharply, forcing a steadiness into my voice that I didn't fully feel.

Lucien hesitated briefly, casting a cautious glance around the drawing room where the rest of the pack had gathered. He exhaled slowly, his voice carefully measured. "We had an incident last night. Someone infiltrated the property. Someone…opened your cell door."

My muscles instantly tightened, tension coiling like a steel spring in my gut. My jaw clenched painfully, eyes flicking immediately toward Seraphina, whose delicate frame seemed to shrink even smaller under my accusing stare.

"Explain," I demanded quietly, the word practically a growl.

Seraphina's voice trembled, barely audible. "It was me. I—I opened the door, Elias. I let you out."

A stunned silence settled over the room. I felt anger spike within me, warring fiercely against disbelief as the dark figure from my cell's doorway came to memory. Seraphina was our healer, our empath—the gentlest soul among us. That she would deliberately betray the pack felt impossible, unimaginable.

"Why?" I finally managed, forcing the question through clenched teeth.

"It was Damian," she whispered miserably, tears spilling silently down her pale cheeks. "He got inside my head. I believed you were in danger. He convinced me...you were dying. He said you needed me to free you or you'd suffer terribly."

My chest tightened, fists clenching involuntarily as rage surged dangerously close to the surface. Damian. Of course it was him—always twisting others to his will, manipulating the vulnerable. Seraphina had always been a soft target, her heart too open, her empathy easily manipulated. Damian had clearly known exactly how to exploit that weakness.

"Did I hurt anyone?" I asked roughly, forcing my voice to remain even despite the fury burning in my veins.

"No," Lucien intervened swiftly, sensing my rising anger. "No one was harmed. But Damian's message is clear—he can reach us, even here, in our own home."

Marcus shifted closer, his deep voice calm yet authoritative. "Our defenses are compromised, Elias. Damian made that abundantly clear. He manipulated Seraphina with precision, exactly as Elowen warned."

At the mention of Elowen's name, a fresh pang of guilt twisted my gut. She'd warned me, cautioned me clearly against ignoring the intensity of the bond. Yet here I was, caught in precisely the trap she'd feared—losing control, endangering everyone around me.

I exhaled slowly, meeting each set of eyes in the room. "This ends now," I said quietly, firmly. "Damian has drawn his line. It's time we draw ours."

Lucien nodded solemnly. "Agreed. And Harper?"

I swallowed hard, her face immediately filling my thoughts— vulnerable, trusting, heartbreakingly innocent. "Increase security around her. Damian's already proven he'll stop at nothing to hurt me through her. We can't afford another mistake."

Lucien gave a curt nod, already turning to issue orders. Isabella stepped closer to Seraphina, offering quiet comfort with a reassuring hand on her shoulder. As my pack sprang into action around me, I stood silently for a long moment, heart heavy with the weight of responsibility and guilt.

Elowen's words echoed hauntingly in my mind: *You cannot protect what you refuse to claim.*

I knew, deep in my bones, that my hesitation had invited this chaos. Damian was simply exploiting the vulnerabilities I'd exposed — vulnerabilities created by my own stubborn refusal to accept the truth.

"Elias," Lucien spoke again softly, lingering briefly by my side. "Go rest. You're still recovering."

I shook my head slightly, stubborn pride warring with reluctant gratitude. "Soon. Right now, I need to see her."

He didn't press further, understanding my need to reassert control, even if only briefly. I turned toward the window, staring out into the darkness beyond the estate grounds, feeling the weight of every choice I'd ever made pressing down on my shoulders.

And somewhere out there, waiting like a dark promise, was Damian and whoever was possibly pulling his strings — whose recklessness had finally pushed me to my breaking point.

Tell Me The Truth

Elias

I softly opened the door, fear of awaking her at this hour. I paused at the threshold, my breath catching painfully in my chest at the sight before me. The moonlight filtered gently through sheer curtains, caressing Harper's sleeping form in a silver embrace, turning her skin into something ethereal, almost otherworldly. She lay curled beneath the covers, her chest rising and falling slowly, the delicate lines of her collarbone and shoulders illuminated like porcelain against the shadows.

Quietly, carefully, I stepped closer, drawn by something stronger than logic or self-preservation. My heartbeat quickened with every silent footstep until I stood beside her bed, looking down at her peaceful expression—a stark contrast to the turmoil she'd unknowingly caused within me.

Her lashes fluttered gently against her cheeks, lips parted slightly as she breathed steadily, unaware of my presence or the way my entire body strained toward her. It would be so easy, too easy, to reach out—to touch, to hold, to claim. The thought of her waking to find me here, weakened by the moon, desperate and needy, made my stomach clench with bitter self-loathing.

I took a steadying breath, forcing back the impulse that threatened to override my carefully built control. Carefully, I lifted the blanket, gently pulling it up to cover her exposed shoulders. She stirred slightly, a soft sigh slipping through her lips as she nuzzled deeper into the pillow, my scent unconsciously soothing her in sleep.

"Sleep well, Harper," I murmured softly, the words carrying a quiet promise of protection, even if she couldn't hear them. "You're safe now. I swear it."

Turning reluctantly, every step away from her felt heavier than the last, but I knew I had no other choice. Harper Wells was a risk, a temptation—one I couldn't afford to indulge.

I froze at the sound of her voice, my hand gripping the door handle so tightly I feared I might crush it. Her words, soft and hesitant, hung in the air behind me, and I knew with absolute certainty that if I turned around, the thin thread of control I'd clung to all night would unravel entirely.

"Harper," I whispered, barely trusting my voice. "It's late. You should rest."

I could hear the rustle of sheets behind me, followed by the gentle padding of her bare feet across the plush carpet. Her scent, warm and inviting, wrapped around me as she drew closer, causing my pulse to pound mercilessly in my ears.

"Elias," she said softly, and I felt her hand—light as a feather, warm and trembling slightly—touch the center of my back. I closed my eyes, fighting desperately against the surge of longing her simple touch awakened in me. "Look at me."

I hesitated, my breath ragged, muscles coiled in painful restraint. "Harper, you don't know what you're asking."

"Maybe I do," she whispered, a tremor of uncertainty mingling with an edge of defiance in her voice. "Maybe I don't care."

I turned slowly to face her, breath hitching sharply in my chest as my eyes fell on Harper standing in front of me, bathed softly in the silvery light filtering in from the terrace. She wore nothing but an oversized t-shirt—its neckline slipping carelessly off one delicate shoulder, revealing the soft, smooth curve of her skin beneath. The hem stopped mid-thigh, exposing just enough of her toned legs to make my pulse quicken painfully.

My gaze trailed helplessly downward, taking in the way the thin fabric clung gently to the curves of her body, hinting at every tempting contour beneath. Her hair was tousled from sleep, a tangled cascade of silk and shadow around her face, framing wide eyes that stared up at me with a vulnerability that cut deeply into my chest. Her cheeks flushed slightly under my scrutiny, but she didn't move, didn't shy away—just stood there, achingly close yet impossibly far, as though daring me to cross the boundary we'd both silently drawn.

Heat surged through me, pooling low in my gut, a relentless ache tightening my muscles until I could barely breathe. Every instinct screamed at me to touch her, taste her, claim her as mine—but I resisted, fists clenched painfully at my sides, jaw tightening with the effort of maintaining control.

She shifted slightly, the fabric of her shirt brushing tantalizingly against her bare skin, and my restraint wavered dangerously.

"Harper," I whispered hoarsely, voice barely recognizable even to my own ears, raw with barely contained desire. "You should go back to bed."

But even as I spoke, my body betrayed me, stepping instinctively closer to her warmth, drawn inexorably into the orbit of her presence. Her eyes softened as she reached out hesitantly, fingers trembling as they lightly traced my chest, leaving a burning trail of longing in their wake.

"You were hurt?" Confusion settled in as her hands ran across my chest. "I saw you?"

Her words hit me harder than any physical blow, shattering what little resolve remained. The soft tremble in her voice was like a blade against my heart, slicing deep and raw. Her eyes searched mine desperately, confusion and concern swirling in their depths as she struggled to grasp what was happening.

"You saw me," I admitted quietly, voice tight, rough with shame and vulnerability. My gaze dropped briefly, unable to meet the intensity of hers. "You weren't supposed to."

"I don't understand," she whispered softly, stepping back, the gentle warmth of her hand still burning against my chest. "You were—hurt, Elias. Badly. You still are. But you're standing here like nothing happened."

I exhaled slowly, battling the overwhelming urge to pull her closer, to erase the worry from her eyes. My gaze drifted downward, tracing the delicate slope of her collarbone, the tantalizing outline of her body beneath the thin fabric of her shirt. Her scent enveloped me completely, sweet and intoxicating, clouding my mind and intensifying the deep, possessive ache I felt for her.

"You're not supposed to see this part of my life, Harper," I murmured hoarsely, finally meeting her wide, uncertain gaze again. "This—this isn't for you."

"Isn't for me?" she echoed quietly, a hint of defiance and hurt threading through her tone. "Elias, you showed up at my door. You pushed me against a wall, and now you're standing in my room at—" she glanced toward the clock on the nightstand, "—four in the morning. I'd say we're way past the point of secrets."

I swallowed thickly, jaw tightening, emotions twisting painfully inside my chest. "You're right. We are. And I shouldn't have—"

Her fingers pressed softly against my lips, silencing me immediately, sending a rush of fire racing through my veins. Her gaze softened, eyes full of an emotion I couldn't place, making it nearly impossible to breathe.

"Don't," she whispered softly. "Don't tell me what you should or shouldn't do. Just tell me what's going on. Please."

I stared at her helplessly, torn between wanting to shield her from the darkness and needing her to understand. My heartbeat thundered. She deserved the truth—but how could I explain the impossible without losing her forever?

"You were hurt, Elias." she repeated gently, eyes searching mine desperately. "You were bleeding. I saw it."

I exhaled sharply, the truth falling heavily from my lips. "Yes, Harper, I was."

She shifted closer, gaze intense and pleading. "Then tell me why— how? What happened to you?"

I hesitated, knowing the truth would shatter whatever fragile reality she'd built around me. And yet, the quiet resolve in her eyes offered a strength I'd never expected to find.

"Because," I finally murmured, voice strained with uncertainty, "the truth might change everything you think you know about me."

She held my gaze, her hand still resting warmly against my chest, heartbeats tangled fiercely in the silence between us.

"Then let it change," she whispered, resolve clear in her voice. "Because not knowing feels a hell of a lot worse."

Harper

I didn't know what else to do. His unwillingness to be honest—especially when I knew something was so clearly wrong—was driving me to a brink of frustration that made my heart ache in unfamiliar ways. Yet, standing this close, feeling the heat radiating from his bare skin, my pulse quickened and my frustration gave way to something far more reflexive and immediate.

I stared up at him, eyes tracing the intricate paths of his tattoos, following the dark lines that curved sensually across his muscular chest and shoulders, each symbol a mystery I desperately wanted to unravel. The intensity in his golden eyes burned through my defenses, leaving me exposed and vulnerable, yet strangely emboldened.

"Fine," I whispered defiantly, feeling my heart thunder in my chest as I slowly rose onto my tiptoes, closing the distance between us. "Don't tell me."

I pressed my lips softly to his chest, right above the steady, powerful rhythm of his heartbeat. His skin was warm, radiating strength and tension beneath my gentle touch. My lips brushed tenderly over a fresh scar, feeling the slight tremor that moved through him in response.

"I'll take the pain away," I murmured, tracing another kiss along the contours of his chest, following the lines of his tattoos, tasting the faint, lingering saltiness of sweat and the scent of herbs still clinging stubbornly to his skin.

Elias exhaled sharply, a deep, shuddering breath escaping him as his fingers instinctively threaded through my hair, holding me firmly yet tenderly in place. I felt his heartbeat quicken beneath my lips, the powerful, rhythmic pulse matching my own, driving me onward, urging me closer.

"Harper," he rasped, voice rough with desire and conflicted emotion, his body visibly tensing with restraint, as if he were barely holding himself back from surrendering completely.

I glanced upward, meeting his burning gaze, feeling both vulnerable and empowered beneath the weight of his stare. "Let me help you," I whispered softly, my breath ghosting across his skin. "Let me be your truth tonight."

He hesitated for only a fraction of a second, eyes darkening to molten gold, before finally surrendering with a low, possessive growl that resonated deep within my bones.

I didn't know how we got here, but suddenly the world had condensed down to just Elias and me—our breaths mingling, our pulses racing in tandem. In an instant, I was lifted effortlessly into his arms, my legs instinctively wrapping around his waist, our bodies fitting together perfectly as he carried me toward the bed. His face buried itself in the curve of my neck, inhaling deeply, almost desperately, as though he were breathing in his very reason for existence.

"You have no idea what you do to me," he growled roughly, the sound vibrating against my skin, sending chills rippling down my spine. The noise was deeper, more raw, more animalistic than I'd ever heard from him before.

My fingers tangled into his dark hair as his hands roamed possessively along my bare thighs, fingertips digging gently into my skin, igniting trails of fire with every touch. My nails raked lightly down his broad, muscular back, eliciting another growl—a guttural sound that thrilled and terrified me simultaneously.

He lowered me gently onto the soft mattress, eyes locked fiercely onto mine, glowing with a heat that consumed every last fragment of doubt or resistance I had left. My breath caught in my chest, heart thundering wildly as he slowly, deliberately peeled away my shirt, exposing skin to the cool night air.

His gaze darkened hungrily, tracing every curve, every rise and fall of my body with an intensity that left me trembling. My bare chest rose and fell rapidly, anticipation and vulnerability warring within me, as his eyes lingered appreciatively, leaving no doubt about the depth of his desire.

"You're beautiful, Harper," he whispered, voice hoarse with longing, fingers trailing reverently over my bare stomach, igniting goosebumps in their wake. "More beautiful than I ever imagined."

My heart squeezed painfully at his words, emotion swelling dangerously in my throat, making it impossible to speak. Instead, I reached up, cupping his face gently, guiding him down until our lips finally met in a ferociously deep kiss—filled with longing, passion, and unspoken promises.

His body pressed against mine, strong and commanding, yet heartbreakingly tender. I wrapped my arms around him, surrendering completely to the intoxicating pull of Elias Blackwell—a man who was both my undoing and my salvation.

His touch was like fire against my skin, branding me with a possessiveness I couldn't—and didn't want to—escape. Elias's fingers slid gently along my thigh, warmth igniting every nerve as he traced paths I hadn't known existed. My breath came in shallow gasps, each sensation heightened, every touch impossibly intimate.

I felt him pause, hesitation evident in the sudden tension of his body pressed tightly against mine. My heart raced wildly as I met his gaze in the pale moonlight, eyes darkened with longing and something far deeper—an emotion neither of us dared to name aloud.

When he finally moved again, his touch was achingly gentle yet commanding, claiming parts of me I'd unknowingly offered from the moment I first saw him. I closed my eyes, surrendering to the rhythm of his fingers careful exploration, the low growl deep in his chest mingling perfectly with my own whispered moan.

In that moment, no secrets existed between us. No fear. Just Elias, me, and the undeniable truth of everything we felt—and couldn't deny any longer.

Elias

My heart hammered erratically in my chest as I held Harper close, feeling her warmth, her softness pressed against me—every part of me aching with relentless need. The room was shadowed, cloaked in moonlight filtering softly through the sheer curtains, outlining her body beneath mine in hues of silver and blue.

My fingers brushed gently along her thigh, feeling her tremble beneath my touch. Her breath hitched softly against my cheek, her body arching instinctively, guiding my exploration. Carefully, tenderly, I moved her panties aside, feeling her tense in anticipation, the heat of her body impossibly inviting. My fingers slid into her warmth slowly, one at first, then two, exploring the depths of her desire, moving with careful, rhythmic precision.

Her moan filled the quiet of the room, raw and honest, a sound that resonated deep within me. Her hips rose instinctively to meet my touch, her hands gripping my shoulders tightly, nails biting into my skin. It ignited something feral within me, and I let out a low, guttural growl, feeling her body tense deliciously beneath me.

"Elias," she whispered breathlessly, her voice quivering with need. "Please..."

My name on her lips was a plea, a prayer, a command that I was powerless to resist. Gently withdrawing my fingers, I moved downward, trailing soft, reverent kisses across her smooth stomach, savoring the taste of her skin—sweet, intoxicating. Settling between her thighs, my breath washed hotly over her sensitive flesh, eliciting a soft gasp.

I tasted her slowly, worshipfully, each movement of my tongue drawing another shuddering breath from her lips. Her fingers tangled desperately in my hair, guiding me as her hips moved in rhythm with my touch. Her cries grew louder, her body arching toward me until she reached the brink of release. Her thighs trembled against my shoulders as her climax overwhelmed her, leaving her breathless, trembling, utterly undone beneath me.

Rising slowly, I met her gaze, her eyes darkened with desire, pupils wide and inviting. Positioning myself carefully, I entered her in one deliberate, achingly slow thrust, her warmth enveloping me completely. We moved together seamlessly, bodies entwined, each thrust deepening our connection, building inexorably toward a shared, inevitable climax.

Harper

Every nerve ending in my body seemed lit on fire, electric with a wild intensity I'd never imagined possible. His touch wasn't gentle—it was raw, possessive, primal in a way that shattered every previous experience I'd ever had. Each thrust felt like a declaration, a promise, a claim. He was taking me, marking me as his own, and God help me, I wanted nothing more than to surrender completely.

My fingers dug desperately into the taut muscles of his back, feeling the power of him ripple beneath my touch, his skin hot and damp with sweat. Elias buried his hands roughly in my hair, pulling my head back to expose my neck fully to his wandering mouth. His teeth grazed my sensitive skin, the sensation sending a delicious shudder through me. A moan escaped me, helplessly loud, as his hips drove deeper, harder, his rhythm commanding, relentless.

"Elias," I gasped, the sound raw, pleading. He growled in response, a guttural sound so deep and wild it seemed to vibrate through the very walls around us. His hand twisted gently in my hair, holding me still as his lips crashed onto mine, hungry and demanding, stealing my breath away. His teeth grazed my bottom lip, just on the edge of painful, sending waves of pleasure cascading through my entire body.

This was nothing gentle, nothing careful or reserved—it was fierce, consuming. Yet beneath that raw intensity, there was a tenderness in the way his fingertips traced the curve of my jaw, the softness of his lips as he kissed my forehead, my temple, my neck. Rough but gentle. Savage yet reverent.

He tugged my hair, tipping my head back as his mouth claimed mine once more, swallowing my cries of pleasure. His grip tightened possessively, every motion driving us closer to the edge, closer to a climax so intense it threatened to consume us both.

The release hit me with the force of a hurricane, pleasure crashing over me in waves so powerful, so overwhelming, that I cried out again, louder, unfiltered. Elias followed moments later, my name ripped from his lips like a battle cry, echoing between us, branding me deeper than any physical mark could.

As we collapsed together, breathless, trembling, I knew with absolute certainty: I'd been irrevocably changed. This wasn't simply passion—this was something deeper, more dangerous, and infinitely more terrifying.

I'd given him a part of myself I couldn't take back—and strangely, terrifyingly, I didn't want to.

In that moment, all boundaries dissolved. There was only Elias—his breath mingled with mine, his body pressed against my own, his heart beating wildly against my chest. He was mine, and I was irrevocably, dangerously his.

The Morning After

Elias

I couldn't begin to put into words the profound relief I felt as I held Harper against my chest, her soft breaths gently warming my skin. It wasn't just about the physical pleasure, though God knew that was unlike anything I'd experienced in lifetimes. It was more—the indescribable feeling of connection, deeper and more profound than I'd thought possible.

I gently brushed my fingers along the soft curve of her shoulder, marveling at the way her body fit perfectly against mine, as if she'd always belonged there. Her breathing was slow, peaceful in sleep, and something deep within me—something ancient and impulsive—settled quietly at last.

My wolf had chosen her, long before my rational mind had acknowledged it. For weeks I had resisted, fighting against instincts that were impossible to ignore, fighting against a bond that had formed without permission, beyond reason. But now, holding her in my arms, her warmth seeping into my chest, quieting the relentless, angry voice inside me, I knew fighting was pointless.

I tightened my arms around her gently, breathing deeply the sweet, intoxicating scent of her skin. She shifted slightly in her sleep, murmuring softly, contentedly, nestling closer into my chest. My heart skipped sharply, possessiveness swelling through me again, primal and fierce, yet softened by an aching tenderness I hadn't felt in decades.

My wolf had chosen her—claimed her as its own—and my human side finally surrendered, exhausted and relieved. Harper Wells had burrowed beneath my skin, tangled herself irreversibly around my heart, and now there was no going back.

Closing my eyes, I pressed a lingering kiss to the crown of her head, inhaling her scent deeply, letting it settle and soothe the deepest parts of my soul. It was terrifying and exhilarating, vulnerable yet freeing.

For the first time in decades, I felt grounded, calm, and whole. Because of her.

A faint rustling sound from the terrace snapped me violently from my reverie, shattering the fragile moment of peace I'd allowed myself to indulge in. My senses sharpened immediately, every muscle in my body tightening in primal alertness. Gently disentangling myself from Harper's warmth, I rose swiftly but silently, moving toward the terrace doors with cautious steps.

Moonlight painted ghostly patterns on the stone balcony as I approached, the familiar weight of dread twisting deep inside my gut. Before I even stepped fully outside, a voice I'd hoped never to hear again shattered the illusion of peace.

"Hello, Eliaston."

The soft, lilting tone was deceptively gentle—sweet poison dripping from each syllable. The use of my ancient name was deliberate, taunting, a direct strike at the vulnerabilities I'd spent centuries burying. The past rushed at me in a wave, memories bitter and sharp.

There she stood, Lycina Duskbane, the dark queen of the southern pack, framed by moonlight, as dangerously beautiful as ever. Her pale silver hair fell in silken waves down her back, eyes a sharp violet, luminous and cunning in the shadows. Beside her stood Damian, smirking arrogantly, his presence an irritating echo of recent events that made my blood boil.

"How dare you set foot on my land," I growled, my voice vibrating with barely controlled rage, fists clenched at my sides.

Lycina tilted her head gracefully, the faintest of smiles tugging at her lips. She stepped closer, fearless, her movements feline and predatory.

"Oh Eliaston, always so territorial," she purred mockingly, gaze flickering past me to the bedroom behind. "I see you have new... interests. That was...quite the show."

My teeth ground together painfully, my jaw rigid with barely restrained fury. "This is my home, Lycina. You have no business here."

She laughed softly, a musical yet sinister sound that clawed beneath my skin. "Oh, Eliaston, we both know that's not true. Your pack's recent troubles are very much my business." She glanced pointedly at Damian, the amusement fading into something colder, crueler. "Though I'll admit, my associate here took matters further than instructed."

Damian stepped forward boldly, smirk widening. "No hard feelings, Blackwell. Nothing personal—just business."

"Everything between us has always been personal," I snarled, fists clenched tight enough to draw blood.

Lycina lifted a slender hand, halting Damian's next words. Her eyes met mine, glinting with dark, unspoken threats. "Consider this visit a friendly reminder, Eliaston. Your control is slipping. Your pack grows restless, your hold tenuous at best. I'd hate to see such a legacy… fall apart."

Before I could respond, Harper's soft voice drifted from behind me, confusion and sleepy vulnerability in her tone. "Elias? Is everything okay?"

Lycina's lips curled into a knowing smile, her eyes gleaming with malicious triumph as they drifted pointedly toward the open door behind me.

"We'll talk again soon, Eliaston." Her voice was smooth, lilting, dripping with dark amusement. "In the meantime, do take care of your little human. She seems quite fragile." Her gaze flickered once more to the doorway, lingering with predatory delight. "I'd hate for something…unfortunate to happen to her…the way something unfortunate happened to my Lionel."

My fists clenched tightly, muscles flexing painfully beneath my skin as protective fury roared through my veins. Before I could move, before I could even speak, Lycina tilted her head toward Damian, giving him a subtle, silent signal.

Damian stepped forward, smirking coldly as he produced a small vial, tossing its purple, iridescent contents directly at me. The glass shattered against my chest, the liquid searing my skin instantly. Pain burned through me, sharp and unnatural, wrenching a startled gasp from my throat. My vision blurred momentarily as dizziness gripped me, making my knees buckle.

"What did you do?" I growled hoarsely, voice thickening as agony spread rapidly through my limbs, igniting a forceful surge I'd fought so long to control.

Damian smiled coldly, eyes glinting with cruel amusement. "Just a little something to speed things up. Let's see how your little human enjoys your...true nature."

My heart pounded violently in my chest, panic and anger colliding with an overwhelming, savage desperation. Lycina's laughter echoed faintly as she stepped backward into the shadows, her victorious gaze fixed wickedly on Harper's sleepy form silhouetted in the bedroom doorway behind me.

"No—" I groaned roughly, the sound torn from deep within my chest as my bones cracked painfully, realigning beneath burning skin. Fur sprouted in patches, dark and thick, as my teeth sharpened, fangs lengthening with terrifying speed.

"Elias?" Harper's soft voice trembled with confusion, fear threading unmistakably through her words.

I turned slowly, agonizingly, eyes blazing gold as I fought desperately to maintain some shred of humanity. But the shift was unstoppable, forced upon me by whatever dark magic they'd unleashed, a vicious manipulation designed specifically to shatter everything I'd built with her.

"Run, Harper," I rasped desperately, voice barely recognizable as my humanity slipped away piece by agonizing piece. "Now."

The war I'd feared had officially begun.

Harper

My breath caught sharply as I stumbled back, heart hammering so loudly I could feel it in my throat. Elias staggered backward, his muscles rippling violently beneath his skin, each contraction accompanied by the horrifying sound of bones snapping and rearranging. Pain twisted his features grotesquely, his normally stoic face contorted in agony.

"Harper—" he gasped, his voice cracking under a pain that sounded otherworldly.

"Elias?" I whispered, eyes wide with shock, feet rooted helplessly to the floor as fear surged through me, ice-cold and paralyzing.

Before I could move, Lucien burst through the doorway, Isabella and Marcus on his heels, faces grim and frantic. Lucien took one look at Elias, his face paling, his usual calm demeanor shattered.

"Harper, move—now!" he barked, grabbing my arm roughly, pulling me sharply toward him.

"But—Elias—" I protested weakly, still dazed, eyes fixed helplessly on the man I'd only moments ago been so close to, now doubled over and groaning in unbearable agony. Lucien didn't wait for a response, instead gripping my arm firmly, nearly dragging me from the room.

"What's happening?" I gasped frantically, stumbling after him down the hall, Isabella close behind us. Elias's screams echoed behind us, growing deeper, harsher, until they weren't screams at all, but feral roars—animalistic, agonizing howls that tore straight into my soul.

"Don't look back," Isabella urged sharply, her voice tense with urgency as she hurried alongside us, her usually composed face twisted with fear. Marcus fell in behind her, his expression hard and grim.

We moved swiftly through winding corridors until Lucien threw open a heavy wooden door leading down into a darkened stairwell. Cold air rushed upward, tinged with a strange metallic scent that made my stomach turn.

"This way," Lucien barked urgently, guiding us quickly down into the darkness. I followed blindly, pulse hammering painfully in my ears. As the door slammed shut behind us, another heart-wrenching scream echoed down the halls, raw and guttural—less human, more animal. The sound made my blood run cold, tears stinging my eyes as we descended deeper into darkness.

The basement room we entered was ancient and windowless, stone walls damp and oppressive. Lucien quickly secured the door behind us, bolts clicking into place with an unsettling finality. I pressed my back to the wall, struggling desperately to steady my shaking hands.

"What the hell is happening, Harper?" Lucien demanded, his voice sharp and urgent, eyes wide and frantic. For the first time, I saw genuine panic flicker behind his usually unreadable gaze.

I stared at him incredulously, heart still pounding painfully in my chest. "You're asking ME?"

Lucien exhaled sharply, clearly trying to regain his composure, though his eyes were shadowed with unmistakable dread. Isabella paced restlessly behind him, arms crossed tightly, worry etched deeply into her elegant features.

"You were the last one with him," Lucien pressed urgently, stepping toward me. "Did something happen? Did he—"

"Did he what? Turn into a werewolf and chase me around the room?" I snapped, hysteria bubbling close to the surface, my voice shaking as disbelief and panic blended dangerously together. "No, Lucien, he just turned into a giant freaking wolf right in front of me without any warning!"

Isabella froze, her eyes widening slightly, exchanging a quick, meaningful glance with Marcus. Lucien took a steadying breath, clearly wrestling with what to say next, his voice calm but strained. "Elias is going through something… difficult right now. Something he didn't want you involved in."

"Oh, you don't say," I retorted sarcastically, my voice edged with fear and anger. "Well, a heads-up would have been nice!"

Lucien shook his head, frustration flickering behind his eyes. "We thought he was contained. Clearly, we miscalculated."

Marcus stepped forward, expression grim. "It's Damian. He's manipulated this situation perfectly."

Isabella's jaw tightened sharply. "We have to get Elias back under control—now. Before he hurts someone or himself."

I glanced around frantically, my chest tightening painfully. "Control? Did you not hear what just happened up there? That wasn't Elias—it was—"

A feral, heart-stopping howl echoed through the walls, reverberating through the heavy stones around us. It was raw, angry, and unmistakably Elias, yet utterly inhuman. A sound so powerful it rattled through my bones and stole my breath.

"What the hell is going on?" I whispered desperately, my voice cracking with panic and confusion. "Someone please tell me something!"

Lucien's expression softened briefly, the tension in his posture easing slightly as he looked at me with quiet, sincere compassion. "Harper, there's so much you don't yet understand. And I'm sorry you had to find out like this. Elias will explain everything—"

Another haunting howl echoed distantly above us, reverberating ominously through the thick walls. The sound pierced my heart, sending another chill cascading through me. Lucien sighed heavily, his tone deeply weary, betraying centuries of guarded secrets.

"But first, we need to survive this night."

"Lycina!" I suddenly shouted, my voice echoing sharply off the stone walls, cutting through the tense silence. Three startled gazes snapped toward me simultaneously, their confusion palpable.

"What?" Lucien demanded, eyes narrowing sharply, his voice a mixture of surprise and urgency.

"Elias called her Lysandra—I think. At least, I think that's what he said," I stammered, breath coming in short, frantic bursts. "That woman with Damian on the terrace. Her name was Lycina, or something like that."

Isabella's face went rigid, her expression shifting from confusion to something darker—recognition, perhaps dread. "Wait. Lysandra? You're sure?"

"Pretty sure," I replied quickly, anxiety edging my voice. "It was hard to hear clearly over the growling and threats."

Lucien exchanged a meaningful glance with Marcus, tension

thickening the air around us. Marcus looked away briefly, clearly processing this new, unsettling information. Lucien turned back to me sharply, urgency burning fiercely behind his usually calm demeanor. "Why didn't you mention this sooner, Harper?"

My mouth fell open, indignation rising swiftly alongside my panic. "Oh, I'm sorry, Lucien. At what point exactly should I have mentioned it? When we were sprinting down the hallway? Or maybe while we were fleeing into your creepy underground dungeon? I don't exactly make small talk a priority while running from giant werewolves!"

Marcus coughed softly into his fist, clearly suppressing amusement at my outburst, but even his eyes held a flicker of unease.

Lucien raised a hand in surrender, sighing deeply. "Fair enough. But you're certain Damian was there too?"

"Yes!" My voice rose sharply, frustration tinged with lingering fear. "I may not have all the details straight, but I'm not blind—or deaf. Elias said her name. And Damian was definitely with her."

Marcus shifted uneasily, his usually stoic face darkening further. "Then it's worse than we feared. It's *Lycina* Duskbane and she doesn't make house calls without a reason."

I swallowed hard, the tension thickening around us like smoke. "Well, that's fantastic. But maybe next time, warn me that I'm going to be stuck in the middle of some supernatural family feud. Because, seriously, running for my life from werewolves was not listed in my job description!"

Lucien exhaled sharply, pinching the bridge of his nose in exasperation. "Believe me, Harper, none of us expected things to escalate this quickly."

"Well, they did," I retorted, crossing my arms stubbornly, my voice trembling only slightly as adrenaline finally began to fade, leaving behind an exhausted ache in my bones. "Now would someone please start explaining what the hell is actually going on?"

"Well," Lucien started. "Obviously, Elias is a werewolf."

"Clearly…"

"And so are we." Isabella added.

"Wait—we as in you three? Or 'we' as in me 'we'? Because we only had sex once, and if that's all it takes, someone should've warned me!"

Lucien's lips twitched into an involuntary smile, despite the seriousness etched deeply into his expression. "No, Harper, it doesn't quite work like that."

"Oh, thank God," I muttered, sagging dramatically against the cold basement wall, my heart still racing a frantic rhythm. "Because let's be real, that would've made for a very awkward HR conversation."

Isabella rolled her eyes sharply, arms folded tightly as she regarded me with a mixture of irritation and reluctant amusement. "Can we focus, please?"

"Fine," I conceded, waving her on impatiently. "Continue with the werewolf 101 lesson."

Lucien sighed again, his voice calm but strained beneath the thin veneer of patience. "Elias, Isabella, Marcus, and myself—we're part of Elias's pack. He's our Alpha. Lycina Duskbane is from a rival pack. She's dangerous, manipulative, and very good at causing chaos. Damian is her… protégé, I suppose you'd say."

"Oh. Wonderful. I just hooked up with the werewolf mafia's junior hitman. Good job, Harper," I muttered bitterly to myself, pinching the bridge of my nose in frustration.

Lucien's eyes narrowed slightly, clearly unamused by my flippancy. "Damian's a witch, Harper, not a werewolf. He specializes in manipulation—particularly emotional and physical attraction."

My mouth dropped open in horrified disbelief. "You're saying I got magically roofied? Well, that explains so much about my recent decision-making skills."

Isabella snorted softly, clearly fighting a reluctant smile. "Unfortunately, yes. Damian's very good at what he does. He manipulates emotions, influences decisions—basically, he's a walking, talking mind-control drug. You didn't exactly stand a chance."

I groaned loudly, slumping against the nearest wall. "This explains so much. I thought I was just really desperate—or really, really lonely."

Marcus shifted uncomfortably; his voice low but reassuring. "Harper, this isn't your fault. Damian was targeting you deliberately—to get to Elias."

I sighed dramatically, flinging my arms upward. "Perfect. So, I'm bait now. Human bait. Exactly how I envisioned my life at twenty-five."

Lucien approached cautiously; his expression gentle. "Harper, Elias chose you. That complicates things—dangerously. Especially now that Lycina knows."

I blinked in surprise, confusion washing through me. "Chose me?

What does that even mean?"

"It means," Isabella clarified bluntly, "that your little night together wasn't just recreational. Elias's wolf marked you, Harper. You're bonded now—whether either of you likes it or not."

I stared blankly between them, pulse pounding frantically, heart skipping unevenly in my chest. "Well, that would've been good information before the whole bedroom thing."

Lucien's eyes softened sympathetically. "We didn't realize he'd bonded to you this quickly. Elias isn't exactly known for emotional impulsivity."

"Really?" I snapped sarcastically; my voice tinged with panic. "Because showing up drunk at 1 AM and pinning me against my apartment door was totally rational behavior."

Marcus cleared his throat uncomfortably, glancing at Isabella, who was now hiding a smile behind her hand.

"Okay," Lucien interrupted firmly, clearly desperate to keep us on track. "Bottom line, Harper—you're part of this now, whether you like it or not."

"Fantastic," I sighed deeply, head dropping back against the wall in exhaustion. "Just great."

"Lycina and Elias were involved in a war," Lucien began cautiously, choosing his words as though stepping carefully through a minefield. His eyes flickered to Isabella, whose expression had hardened into something unreadable. "Around 1892, if memory serves."

My mouth dropped open slightly, disbelief momentarily stealing my voice. I blinked several times, struggling to process what he'd just said. "Wait—did you just say 1892?"

"Yes," Isabella confirmed gently, eyeing me with a guarded expression. "1892."

I gave a short, incredulous laugh, nervously tugging at a strand of my hair. "Okay, so either you're both crazy, or I'm suddenly trapped in an episode of 'The Twilight Zone.' Let me just pick my jaw off the floor really quick, because clearly, you're talking about Elias's great-grandfather or something, right?"

Lucien's expression softened, a hint of sympathy creeping through his careful composure. "Not exactly, Harper."

I stared at him blankly. "What do you mean, 'not exactly'? Are you trying to tell me Elias was alive in 1892? Like alive-alive? Breathing, walking, growling?"

Lucien nodded calmly, entirely serious. "Precisely."

My heart pounded erratically, pulse hammering so loudly I could barely hear my own thoughts. My voice was tight, half skeptical, half terrified. "Lucien, that would make Elias—"

"Very old," Isabella supplied dryly, a hint of amusement in her eyes at my obvious panic. "Much older than you probably realized."

I sucked in a shaky breath, stumbling backward until my legs bumped against a chair, forcing me to sit before my knees gave out entirely. "And exactly how old is 'very old'? Because 1892 already feels way beyond ancient."

Lucien exchanged a careful glance with Isabella, clearly debating how much more to reveal. Finally, Isabella sighed softly, her voice gentle but firm. "Elias was born in 1687, Harper."

I stopped breathing entirely for a moment, my entire body froze as her words sank in. "Excuse me—did you just say 1682? Like, he's older than electricity? Older than sliced bread?"

A flicker of amusement briefly softened Lucien's usually stoic face. "By a considerable margin, yes."

I exhaled sharply, pressing my hand over my rapidly beating heart, head spinning with disbelief and shock. Elias Blackwell, my brooding, frustrating, infuriatingly attractive boss—was over a hundred freaking years old. A hundred and something. Math was escaping me, and honestly, I didn't even have enough brain cells left for simple arithmetic at this point.

"You might have warned me about this sooner, you know," I accused weakly, glaring between them. "Like, hey Harper, your boss predates electricity and the Titanic."

Marcus shrugged lightly, unrepentant. "You didn't exactly ask."

"I didn't—" I shook my head quickly, laughing incredulously, eyes wide. "Right. I forgot the standard interview question: 'So, is my employer immortal, or should I expect him to retire sometime this century?'"

Marcus' mouth quirked up into an amused smirk. "Noted for future hires."

I leaned forward, elbows on my knees, staring blankly at the floor. "1892..." I murmured softly, still struggling to process the impossible truth they'd dropped on me. My voice grew quieter, curiosity and a hint of anxiety threading through my tone. "So, this Lycina—why exactly does she have it out for Elias? I mean, besides the fact he's apparently older than dirt?"

Another silent, uneasy glance passed between Lucien and Isabella, clearly hesitating again. I narrowed my eyes sharply, frustration boiling up anew. "Oh, come on! After dropping a bomb like that, you don't get to keep secrets anymore."

Finally, Lucien sighed, leaning forward, his voice low and measured. "Lycina and Elias have history—a long, bloody one. In 1892, Lycina lost someone she cared deeply about, and she blames Elias."

I swallowed hard, a chill snaking up my spine. "Lost someone?"

"Yes," Isabella added softly, voice tinged with something like regret. "Her mate."

"Oh," I whispered faintly, heart tightening with sudden sympathy even as confusion and worry tangled painfully in my chest. "That explains… a lot."

"Indeed," Lucien murmured grimly. "And it's why this won't end peacefully."

I nodded slowly, realization settling heavily over me. Elias's past was tangled with loss, violence, and grudges older than anything I'd ever imagined. The picture was becoming clearer, though far darker than I'd anticipated. Elias, powerful yet vulnerable, carrying centuries of secrets—and now, I was caught squarely in the middle.

Somehow, instant noodles and overdue bills suddenly seemed the least complicated parts of my life.

The Revelation

Elias

Sunlight burned mercilessly against my eyelids, forcing me awake. I lay for a long moment, disoriented and aching, trying to piece together the fragmented memories scattered through my mind. Pain surged through my muscles as I slowly sat up, realization dawning coldly that I was lying outside, in the dew-covered grass of the courtyard.

I lifted my head carefully, grimacing as a sharp throb radiated from my temples, images flooding back in disjointed bursts: Lycina's smug smile, the sickeningly sweet scent of magic, Damian's arrogant smirk, and Harper—God, Harper. Panic surged, tightening my chest painfully. Had she seen everything?

Scrambling unsteadily to my feet, heart hammering against my ribs, I ignored the protests of my battered body. Cold dread pooled in my gut, choking off my breath. If I'd hurt her—or worse—I'd never forgive myself.

"Harper!" I roared, voice rough and frantic as I charged back toward the house. The grand doors burst open under my urgency, echoing loudly through empty corridors. My pulse pounded relentlessly as fear clouded rational thought, primal instincts fraying the thin edge of my control.

"Lucien! Isabella!" My voice echoed again, desperate and raw, the names reverberating against marble walls. "Answer me, dammit!"

I stumbled into the foyer, breathing ragged, barely registering the torn remnants of clothing hanging loosely from my frame. Panic surged anew as I called out again, voice echoing harshly. "Lucien! Isabella!"

Footsteps rushed toward me, quick and familiar. Lucien appeared first, his expression grim yet steadying, eyes wary but reassuring.

"Elias, thank God," he breathed, visibly relieved. "You're back."

"Harper," I ground out hoarsely, my voice breaking, frantic eyes searching past him. "Tell me she's safe."

Lucien stepped closer, placing a calming hand firmly on my shoulder. "She's safe. She's downstairs. You didn't hurt her."

I exhaled raggedly, tension draining slightly from my rigid posture, relief making me weak. "I need to see her."

Lucien hesitated briefly, a flicker of caution crossing his face. "Give her a moment. Last night was...a lot for her to handle."

I clenched my fists tightly, guilt twisting sharply in my chest. "It was Damian. And Lycina. They did something—forced me to shift."

"I know," Lucien said quietly. "Harper knows. She saw everything."

My jaw tightened sharply, shame and anger warring fiercely within me. "She wasn't supposed to see that. Not yet."

Lucien placed a reassuring hand on my shoulder, squeezing gently. "She handled it better than expected. Harper is tougher than you think."

I nodded slowly, though my gut twisted with regret. The secret I'd worked so carefully to conceal was now brutally exposed. Harper knew—and nothing between us would ever be simple again.

I made my way slowly toward the lockup beneath the house, each heavy step echoing sharply against stone walls still damp from the morning chill. My chest tightened with anxiety, an ache settling deep in my gut the closer I came. My heart thundered painfully, a mixture of dread and desperate longing driving me forward, even as fear whispered warnings in the back of my mind.

When I reached the reinforced door, I paused, gripping the handle tightly as though bracing for impact. Swallowing hard, I pushed it open cautiously, breath catching in my throat as my eyes adjusted to the dimness inside.

Harper sat huddled on the narrow cot against the far wall, knees drawn protectively to her chest. My heart twisted painfully at the sight of her—so small, vulnerable, and achingly fragile. She wore only an oversized T-shirt that barely covered her thighs, leaving her smooth legs bare and exposed in the cold gloom. Her hair spilled in messy waves over her shoulders, tangled and wild, framing a face pale with exhaustion, marked with the lingering shadows of fear.

She'd never looked more beautiful—or more broken.

My instincts screamed at me to go to her, to wrap her in my arms, to erase every ounce of pain she'd suffered because of me. But as her eyes lifted slowly to meet mine, wide and uncertain, the haunted wariness in her gaze stopped me in my tracks.

"Harper," I murmured softly, voice barely audible over the pounding of my heart. "God, are you okay?"

She didn't answer, just stared, her trembling fingers twisting anxiously together in her lap. The thin T-shirt slipped slightly from one shoulder, exposing skin I'd worshipped only hours ago—now bruised from our frantic escape. Shame tightened painfully in my chest.

"Harper," I tried again gently, stepping carefully toward her. "I'm sorry. I didn't want you to see—"

Her body flinched visibly at my approach, fingers gripping tighter around her knees, knuckles turning white. Her reaction struck me harder than any physical blow I'd ever suffered. The realization hit like ice water, sobering and devastating in equal measure. She was afraid—terrified—of me. And the knowledge cut deeper than any injury I'd sustained.

I immediately halted my movement, my hands falling helplessly to my sides. Her fear hung heavily between us, suffocating me more than any chains ever could.

"I won't hurt you, Harper," I whispered, voice strained with a desperation I'd never known. "I swear—"

"I know," she finally interrupted softly, her voice thin and shaking. "I know, Elias. But...I just—need a minute. Please."

I nodded slowly, backing away a step, swallowing down the lump tightening my throat. "Take all the time you need."

But even as I spoke the words, a deep, gut-wrenching ache settled inside me. My wolf clawed restlessly beneath my skin, anger and pain blending into a tormenting cocktail of helplessness. I'd never imagined a single look from Harper could shatter me so completely.

Yet here I stood, utterly broken, willing to wait forever if that's what it took to regain her trust.

Harper

The truth was, I didn't know what I felt anymore. Part of me had spent the last few hours desperate to see Elias again, to throw myself into his arms, to feel his solid strength reassuring me everything would somehow be alright. Yet, the moment he stepped through that door, the image of the wolf surged back into my mind, blindingly vivid. My breath hitched painfully as fear flooded my veins, chasing away any rational thought.

My eyes traveled slowly over his powerful frame—now fully human again but still haunted by shadows of what he'd become. I remembered every agonizing detail of watching his body contort, muscles rippling grotesquely as bones shifted, his eyes wild and golden, pleading with me even as his voice had rasped desperately, telling me to run.

Run from him.

A shiver tore through me, uncontrollable. Elias hesitated, sensing my discomfort, and for a brief second, I saw something flicker behind his eyes, a deep, gut-wrenching hurt. It twisted sharply in my chest, knowing I'd caused it.

Yet, even with my heart screaming to soothe his pain, my instincts screamed louder to protect myself.

"I just..." My voice broke, weak and trembling. "I just need a minute, Elias."

His jaw clenched, the muscles visibly tightening beneath the smooth bronze of his skin, dark tattoos rippling as his shoulders stiffened. His gaze dropped, unable or unwilling to meet mine, though the quiet devastation was clear enough in the tense line of his body.

"Of course," he murmured quietly, voice rough with suppressed emotion. He stepped back, withdrawing immediately, giving me space even though every inch of him seemed to scream with the urge to reach for me, to bridge the gap I'd suddenly put between us.

He lingered only a moment longer, eyes briefly locking onto mine one last time. In that instant, I saw raw vulnerability, something I'd never thought Elias Blackwell capable of. And then he was gone, the door clicking quietly behind him, leaving me alone in a silence heavier than anything I'd ever known.

I drew a shuddering breath, my fingers trembling as I clutched the thin fabric of my shirt. This wasn't a rejection, no matter how it felt to him. I just needed time—time to process, to understand, to decide whether the man I'd begun to fall for was a man at all, or something far more dangerous.

"I'm sorry, Elias," I whispered to the empty room, closing my eyes as a single tear slipped down my cheek. "Please forgive me."

Elias

My body trembled with every step as I slowly moved away from Harper, each footfall echoing the hollow pain that surged through my chest. The rejection wasn't intentional, I knew that. But her fear pierced me deeper than any blade, and it took every ounce of strength I had left just to leave her there, alone, shivering in the chill of my shadow.

I made it halfway down the corridor before my legs buckled beneath me, knees slamming painfully into the marble floor. My vision blurred, and a strangled sound tore from my throat—anguished, raw, like the howling of a wounded animal. My fists clenched tight at my sides, shoulders shaking uncontrollably as grief broke through every carefully built wall inside me. The emotions came swift and merciless, flooding past my defenses, centuries of control crumbling in an instant.

Footsteps echoed rapidly down the hallway, urgent and confused. I heard the stunned silence as Marcus, Lucien, and Isabella arrived, stopping abruptly, unsure how to approach the sight before them. Their Alpha—the unshakeable, uncompromising leader who'd never once faltered—was kneeling on cold marble, breaking apart at the seams.

"Elias?" Lucien's voice was cautious, hesitant, concern and shock coloring his usually measured tone. "What's happened?"

My only answer was another strangled sob, shoulders shaking violently as tears I hadn't shed in over three centuries cascaded down my face, hot and shameful. My chest burned, heart thundering wildly, the ache raw and unfamiliar.

"She's afraid of me," I choked out hoarsely, barely able to force the words past the tightness gripping my throat. "Harper…she's terrified, and I caused that."

Isabella moved first, dropping swiftly to her knees beside me, her usual fierce reserve melting into something tender, almost motherly. Without a word, she wrapped her arms gently around my shaking shoulders, holding me tightly, silently offering comfort I hadn't felt since childhood.

"Elias," she whispered softly, her voice breaking slightly. "It's okay. She'll understand. Just give her time."

Marcus and Lucien exchanged worried, bewildered glances before they, too, moved closer, hesitantly sinking to their knees beside us. Marcus laid a comforting hand firmly on my shoulder, his touch steady and reassuring. Lucien placed his hand on my back, strong and grounding, his silent strength holding me from completely unraveling.

"She won't," I whispered brokenly, agony cracking every syllable. "How could she? She saw me—I was a monster. I broke our trust."

"Elias, she's strong," Lucien said gently, conviction underlying his soft tone. "If she truly knows you, she'll see beyond this."

Isabella tightened her arms around me, the warmth and closeness of my pack anchoring me even as my body shuddered, each sob more wrenching than the last. "You're allowed this moment," she murmured soothingly against my hair, her usually sharp voice gentle with compassion. "You've been strong for too long. Let it out."

I did. In the silence that followed, with their quiet strength surrounding me, I allowed myself to feel every painful, devastating emotion I'd suppressed for centuries. For the first time since my mother's death, I wasn't standing alone against the darkness.

For once, I allowed myself to break.

Harper

I slipped quietly from the lock-up, my heart aching and my thoughts swirling chaotically as I ascended the stone staircase. Every step felt heavier than the last, my mind a storm of conflicted emotions, fear, confusion, and beneath it all, an undeniable ache that tugged relentlessly at my heart.

As I turned down the long corridor, heading toward the safety and solitude of my temporary room, a soft voice stopped me.

"Harper?"

I jumped slightly, startled out of my thoughts, turning quickly to see Isabella standing by one of the tall windows, moonlight bathing her striking features in an ethereal glow. Her eyes softened with genuine concern as she took a slow step forward.

"Hey," I whispered awkwardly, trying to gather what little composure I still possessed. "I was just—"

"Are you alright?" she asked gently, moving toward me with surprising tenderness. Her sharp gaze softened considerably; the usual edge of suspicion replaced by a quiet empathy I hadn't expected.

I hesitated, heart hammering in my chest. "Honestly? I don't even know anymore. This is all just…a lot."

Isabella nodded thoughtfully, eyes carefully assessing me. "I understand. It's a world you weren't meant to see—at least, not yet. But here you are, still standing."

"Barely," I murmured weakly, rubbing my forehead tiredly. "I just watched your brother scream and shift into something out of a horror movie. So yeah, I'm having a bit of a moment here."

A faint, sympathetic smile curled her lips. "Fair enough."

We stood quietly for a moment, the silence stretching with awkward uncertainty until Isabella broke it gently. "How do you feel about him?"

Her question caught me entirely off guard. I opened my mouth, then snapped it shut again, struggling for the right words. My cheeks flushed hotly under her patient, unwavering gaze. "I—honestly, I don't even know. Elias is just…"

"Complicated?" she supplied knowingly, raising an eyebrow in amusement.

I laughed despite myself, feeling some of the tension easing from my shoulders. "Very. But also…I don't know, Isabella. I'm drawn to him. There's something about him I can't shake, no matter how hard I try. And believe me, I've tried."

Isabella's expression softened further, her voice low and thoughtful. "That's because Elias isn't someone you can easily walk away from. Trust me, I know. He's intense, fiercely protective, deeply complicated, and undeniably infuriating. Her eyes sparkled knowingly. "But when he cares—really cares—he's devoted beyond reason. I've never seen him lose control like he did tonight. You matter to him more than you probably realize."

My breath caught in my chest, emotions swirling chaotically inside me. I shook my head slowly, a nervous laugh bubbling up. "I don't know if that's comforting or terrifying."

"Maybe both," Isabella offered gently, giving my arm an affectionate squeeze. "But for what it's worth, I think he needs you now. More than he'll ever admit."

I hesitated, looking at her uncertainly. "But earlier…he seemed—"

"He was wounded, Harper. Physically and emotionally," she interrupted softly, eyes intense with meaning. "He's not himself right now. If you're willing to face that—to see past this moment—I think you could find something truly worth holding onto."

"Where is he now?" I asked quietly, heart fluttering nervously at the thought of confronting him again.

"In the courtyard," she replied softly, a knowing gleam in her eyes. "He goes there to clear his head. If you're looking for him, that's where he'll be."

I exhaled shakily, feeling a sudden rush of determination mingling with my fear. "Thanks, Isabella."

She nodded gently, stepping back as I turned to head toward the courtyard. My pulse quickened with every step I took, unsure of what I'd find, or what Elias would say. But despite everything, one thing remained clear—I couldn't stay away from him, even if I tried.

Elias

I stood quietly at the far end of the courtyard, the gentle hum of evening insects a soothing backdrop to my chaotic thoughts. Moonlight spilled generously over the stone paths and neatly trimmed hedges, washing everything in a soft, silver glow. The courtyard had always been my refuge—a sanctuary tucked away from prying eyes, surrounded by towering ivy-covered stone walls and ancient trees that whispered centuries-old secrets to those willing to listen. Here, beneath the starlit sky, I usually found clarity, the kind that eluded me now.

Lucien approached silently; his footsteps barely audible against the mossy stones. "Now that we know what and who we're dealing with, it's just a matter of time before the matter is resolved, sir."

Lucien's voice remained steady and reassuring. "They've shown their hand too soon."

I nodded slowly, though my mind still felt restless, burdened by far more than just the immediate threat. "Thank you, Lucien. Keep me informed."

He inclined his head respectfully. "Of course, sir. I'll ensure extra patrols until this situation is fully contained."

As Lucien stepped away, a soft breeze rustled the leaves overhead, carrying with it a familiar, comforting scent—Harper. I turned instinctively, my heart immediately quickening at the sight of her standing uncertainly near the entrance, her silhouette illuminated faintly by moonlight. Her hair cascaded loosely around her shoulders, catching the silvery light and amplifying the vulnerability radiating from her slender frame.

"Harper," I breathed quietly, surprised she'd even ventured to seek me out after everything she'd witnessed.

She stepped forward hesitantly, wrapping her arms protectively around herself. "Hi."

Her voice, gentle and cautious, reached me through the quiet stillness. My heart quickened sharply, every muscle tensing, a familiar possessive ache tightening within my chest. I resisted the urge to close the space between us, sensing her hesitation and not wanting to frighten her further.

"I wasn't sure you'd still be here," I admitted softly, my gaze searching hers carefully.

Her lips quirked faintly; a ghost of the usual humor I adored flickering across her expression. "Yeah, well, I guess I'm stubborn. Comes with the territory."

I allowed myself a small smile, warmth briefly easing the tension coiled tightly in my chest. "I've noticed."

She shifted uncertainly, eyes flickering nervously toward Lucien, clearly uneasy with the seriousness of our conversation. Lucien discreetly stepped away, quietly excusing himself and granting us privacy. I took a slow step closer, heart pounding steadily louder with every inch I closed between us.

Harper's gaze softened, eyes wide and filled with a wary tenderness that unsettled and excited me simultaneously.

"You're not afraid?" I asked cautiously, voice thick with uncertainty.

"Oh, I'm plenty afraid," she admitted quietly, stepping closer still, her gaze never wavering. "But apparently not enough to leave."

I exhaled slowly, relief and gratitude washing through me as I held her gaze. "Good. Because I don't think I could handle losing you right now."

The honesty slipped past my defenses before I could catch it, but Harper simply smiled, understanding far more than I'd intended to reveal.

Harper

I could no longer hold it. In an instant, my restraint shattered like fragile glass, and suddenly, I was moving. Running toward him, closing the distance in frantic strides, propelled by a desperate need deeper than anything I'd ever felt. I leapt into Elias's arms, my legs locking firmly around his waist as his strong arms immediately caught me, tightening protectively around my body.

His warmth surrounded me like a safe haven, his bare skin radiating heat that seeped through my clothes and melted away the tension I'd been carrying. Pressing my face desperately into the curve of his neck, breathing him in—spice, musk, and something wild and undeniably him—I finally allowed myself to break. Tears burst forth, uncontrollable, hot and raw, shaking my entire body as I sobbed openly, trembling in his embrace.

"I am so sorry, Harper," Elias whispered roughly, his voice breaking under the weight of genuine remorse, deep anguish trembling beneath the surface. "I am so, so sorry."

I held onto him tighter, fingers gripping the tense muscles of his shoulders, tears wetting his skin as he gently cradled me, strong yet infinitely careful. His hand moved soothingly along my back, comforting, apologetic, and filled with unspoken promises.

"You're safe now," he murmured softly, voice thick with emotion, breathing ragged against my ear. "I promise, you're safe. I'll never let anything happen to you again."

I pulled back slightly, just enough to meet his gaze—fierce, golden, and shimmering with unshed emotion. With trembling fingertips, I cupped his face, forcing him to meet my eyes.

"I don't want to be safe if it means being away from you," I whispered brokenly, watching as surprise, relief, and deep, raw emotion softened his gaze. "Just…please, Elias. No more secrets."

He pressed his forehead tenderly against mine, closing his eyes briefly as if my words were both relief and torment. "No more secrets," he vowed softly, his voice rough, urgent. "I promise."

"You kind of smell, though," I sobbed softly, my voice muffled against the curve of his neck as tears mingled with a reluctant laugh, releasing some of the tension that had wound itself painfully tight in my chest.

Elias stilled briefly, then chuckled deeply—a sound that resonated from somewhere deep within his chest, vibrating pleasantly against my body and sending a comforting warmth cascading down my spine. It was a rare, genuine sound; a carefree laugh utterly unlike anything I'd ever heard from him before. It was intoxicating, making my pulse flutter and my heart ache simultaneously.

"I suppose I deserve that," he murmured, amusement lingering softly in his voice, tightening his arms around me as he pressed me closer, as if reluctant to let go even for a second.

"Seriously," I muttered playfully, lifting my head to meet his eyes, feeling the smile that tugged insistently at my lips despite the remnants of my tears. "I mean, no offense, boss, but it's rough."

His golden eyes sparkled in amusement, softening the severity of his usually intimidating features. He leaned forward, brushing his lips gently across my forehead, his voice warm with quiet humor. "Well, I suppose fighting for my life and turning into a feral beast tends to ruin one's personal hygiene."

I smiled, gently brushing my thumb across his cheek, savoring the softness of the moment. "Maybe you should see someone about that. Seems like a pretty serious condition."

"I'll get right on that, Miss Wells." he murmured, his laughter fading into a gentle, contented sigh as he pressed his forehead softly against mine.

My heart fluttered lightly, the ache and fear replaced by an overwhelming sense of calm and security that felt impossible given the chaos we'd just experienced. As I nestled back into the comforting curve of his neck, breathing him in despite the lingering scent of sweat, dirt, and something distinctly wild, I knew, without a doubt, that I would willingly endure a thousand terrible nights if it meant staying in his arms.

"Don't worry," Elias whispered softly, tightening his embrace as he carried me gently back toward the house. "I'll see about getting a shower before you reconsider staying."

"Good idea," I mumbled sleepily against his skin, feeling more at peace than I had in weeks. "Because you definitely owe me hazard pay after tonight."

Elias

Carrying Harper to my bedroom felt surreal, like I'd stepped into a fragment of a dream—one I never imagined I could have again. Her delicate body clung tightly to mine, arms looped softly around my neck, legs holding firmly around my waist. She felt so impossibly warm, so right pressed against me; it was almost too much to bear. I inhaled deeply, absorbing her scent, feeling it calm the lingering chaos that roared inside my chest.

As I moved slowly through the main hall, the tension I'd been carrying for days—maybe centuries—began easing, melting under the weightless comfort of Harper's embrace. Her presence soothed something primal within me, something I hadn't known needed soothing until this moment.

Isabella glanced up from the fireplace as we passed. Her eyes softened knowingly, lips curling into a subtle smile as she offered a quiet nod of approval. It was a rare gesture from my sister, and it warmed me more than I cared to admit.

Harper shifted slightly in my arms, murmuring softly, her face nestled trustingly against my neck. I tightened my hold, savoring the protective surge that flooded my chest. This moment—her trust, her vulnerability—was precious beyond measure. I ascended the winding staircase to the west wing, my steps steady despite the exhaustion still pulling at my bones.

The journey was too short. I didn't want to let her go, didn't want to break this spell of warmth and quiet intimacy. Yet, as I reached my room and carefully laid her onto the soft sheets, her eyelids fluttered sleepily open, eyes finding mine in a gaze filled with tenderness and something deeper, more profound than I dared name.

"I'm right here," I whispered softly, brushing her hair gently back from her face.

"I know," she murmured sleepily, reaching out to lace her fingers gently through mine. "And that's exactly where I want you."

Stepping into the shower was cathartic, each droplet of steaming water cascading down my battered skin, slowly washing away the chaos, fear, and anger that lingered like dark stains from the night before. I closed my eyes, leaning my forehead against the cool tile wall, breathing deeply as the heat seeped into tired muscles, soothing me physically but doing little to quiet the storm brewing relentlessly beneath my skin.

My fists clenched involuntarily at the memory of Lycina's taunting voice, Damian's mocking smile, and the realization of how dangerously close Harper had come to being harmed because of me. The thought alone was enough to set my blood boiling again, a low growl threatening to rise from deep within my chest.

I forced myself to breathe, to let the water soothe away the edges of my fury, even as I silently vowed that their punishment would come swiftly. Lycina and Damian would pay, and the thought of their pain brought me grim satisfaction. But for now, I need to remain steady, calm. Harper needed stability, not more violence.

Almost as if she sensed my thoughts, Harper's familiar scent curled through the steamy air, winding gently around my senses. My breath hitched, my pulse quickening instantly as I turned toward the glass enclosure just as the door softly opened.

There she stood, her delicate frame bared to me, utterly breathtaking in her vulnerability. The glow of the steam caressed every graceful curve, the soft lighting in the bathroom highlighting the smooth contours of her skin, drawing my gaze in helpless admiration. Her eyes held mine boldly, with an intensity that instantly pulled me toward her, undoing every carefully constructed wall I had built.

"Harper," I murmured hoarsely, my voice thick with a mix of astonishment, desire, and relief. Her eyes sparkled with a quiet, unwavering strength, even as uncertainty lingered softly behind their depths.

Without a word, she stepped inside, letting the warm spray embrace her body as she moved toward me. My chest tightened painfully, every muscle in my body responding to her presence. Her closeness both soothed and inflamed, calming the raging storm within while igniting another, deeper need; instinctive and undeniable.

I reached out gently, hesitating only a heartbeat before pulling her against me. Her arms circled my waist, fingers tracing the muscles of my back, my hands instinctively wrapping around her smaller frame. She pressed her cheek against my chest, her soft breath washing over my skin, causing a shiver that resonated to my core.

"I'm here, Elias," she whispered softly, her voice barely audible above the rhythmic fall of the water. "I'm not going anywhere."

Something broke free in me then, a feeling deeper than desire, more profound than relief—a fierce, protective certainty that this woman belonged in my arms, beside me, now and always. My grip tightened, pulling her closer as I pressed my lips gently to the crown of her head, breathing in her scent, memorizing every nuance, every heartbeat, every whispered breath.

"You're mine, Harper," I growled softly, possessively, unable to hide the intensity that surged through me. "I won't let anything happen to you again."

She tilted her head back, eyes wide, trusting, and full of quiet determination. "I know."

And in that moment, with her body pressed against mine, water washing away the darkness, I felt something powerful shift within me. Harper wasn't just someone to protect, she was my strength, my weakness, my very heartbeat. She was the grounding force I never knew I'd needed, and I'd move heaven and earth to keep her safe.

Steam filled the shower, swirling around us like a delicate mist, but nothing was more intoxicating than Harper kneeling before me, eyes locked onto mine, impossibly wide, trusting, and utterly disarming.

She pressed her lips softly against my abdomen, her warm breath ghosting over the intricate tattooed vines that stretched across my ribs, descending slowly as if each kiss traced a promise onto my skin. My muscles tightened involuntarily beneath her gentle touch, breath hitching, my fingers instinctively threading into her damp hair, guiding her without force, yet craving her closeness.

"Harper," I whispered roughly, a tremor escaping into my voice, betraying how deeply she was affecting me. "You don't have to—"

"I want to," she murmured softly, voice barely audible over the cascading water around us. The sincerity, the willingness in her tone unraveled what little remained of my control.

Her fingertips traced over my hips, tentative yet deliberate, as if she were learning every inch of me, memorizing every scar and marking along my body. Heat surged sharply through my veins, a mixture of longing and something far deeper—a tenderness that startled me.

I cupped her face gently in my hands, thumbs brushing tenderly over her cheeks, silently asking once more if she was sure, if she understood what this meant, what this act would signify between us. In response, she smiled softly, eyes shining brightly with trust and a vulnerability that humbled me deeply.

Slowly, reverently, she lowered herself to her knees, water soaking her hair, droplets cascading down her face and shoulders. Her gaze never left mine, an intimate connection that felt as powerful as her touch.

The ache inside me intensified sharply, desire coiling fiercely in my gut. I reached down, gently cradling the back of her head, my breathing ragged and uneven.

"Harper," I whispered roughly, her name a plea and a warning intertwined.

She leaned forward, closing the distance between us, and as the warmth of her mouth enveloped me, the world around me fractured, fading away into nothing but heat, water, and the breathtaking certainty that this woman, this fierce, gentle, maddeningly brave woman, had irrevocably claimed my soul.

The water cascaded relentlessly around us, steam fogging the glass of the shower, enclosing us in our own private sanctuary. I pressed one hand firmly against the cool surface, fingers splayed wide, bracing myself as sensation overwhelmed every rational thought. My other hand remained buried in Harper's wet hair, cradling the back of her head gently, guiding without pressure as every muscle in my body tightened, breath ragged and uneven.

"Harper," I groaned softly, her name escaping like a sacred mantra, reverberating through me, anchoring me even as reality slipped away. "Harper...Harper..."

Heat surged fiercely, building unbearably within me, her touch and warmth driving me closer to the edge with every passing second. Her fingertips dug gently into my thighs, grounding herself as she responded intuitively, moving in rhythm with my urgency. Her presence was overwhelming, an intoxicating instinctive claim that left me powerless, surrendered to the overwhelming intensity of this moment.

"Harper," I repeated, louder this time, voice breaking slightly, desperation woven deeply into each syllable as pleasure surged forward relentlessly. The glass wall steamed under my palm, and the heat of the shower mixed with the burning ache inside my chest, leaving me gasping, trembling beneath the strength of her tenderness.

My heart raced wildly, blood pounding fiercely in my ears as the pressure mounted, muscles tensing, spiraling rapidly toward release. Everything blurred around me, leaving only her soft warmth, the delicate strength of her, the trust she placed in me even now.

"Harper," I rasped again, voice shattering into something raw, unrestrained, begging for release and forgiveness, passion and promise interwoven until nothing else mattered except her. "Harper…Harper…"

Then everything inside me unraveled completely, a cry tearing from my chest, guttural and fierce, echoing off tile and glass. My body shook violently, knees nearly buckling, hand pressing harder against the glass as the rush of pleasure tore through me, deep and all-consuming, leaving me helpless and vulnerable.

And as the intensity slowly ebbed away, leaving my body trembling and breathless, clarity came crashing in with undeniable force:

Harper wasn't just in my arms, she had claimed every hidden, vulnerable part of me, binding herself permanently to my very being.

Chapter 13

The Confrontation

Harper

It's almost surreal how deeply attractive Elias is—not just because of the dangerous, thrilling allure surrounding whatever the hell he is, but his body, *my god.*

He lay beside me, peacefully asleep for once, his chest rising and falling rhythmically beneath my fingertips. My hand moved slowly, delicately tracing the intricate patterns inked onto his skin, the dark, swirling vines and symbols beautifully etched across firm muscle, telling stories I didn't yet understand. Each elegant twist and swirl of ink seemed deliberate, almost alive, like secrets whispered against his flesh.

I exhaled softly, my heart skipping every time my fingertips brushed a sensitive spot, and his muscles involuntarily tense. The warmth of his skin radiated beneath my touch, stirring memories of what had just transpired between us. I still couldn't fully wrap my head around what I'd done, how boldly I'd acted—yet I didn't regret a single moment of it.

The image replayed vividly: his eyes locked fiercely on mine, the low growls, the urgent way he'd moved against me, untamed yet controlled. My cheeks flushed, heat pooling low in my stomach at the memory. His scent lingered everywhere, clinging stubbornly to my skin, my sheets, my senses—marking me as surely as his touch.

I couldn't help myself—I leaned in closer, pressing my lips softly to the intricate ink on his shoulder. The way he shivered slightly beneath me, even asleep, sent a pulse of heat through my veins, deepening the ache I felt for him. I pulled back, my breath coming faster as my heart fluttered nervously, knowing something had irrevocably shifted between us.

Yet beneath the thrill and desire, questions lingered: What was Elias hiding from me? Could I handle the darkness that clung to him, barely concealed beneath the surface?

My heart ached softly with uncertainty, but as I nestled into his warmth, pressing my cheek against the steady rhythm of his heart, one thing was perfectly clear: I was irrevocably, dangerously his.

"What are you deep in thought about?" Elias's voice was soft, a low rumble vibrating gently through his chest beneath my cheek.

"Did I wake you?" I asked, startled and slightly embarrassed at having been caught staring at him so openly.

"Not at all," he replied smoothly, though his voice was still thick with sleep.

I raised an eyebrow skeptically, unable to suppress a playful smirk. "Liar."

His lips curved into a faint, sleepy smile, eyes opening slowly, golden gaze capturing mine with lazy intensity. "You didn't answer my question."

I hesitated for a moment, fingertips continuing their absent-minded path along the elegant swirls of ink decorating his chest. "I was just wondering...about your tattoos. They seem special—like each one has a story. What do they mean?"

His eyes softened slightly, a flicker of vulnerability surfacing briefly before disappearing behind his carefully composed expression. "They do have meaning, each one. Moments, memories...reminders."

"Good memories or bad?" I asked softly, my curiosity deepening as I gently traced the swirling patterns that wove down his ribs.

"A bit of both," he admitted quietly, his gaze lingering on me thoughtfully. "But lately, they've taken on a new meaning entirely."

"Oh?" I whispered, warmth flooding my cheeks at the intensity in his gaze. "And what's that?"

He shifted slightly, bringing his hand up to gently cup my face, his thumb brushing tenderly against my cheek. "They remind me that even after centuries, there are still things that can surprise me."

I felt my heart flutter wildly, warmth flooding my chest as I leaned into his touch. "I'm glad I could contribute to your tattoo meanings," I teased gently, attempting to lighten the intensity of the moment, though my voice was far softer than intended.

He chuckled softly, a low, rumbling sound that sent pleasant chills down my spine. "You've done far more than that, Harper."

I fell silent, meeting his gaze once more, the seriousness in his eyes resonating deep within me. "Elias—"

"Shh," he whispered gently, pulling me closer until my head rested comfortably against his chest again. "Rest. We have plenty of time for stories later."

And for once, I didn't argue.

Elias

Sunlight streamed gently through the sheer curtains, casting golden streaks across Harper's sleeping form tangled gracefully in the white sheets. Her soft breathing echoed gently in the silence of the room, and for a moment, I allowed myself the indulgence of simply watching her. She looked impossibly peaceful, her hair fanned out across the pillow, soft tendrils framing her face. A fierce protectiveness surged through me, tightening my chest painfully, and I knew in that instant I would stop at nothing to keep her safe.

Quietly slipping from the bed, I reached for my clothes, swiftly dressing without disturbing her rest. As I buttoned up my shirt, I cast one last lingering glance at her—committing every detail of her sleeping form to memory before silently stepping out into the hallway.

Lucien waited at the foot of the stairs, his expression dark with urgency. "Elias," he said, his eyes piercing with a gravity I couldn't ignore. "We have a situation," he continued, his voice low but insistent. "We need to go. There's something you need to see—immediately." I frowned, eyes narrowing slightly, a familiar sense of unease curling tightly in my gut. "What's happened now?"

Lucien glanced briefly over his shoulder at Marcus and Isabella, who stood quietly near the entrance to the living room, their expressions unusually grim. Isabella stepped forward, gently touching my arm to draw my attention.

"Marcus and I will keep Harper safe," she assured me firmly, her dark eyes softening with understanding. "We've already tightened security— nothing will touch her here."

I nodded; my jaw set tight. "Good. If anything happens."

"It won't," Marcus interrupted confidently, placing a reassuring hand on my shoulder. "We won't leave her side."

Lucien cleared his throat impatiently, urgency radiating from his posture. "We need to go now, Elias. It can't wait."

With a final lingering glance back toward the room where Harper still slept peacefully, I reluctantly followed Lucien to the sleek black car waiting in the driveway.

The drive was tense and heavy with silence, Lucien gripping the steering wheel tightly, his eyes narrowed in careful concentration. After several long minutes, I finally broke the uneasy quiet.

"Lucien," I demanded sharply, my patience thin. "Tell me what's going on. Now."

He glanced quickly in my direction before turning his attention back to the road. "Damian was caught early this morning by our scouts, trying to slip back into the city. We have him secured at a facility just across the river—isolated enough that we won't be disturbed."

My pulse quickened; muscles instinctively tense. "He's alive?"

"Barely," Lucien admitted, a hint of grim satisfaction coloring his voice. "He was severely wounded, but he insisted on speaking directly to you. He knows more than he's told us so far, I'm certain of it."

The surge of fury that rushed through me was visceral, hot, and damning. Damian—the man who had dared touch Harper, who had violated her trust, had manipulated her mind—now demanded an audience with me? The thought made my knuckles whiten, a low growl rumbling involuntarily from my chest.

"He's a dangerous bastard, Elias," Lucien continued carefully, sensing my rising anger. "But he's a hired weapon. Lycina is the hand holding him, and if we can break his loyalty, he'll give us what we need to end this."

"Or he'll try to manipulate us further," I muttered darkly, staring out the window as city lights blurred past, my thoughts drifting back helplessly to Harper. "How did she react, Lucien? To everything?"

He hesitated briefly, clearly uncomfortable. "Confused, upset. Afraid. But mostly worried about you, Elias. More worried about your safety than her own."

My heart twisted painfully, both warmed and wounded by his words. "She doesn't deserve to be caught in the crossfire."

"None of us do," Lucien replied firmly, slowing as we approached a secluded building hidden by dense trees, guarded by armed men who stepped aside quickly to let us pass. "But Harper is resilient—perhaps even more than you've given her credit for."

As we parked and stepped out into the cool night air, Lucien turned toward me, eyes piercing in their intensity. "Keep your head, Elias. Remember, he's not our ultimate target, just a tool. We need information, not vengeance."

I clenched my fists tightly at my sides, nodding sharply as we entered the building. Every muscle in my body screamed for release, for action, for violence—but I swallowed it down, knowing that answers were more important than revenge.

Still, the image of Harper's sleeping form remained stubbornly vivid in my mind, a powerful reminder of why I was here, and why failure simply wasn't an option.

The heavy steel door of the interrogation room groaned as Lucien pushed it open, revealing a scene bathed in harsh fluorescent lighting. The sterile glare illuminated cracked concrete walls streaked with stains of old blood, a grim testimony to past interrogations. At the center of it all, Damian slumped in a metal chair, wrists bound tightly behind his back, glowing faintly with silver runes powerful magic preventing any hope of escape.

My jaw clenched as I took in his battered state. His face was marred by bruises, a deep purple swelling beneath one eye and a fresh gash on his lower lip dripping blood onto the torn collar of his once-immaculate shirt. Despite his obvious pain, Damian managed a mocking smile, his sharp eyes filled with defiant amusement as they met mine.

"Elias," he drawled weakly, his voice rasping from dehydration or perhaps from a recently broken jaw. "It's been a minute." He said mockingly.

"Not nearly long enough," I snarled, stepping closer, fists clenched tightly at my sides to keep from launching myself at him. "Damian, your first mistake was laying a hand on Harper. Your second was daring to step foot in our home."

Damian's eyes sparkled maliciously, the corners of his lips twisting upward into a cruel, knowing smirk. "She didn't seem to mind my touch at all. In fact, I'd say she enjoyed every second."

Rage surged through me like wildfire, a deep, animalistic growl vibrating in my chest, fingers curling involuntarily into fists, nails biting sharply into my palms. Lucien's steady hand rested firmly on my shoulder, an anchor holding me back, reminding me of the line I couldn't cross—not yet at least.

"Enough games, Damian," Lucien warned evenly, his voice calm but edged with a deadly seriousness. "He's here…like you asked. Tell him what was in the vial. What is Lycina planning? The truth, this time."

Damian shifted painfully in his restraints, expression sobering slightly beneath the force of Lucien's tone. His eyes still danced with spiteful amusement as he slowly lifted his gaze back to mine, a sly smile tugging stubbornly at the corner of his bloodied mouth.

Damian's mouth curved into a sinister smile, and his eyes—dark with hatred and a sickening pleasure, locked onto mine. "Something special, a concoction Lycina spent centuries perfecting, just for you, Eliaston. Wolfsbane, of course; but mixed with something even more potent—a curse designed especially to tear you apart from the inside out."

My jaw tightened painfully, dread pooling like ice in my veins. "Speak clearly, Damian, or I'll tear your throat out with my bare hands."

He chuckled coldly, unbothered by the threat. "It strips away your power piece by piece, Eliaston. Wolfsbane neutralizes your strength, sure—but the blood magic, the curse woven into that potion, it destroys the very thing that defines you. You'll become utterly human, painfully mortal, completely vulnerable."

The blood drained from my face, my throat tightening in disbelief. Human. Mortal. Vulnerable.

"Impossible," Lucien whispered harshly from beside me, his voice strained with disbelief. "Elias, that's—"

"A fate worse than death?" Damian finished, lips pulling back in a triumphant sneer. "Exactly. Lycina figured the best revenge was taking away your precious immortality. No pack, no power, no protection…no throne. You'll watch everything you care about destroyed, starting with your pretty little human."

Rage ignited like wildfire in my veins, threatening to consume whatever rational thought that remained. My body shook, barely containing the beast within—one that would soon abandon me entirely. Damian was baiting me, twisting the knife deeper, savoring my reaction.

My heart thundered dangerously in my chest, a bitter taste filling my mouth as his words sank in. He'd intended for me to lose control — to hurt Harper. The mere thought was enough to ignite a fury so intensely it nearly blinded me.

"You don't believe me," Damian mocked dangerously, "Have you checked your sigils lately?"

My pulse spiked, dread coiling tighter. Quickly, I pulled back the sleeve of my shirt, revealing the intricate tattoos that had marked my skin for centuries. My breath caught sharply in my throat as I saw the edges already faded, disappearing into nothingness.

"They're fading," Damian taunted with vicious satisfaction. "Each mark that vanishes pulls you closer to humanity. When the last sigil disappears, you'll be completely human, entirely powerless."

My blood turned ice-cold, breath freezing in my lungs as Damian's sinister confession echoed through my mind. This wasn't just an attack, it was a targeted strike, calculated and viciously precise. I stared at the fading lines, horror and disbelief battling within me. The once bold and powerful symbols were now turning into ghostly shadows, mocking my vulnerability. Damian watched my reaction, eyes glittering maliciously.

"What's the antidote?" Lucien demanded harshly, stepping forward menacingly, his usual calm shattered by a wave of protective rage.

Damian chuckled weakly, spitting blood onto the grimy floor, his voice tinged with dark amusement. "There isn't one."

My fists trembled with barely restrained fury, the muscles in my back coiled painfully, ready to snap. My control was slipping rapidly — just as Damian had hoped. Every instinct screamed to rip his throat out, but I fought against it, focusing instead on Harper, safe for now but forever at risk because of this man's sick games.

Lucien stepped forward, his eyes cold and uncompromising, yet his tone remained eerily composed. "You're going to tell us exactly how to break this curse, Damian. Or so help me, you'll beg for death before this night ends."

Damian laughed, the bitter, mocking sound echoing harshly against the walls. "You can try. But you won't like the answers."

My patience shattered completely, a snarl ripping from my throat as I lunged forward, grabbing a fistful of Damian's blood-soaked shirt. I slammed him hard against the wall, the chair screeching violently beneath his weight, eyes blazing with murderous intent.

"You listen carefully, Damian," I growled, every word dripping with deadly promise. "You can play your sick games with me, but touch Harper again—"

Damian interrupted with a defiant smirk, bloodied teeth gleaming, eyes flashing dangerously. "It won't be me that touches her."

His taunting words ignited a fury so intense that control shattered entirely. With a roar of pure rage, I hurled Damian violently across the room, watching the chair shatter spectacularly against the far wall, as Damian slumping down to the floor.

The echo of my rage faded slowly, replaced by a deafening silence. My breathing came harshly, chest heaving with barely controlled fury. Lucien's steady hand returned firmly to my shoulder, anchoring me back to reality, grounding me through the haze of anger.

A tense silence filled the room, broken only by Damian's ragged breathing. Slowly, I forced my breathing back under control, turning cold, calculating eyes toward Lucien, who watched me cautiously, assessing every volatile shift in my mood.

"Find a way," I ordered quietly, voice dangerously soft. "Find a way to break this."

Lucien nodded sharply, his eyes burning with determination. "We will, Elias."

As we left the interrogation room and stepped outside, a harsh strangled sound of despair escaped my lips. My heart was pounding, the weight of everything—centuries of power, of strength—crumbling around me. But through it all, Harper's face emerged clearly in my thoughts: beautiful, fragile, precious.

"What happens now, Lucien?" I demanded hoarsely, panic creeping into my voice despite my efforts to suppress it. "How can I protect her if I'm…if I'm nothing?"

"You're not alone, Elias. We'll get through this—as we always have."

My gaze drifted helplessly upward, heart heavy and uncertain. I had been untouchable for centuries—now I was merely human, stripped of power and immortality, desperately vulnerable.

And yet, despite everything, my mind refused to let go of Harper. Her stubborn defiance, the unexpected bravery that shimmered beneath her awkward exterior, even the gentle warmth of her touch—it all haunted me, relentlessly tugging at my thoughts. She'd become my greatest vulnerability, yet also the one thing I'd fight hardest to protect.

Lucien's voice broke through the chaos in my mind, steady and urgent. "Elias, we need to get back. This changes everything."

"I know," I whispered roughly, straightening my shoulders with newfound resolve. "And it changes nothing, Lucien. Human or not, I'll burn the world down before Damian or Lycina ever lay a finger on Harper again."

To Be Continued in *'The Ashen Throne'*

Hey, you. Yeah, you.

You made it all the way to the end. That means something. If you laughed, cried, blushed, or raged alongside Harper, I'd love it if you'd leave a review.

It doesn't have to be fancy—just a few words can make a big difference.

Your voice might just be the reason someone else takes the leap into this story.

Thank you. Truly.

Drop a Review

www.phoenyxjrose.com